Born in Carlisle in the footprints of the Romans, Thelma became fascinated by history at an early age. The past, as well as the present, has always enthralled her; particularly the interweaving of the two together. She has always wanted to share her love of history, and especially the quiet corner of her heart that still lives in Hadrian's country.

Marrying a sailor meant a nomadic lifestyle; something she still embraces. Her occupations have ranged from ESOL teaching in Derbyshire, to steam engine fireman in North Wales, to being in charge of an A & E in New Zealand. She currently lives on The Machars of Galloway

Relative Dating

2nd Edition 2017

T G Hancock

Relative Dating

Also by the same Author:

Tree Dimensional (2009)

ISBN 978 1 8438651 2 4

Diverse Distress (2009)

ISBN 978 1 8438655 8 2

Grave Doubts. (2009)

ISBN 978 1 8438655 7 5

Smokescreen. (2010)

ISBN 978 1 8438664 9 7

Collide and Conquer. (2011)

ISBN 978 1 9034904 8 8

In the Loop. (2011)

ISBN 978 1 8438670 2 9

Timeline. (2011)

ISBN 978 1 8438691 2 2

Enter Two Gravediggers. (2011)

ISBN 978 1 9034906 6 2

Disreputable Truth. (2012)

ISBN 978 1 8438682 9 3

Discarded Images. (2014)

ISBN 978 1 9100771 3 9

Dedication

To Catherine James, with love.

Relative Dating.

Prologue.

HE DIDN'T KNOW IT, but he had less than six minutes to live, which looked at from anyone's viewpoint was a great waste of potential.

'Hi Max, whatya lookin' at?'

His equally dusty and youthful friend looked down at Max crouched on the floor; Max was peering one eyed through a small hole in the roof.

Max looked up, his eye grimily encircled, and grinned wickedly like a one-eyed terrier, 'Well, to tell you the truth, Johno, I'm damned if I know! I can see the excavations and there's this really shifty guy down there.'

He stood up and the pair, with the single-mindedness of youth, headed towards the narrow exit. If John hadn't snagged his duffel bag on the door jamb maybe he would have turned into a really fine architect; on such things is the fate of a man, apparently, decided.

Max clattered down the wooden steps built into the side of the Cathedral wall. Originally used by the monks to light candles in the tri-form, they had been extended to allow access to the top of the vaulted ceiling over the side chapel.

As two keen and budding architectural students, the two mates had received permission to climb up and observe the original mason's work. Max had been peering down through the mason's hole at the apex of the furthest vault when he'd made his comment.

The dust swirled and settled in their wake, falling

in a shower of fine quartz, glittering in such fitful late evening sunshine as managed to get through the cracks, and joyfully run along the joists in thin golden chains.

Max shot out the door like a cork from a bottle and headed towards the open area of wall at the end of the Cathedral where a large amount of disturbed earth declared the frantic activity of archaeologists anxious to salvage what they could before the area was rebuilt. It looked as though giant moles had decided to build a council estate.

'Hi mate; what you up to?' Max shouted down at the crouched figure dressed in jeans and black hoody, who was chipping away, with less than careful strokes, at an area in the pit near the wall. The man, seeing the approaching teenager, lifted a startled scowling face from his task. His stocky figure moved fast as he scrambled across the discarded rubble and dodged around excavations towards the wooden ladders leaning against the top of the hole.

Max headed determinedly down the ladder as the man headed upwards. John later described the events at the inquest as having happened in slow motion; the man climbing and anxious to get away, Max eager to prevent him. The meeting halfway saw a brief struggle with Max pushed and sailing over the man's head into the pit and laying still in the muddy clay with his head at a strange angle. The man appeared to have become glued to the ladder as he looked backwards and downwards.

At the same time John stood frozen at the top. 'Max, are you alright? Max!'

The man, after a frozen minute of his own, had started to climb again and on reaching the top had tried to shove pass, but John had gripped him firmly round a skinny forearm, even while he'd continued to shout down at his best mate, Max. The man turned a white face towards him, pulling on the hand holding him; 'Let me go!'

It was said in a breathless undertone and he began to drag John away from the edge.

John, raising a fist to stop the man in the most efficient way he knew, was only prevented in performing this timely action by the appearance of several people in Wellingtons and anoraks who surrounded the struggling pair. They had been round the corner out of the wind having a quiet break and cuppa and had come to investigate the shouting.

'What's going on?' A tall broad-shouldered man of about thirty five, wearing Wellingtons and looking more like a navvy than the visiting eminent professor he later turned out to be, took in the scene of struggling man, white faced youth, and then the body laying in their newly dug site.

'Charlie, grab this guy! Grace, get the youth! Bob, come with me!'

He'd taken charge efficiently, calling the police and controlling his temper admirably as the precious days slipped by and their archaeological site turned into a crime scene. When the dust had finally settled, one Philip Jardin found himself incarcerated at Her Majesty's Pleasure, sentenced to seven years for manslaughter and attempted theft of Roman artefacts, very few of which made it to the light of day because his actions lost the archaeologists their chance to excavate them.

1

'I FOUND A COIN hoard once.' The voice came from the still figure in the hospital bed and startled Dan, who'd thought she was asleep.

He set down the coin he'd been absently turning over in his hand, trying to read the inscription. 'Are ye in pain?' He questioned softly, even while he reached under the covers for the pump to give an additional bolus of morphine.

'No.' Her hand reached out over his, stilling his movement. 'I fine, I'm just not sleepy.'

'Can I get ye anything; a drink?'

'No, Son,'

Dan smiled at her, 'Son?' he raised an ironical eyebrow.

'Well, when you get to my age everyone looks young.'

'Millie, you are not that old.' He gently turned the warm, paper thin, skinned hand still resting on his and held it warmly between his own two hands. Looking at the frail figure he quietly assessed her. He could feel her pulse in the joint between thumb and forefinger; a little thready, but steady. Her chest, under its covering of white lace and linen, rose and fell evenly, barely disturbing the long grey plait of hair resting across it. He patted the hand and released it.

'Satisfied?' Millie was aware of his little assessment. Dan nodded.

'How old are you, Dan?' She looked at the close cropped skull with the red hair bristling over it, matching in colour the faint five o clock shadow on his cheeks and chin. His bright blue eyes looked across the white cotton sheets at her with a decided twinkle.

'I'm forty-two, Millie, and you are only eighty, which means ye ha' to stop flirting wi' me. It's unethical!'

'I had a beau once, I flirted with him dreadfully, and it was such fun!' she smiled reminiscently. 'He was an American airman. I do like a man in uniform.' She sighed gustily, making them both laugh, then asked; 'Do you miss your uniform?'

Dan looked down at his well worn and very comfortable jeans, and the sweat shirt with Utah University emblazoned on the front. 'Nay then, I might ha' worn khakis for most of m' adult life and I mun admit it did attract the lassies; but I canna say I want to be back in uniform forebye.'

'Why did you leave the service, Dan?'

'Think on, m' time was done Millie. I'd served my 22 and seen the world. I doubt not I could have stayed on; in a teaching capacity ye ken, but professional soldiering is for bairns eager to rough it. Nae doot I've got to the stage where I want more o' life than I can carry in a kit bag. A need some roots.'

'What about your family, Dan?'

'I ha' none Millie; at least none that ha' come and demanded paternity frae me!' His eyes twinkled in the subdued lighting of the bedroom.

'Grace's mine you know?'

Dan thought of the young woman who'd been to visit the evening before, her baggy flannel top and jeans concealing whatever figure she might have underneath. 'I guess she is at that.'

'No. I mean she's mine, my grandchild; I had a child just after the war. It was a terrible thing having a baby when you weren't married, so I told everyone she was my cousin's child. That her parents had died in the war; so many children were in that position so there weren't too many questions. But she was mine! I've got to tell Grace before I go, but I'm not sure how. It's so difficult when you've lived a lie for so long. I don't want to lose her love.' The old hand twitched on the soft pink coverlet of the duvet and gripped Dan's hand again, 'Maybe you could tell her for me?' It was half a question, half a plea.

Dan looked uncomfortable. 'To my mind she'd love ye regardless, but she'd not take that sort of personal news from a stranger, Millie, and a brown job as well. I'm just an ex-army nurse. Look now, she's got a doctorate!'

'What's that got to do with it? I bet you had plenty of authority, you still boss me around!' Millie grinned, then the humour faded away, 'I wish you would, Dan. It's worrying me; she pretends she's so tough but really she's so easily hurt.'

'Och! Millie.' He sighed softly.

'Don't you like her?' Millie looked at him with eyes gleaming with unshed tears. 'She's very shy. It's not that she doesn't like you.'

Millie looked at the strong hand holding hers so gently. 'She does remind me of him; my beau, much more than my daughter ever did. Grace has his eyes and his blonde curly hair. She's got his height too; and sometimes I see a look on her face that reminds me of him when we first met.

'I can see him now! He had one of those Stirling jackets with a fur collar, like you see on Battle of Britain pictures. They always looked so young and devil-may-care in those jackets, Dan. He was standing in the marketplace lighting a cigarette and squinting through the smoke at the air-raid warden, with a look of mischief on his face.' She chuckled.

'He leaned back against the wall and just grinned at the guy who was waving a finger under his nose, all officious and drawled, "What's your beef, Mac?"

'The warden was red-faced and red-nosed and he was always harassing us land girls for all sorts of petty things. It was so good to see my James just standing there grinning at him. Not that he was my James then, but he was later.'

"What's eating you, buddy?" He said and the fat warden just got redder in the face.

"You Americans, don't you know better than to show a light? Endangering civilians this way!" And his voice got all high and squeaky; like a happy mouse sighting cheese! "I want your name, rank and number. I'm reporting you to your senior officer."

"Says you. It's still light, Mac. I don't think my fags gonna bring a bomber down on the town hall at five in the evening, even if it is nearly dusk." He grinned at the admiring circle of girls and then smirked at the warden. Then, deliberately turning his back, linked arms with two of the girls and sauntered away from the spluttering man.

Millie had followed in their wake, too shy to speak herself but willing to be in the crowd as they headed for the tea dance being held in the hall down the street. Sounds of laughter floated out the door along with a medley of mixed accents from the troops stationed in the border town.

"Isn't he dishy, Millie?" The speaker, a twenty year old with a permanent wave that resembled corrugated iron, a skirt that was tight enough to restrict her blood when she sat and daring enough to show the tops of her knees, linked arms with Millie and tugged her along in the wake of the smooth talking Yank.

Millie flushed, "I wish you wouldn't be so coarse, Jen." But her eyes followed the back of the American, admiring the way he walked and the set of the jacket. It was such a contrast to the Tommies

7

in their stiff brown uniforms, with their polite manners and tired eyes.

The girls entered the hall just as a waltz was starting and they hurriedly divested themselves of cardigans and gasmasks and found seats at the tables spaced around the edges of the pocket sized dance floor. They looked expectantly at the men lounging in little groups at the far side of the hall.

The air smelt of Woodbines, strong tea and lavender water. Millie surreptitiously checking her face in a small mirror, patted her hair, and pushed a Kirby grip into place. It held back the bun of soft light brown hair that she was so proud off. Her mother had said her hair was her one true beauty so she kept it unfashionably long, despite the current trend for permanent waves.

Jenny was boldly eyeing the young men, "I'm going to dance. Are you coming?"

"Jen!" the two had been best friends at school but Millie never understood why; they were so different. Jenny was abrasive and sarcastic, a true friend however, she would never knowingly hurt Millie even while she watched her squirming in her seat. She laughed gently at Millie, "I'll bring him to meet you later shall I?" She watched the flush start its journey across Millie's delicate skin. "Never mind, Auntie Jen will get him for you!" She patted Millie's shoulder and grinned impudently at the horrified face of her friend as Millie focused on her.

She looked across the room at the men, but under her lashes her eyes kept being drawn to the young Yank. He stood surrounded by girls and Millie thought he was the handsomest man there. "You can't just go up to a man and demand a dance!" She all but whispered.

"You watch me!" Jenny sashayed her way across the room towards the Yank and held out a cigarette. "Got a light?"

8

The Yank took his cigarette from his mouth and held the tip against Jen's. "There you go little lady; and what's your name?"

Jenny smiled boldly up into his dark grey eyes. "I'm Jen, do you want to dance?"

He nipped his cigarette out, dropping the barely smoked end into an ashtray on the table before taking her hand and leading her forward as he said "The name's James Belsham, from Texas."

Millie, an interested observer, sat tight in her seat wishing she had Jenny's courage. She shook her head at one shy young man who approached, keeping their bags and gas masks tightly gripped on her lap as she watched the couple whirl around to the tinny piano being played with verve by the local librarian.

As the music ended she shifted in her seat, waiting for Jenny to come back.

Jenny approached with the Yank in tow. "This is my friend Millicent Rose Armstrong. Millie meet James Belsham. He's flying escort B19's for the British Air Force."

"Jen!" Millie felt herself blushing as the young man shook hands and looked at her from eyes that reminded her of the Irish Sea on a sunny winter's day, sparkling and stormy by turns. His voice however was surprisingly kind. "And what do you do, little lady?"

"Oh we're land girls." Jen answered for them both.

"Oh Yeah, I've heard about you all. You 'Dig for Victory' don't you?"

Jenny nodded "We're out at Blists Park at the moment sowing potatoes. It ruins your hands." She sighed and looked at the dirt engrained around her fingernails.

"Does it ruin your hands too?" James looked at Millie who nodded wordlessly.

"Well it shouldn't stop you dancing. You do dance don't you?" Millie nodded again.

"Well come on then."

'And that's how we met.' Millie looked at Dan, the sparkle and animation fading from her face. 'I fell in love on that dance floor, Dan. God knows what he saw in me, I was dressed in land girl uniform with green corduroys and a thick green jumper. But we none of us had a lot of clothes. He was big and bold, and kind and caring, and when he went back to the States he didn't know we'd started a baby between us. It's funny really; I always thought Jen would be the one to get into trouble, but of course she was too wise for that; it's always the innocent ones that get caught out.'

Dan, coming back to the present, looked at the old face lying on the pillow. 'I'm glad ye fell in love, Millie. Everyone should have someone special. Let me wipe your face and settle ye on those pillows. Ye can tell me some more of your adventures tomorrow. I enjoy hearing them, but ye need to rest now. Would ye be liking a drink?' He eased her forward, offering a sip of juice and expertly turning the pillow over to provide a cool smooth surface for her head.

'There ye go.' He tucked the soft coverlet over her and quietly pressed the booster to give her a few mil of pain relief to counteract the effects of the movement. He sat holding her hand while he watched her drift off under its influence.

He glanced down at the fob watch on his chest; nearly four, he mentally calculated the effects of the latest bolus and decide he'd be able to let her sleep until maybe seven before he needed to start on the difficult task of bed-bath and dressing changes. He was on duty from nine to nine and he liked to have everything ready for the day shift.

Finally he sat back and picked up the novel he was

reading, but somehow couldn't concentrate. He kept thinking about the story Millicent had told him. He didn't know much about the Second World War, except for the war books he'd read and they mainly dealt with manly men killing other men.

This was a side he'd not really considered; the civilians. Millie had been talking to him all week about her past; it was something people did when they were aware of how short a time they had left, as if they needed to leave a legacy, but Millie, unlike some, was really interesting.

Of course he knew all about the Americans being stationed in England. 'Over paid, over sexed and over here.' his father had bitterly remarked when he'd once asked about it. His Dad hadn't been too happy about him joining the British Army either. But then he'd joined as a nurse and that had been even worse!

The way Dan saw it; it was a damn good job which, until the Crimea, had always been done by men, for men. He was just as capable as a woman of holding someone down and sticking a needle in them and, taken the right way, it was less embarrassing for a man to ask a fellow officer for a bottle to pee in, than to ask some slip of a thing.

But his Dad had never really understood. Accepted yes - but understood? Dan shook his head and grinned as he thought of the conversation when he'd announced his intention to become a nurse. He might as well have told his Presbyterian father he was joining a monastery; he'd have met with almost the same resistance.

'A nurse!' First the note of incredulity, then a horrified look had crossed his father's lined face. 'You're nae,' he paused, nearly choking and going beetroot red over the word as he'd all but whispered, 'Gay!' His father had looked furtively over his shoulder at Dan's mother serenely doing her knitting and watching Coronation Street.

'Nay Dad, I'm not 'Gay'. Dinna fash yersel, I just want to be a nurse.' Dan hadn't lowered his voice and caught the faint twitch of his mother's lips as she watched the TV. He didn't think Ken Barlow had said anything remotely funny. In fact he thought his mother was a lot more flexible than his father.

'For why? Would ye cast me forth if I was?' The question was said half jokingly but Dan, waiting for the answer, found he really wanted to know.

His Dad looked across at him, absently pushing breadcrumbs from their tea around the chenille table cloth with one stubby finger. 'I dinna ken lad. It'ud be damn hard to swallow.' He kept his voice low and looked seriously at his teenage son.

The placid Yorkshire overtones of his wife's voice filled the silence between the men - an odd contrast to their soft Scots. 'You'd love him just the same, Geordie Campbell, make no mistake about that!' His mother had folded her knitting as the theme music for the programme played and came over to the pair of them. She laid a work-roughened hand on each shoulder, looking down at the two serious faces, so similar, turned up towards her. 'Geordie, let be. It's what the lad wants to do; be proud of him, like I am.'

That had been the end of it. Dan had gone away to train and each time he went home he found his latest photo proudly displayed on the mantelpiece for everyone to see. They'd come to his passing out parade and his father, looking incredibly uncomfortable in his Sunday go-to-meeting clothes, which also happened to be a demob suit, had clapped as hard as anyone there. His parents had indeed been proud of him.

Dan sighed and picked up the book again. They'd died still proud of him and he missed their support. They had loved each other very much and showed it; Millie had had the same expression on her face when she'd talked about her James. He wished he'd found someone like that for himself; but it didn't look like it was going to happen now.

GRACE GORDON WAS ALSO at home in jeans, much more so than in the designer label suits she had in her wardrobe. Her first choice of footwear was the wellington, though she did concede that you couldn't beat a good pair of leather boots for dry weather. Today, however, she had had to attend a meeting to try and get more time and funding for the dig, so she'd made an effort and had dressed in her best 'interview suit' of soft green wool.

She'd combed her 'wash and wear' hair down ruthlessly, plastering the curls with water in a vain attempt to subdue them. This treatment had lasted for approximately five minutes, whereupon the curls, drying out, had bounced back to riot around her cheeks and head. It was like froth on a head of ale.

She'd even remembered to use a touch of lipstick, but had chewed it all off her pretty bow shaped mouth while waiting to put her case to the bigwigs; a pair of gold hoop ear-rings swung from dainty earlobes but these signified nothing, since they were a permanent fixture.

It was nearly half five as she entered the bedroom of Millie's tidy little house, bearing a small bunch of pink and gold honeysuckle that she'd found growing near the dig.

'Hi darling, how are you feeling today? You look a bit tired.' She bent and caressed the elderly cheek before planting a kiss on its cool surface.

Millie smiled up from her semi prone position. 'I'm not in the least tired and even if I was I can't waste time sleeping when I have you coming to see me, darling.' She raised a hand and in turn patted Grace's cheek, 'My don't

13

you smell nice.'

'It's not me it's the honeysuckle. I just shot through the shower after I left the dig; I didn't remember to put any scent on.' Grace grinned down disarmingly. She waved the honeysuckle, 'Vases under the sink are they?' Millie nodded and watched her granddaughter leave the room in her usual impetuous fashion.

When Grace returned she gazed around looking for a space to put down the small crystal vase. She noted the neat trolley of spare bedding and dressings pushed to one side behind the door, and the old fashioned dressing table with its large mirror opposite the window. This was reflecting the sunshine back into the room, making the yellow and blue paintwork bright.

'Put them on the window ledge, darling. Then the warm air will blow the scent around.'

Grace wandered across and stood for a moment after she'd set the flowers front and central on the sill. She moved the soft, and faded, velvet curtains, their creamy colour hazy from much washing. 'It's still a beautiful day out there, Aunt Millie. Hopefully it'll dry up some of the mud I've been wading in these last two days.'

'Have you found anything new?' Millie, her honey-gold eyes sparkling, tried to wriggle up the bed a bit more and Grace came over and placed an arm under her, lifting Millie's slight frame effortlessly into a more upright position.

'It's slow work at the moment. We've uncovered several bits of Samian ware and lots of medieval stuff, but nothing else in my line so far.' Grace eased the lace-edged pillow under Millie's shoulders. 'Did you look at the coin?' She shed her suit jacket and sat down on the side of the hospital bed, careful not to jolt Millie.

'Well I looked, but I can't make it out. It's a Pontin of the third century but what it's doing up here in

14

Hadrian's country I don't know.'

Grace sighed, 'Yeah. I'd come to the same conclusion. I'd better take it back and put it with the other finds.' She carefully picked up the coin from the side table and put it in a small plastic box.

'I showed it to Dan.' Millie looked a bit guilty; she knew that she wasn't supposed to let anyone else handle it.

Grace exchanged a conspiratorial looked with her, silver grey eyes flashing mischief, 'Well I won't tell anyone if you don't.' She tucked the box away in her jacket pocket and threw the coat to the end of the bed. 'What did he make of it?'

'He said he couldn't figure out how come the Romans were so careless with their money, always dropping it for people to find millennia later. And he wants to know what the 'point is' anyway.' Millie grinned at Grace, 'Point is!'

'Yeah I got the joke, but it's so feeble and ancient it's a wonder it didn't expire. It's almost worthy of David.'

'Not that he had any idea what a Pontin was, mind.' Millie continued, 'I told him it was a kind of Celtic coin found down south, mainly in the Kent area, and that nobody did know what its point is, though everyone has their own theories.'

They grinned at each other, 'I'm not sure what kind of drugs you're on, Aunt Millie, but they're certainly bad for your sense of humour. Pontins!' She muttered to herself, but the silver eyes glinted as she looked affectionately at her relative.

'I like him, Grace. He's a really good nurse.'

'Hey, only the best is good enough for my favourite aunt.'

Millie felt the now familiar guilt rise up and looked at the serene face of her grand-daughter. 'You know I could

15

have stayed in the hospital for a bit longer, it must be costing you a fortune to have me at home with agency nurses and this special bed.'

Grace looked lovingly at the worried face. 'I knew you wanted to come home and I want what you want.' The smile she offered was a bit crooked, 'We know it won't be a big drain on my finances.'

Millie smiled back equally sadly. They both knew that she wasn't going to recover from the breast cancer; it had gone too far before she'd admitted something was wrong.

'It is nice to be in my own room, with my own things about me, and while Mary is a nice little thing, I do feel safe with Dan. I feel secure when he lifts me.' She paused, then grinned wickedly across the duvet, 'I do like having a man about the place.'

'Well I did have my doubts about a male nurse when the agency sent him. You don't find him doing the personal stuff embarrassing?' Grace cast her a sidelong look.

Millie looked at her with a strange smile. 'It isn't my generation that's straight-laced, darling.' She patted the young hand holding hers and looked at Grace. 'It's all a matter of what you're brought up with, I shared a bedroom with my parents and I bathed in front of the fire. We might have tried to be a bit private but houses weren't big enough to be that prudish!'

She watched the faint colour wash over the pretty high cheeks. 'I know what a man looks like, and I'm past caring what a man thinks of my body, darling.' She grinned 'I don't think Dan would find it that fascinating anyway. And besides; he's always a gentleman.'

Grace smoothed the covers and they sat holding hands. 'OK. But if you get uncomfortable you just say so. I want you happy.'

After a moment Millie smiled 'So, tell me about the progress. You said they had found some Samian ware. Is it all little bits or can you make a guess at what kind of pots you've found?'

'Oh that's not my department. Kate deals with that. Hey, do you want to hear David's latest joke, I don't know where he gets them from,' She grinned, 'it's as terrible as usual.'

Millie looked at her eagerly. 'OK. Tell!'

'He says they've found some hardened criminals in Pompeii Jail.'

'You're right. It is terrible.'

'Well you know David.' They both groaned even while they grinned. Then they settled down to talk about the archaeological dig that Grace was currently working on just outside the town. Millie had been fascinated by Roman remains ever since she was a child and discovered that a Roman fort had been built in her neighbourhood. Granted only a small pile of stones, half-wall, half-path, remained in the Stanwix area, but that was enough for Millie's active imagination. She had passed that love and imagination on to Grace.

Grace loved coins but was actually an osteoarcheologist. The dig had found one femur and the bones of an inner ear. As with all human remains, once the coroner was sure they were ancient, a qualified archaeologist had to remove them. The student who had found them originally had been disappointed but resigned when Grace had taken over the little patch of earth.

It was proving to be slow and painstaking work but finding the stapes had proved that it was worth the effort. Grace was hoping that they might find some more of the human remains but sieving so far hadn't turned up anything else and she was beginning to think that might be all they were going to get.

17

Today's meeting wasn't just to beg for money, but to beg for extra time; the finding of a body might just gain them those extra days. The area was being cleared for redevelopment and while the archaeologists dug the contractors champed at the bit, even if they were being generous in the loaning of heavy plant machines. Grace couldn't help thinking this was just to speed things up.

The few precious bits of human remains so far discovered, however, didn't seem to be in the right area. 'The bones shouldn't have been inside the camp. Romans don't bury their dead inside.' She mused.

'I don't think the area has been robbed out, but I suppose it might have. It's certainly true that the stratigraphy is a bit odd; that could be ploughing, which would explain the state of the Samian ware, or rabbits which wreck any chance of relative dating and leave us to fall back on modern technology.'

She grimaced, 'I've been doing this job for eighteen years and I still hate rabbits and their burrows. They can undo a theory faster than a panel of university professors when they start to burrow through a site.' She smiled down, noting the tired look growing. 'Shall I get some tea, and what could you eat?'

Millie shook her head, 'I'm really not hungry, darling. But you need to eat something; you're still a growing girl.'

Grace looked down at her figure; without the severe tailoring of the jacket the soft blouse emphasised her nicely curved person. The slightly flared skirt was short enough to show off her long shapely legs and the low heels gave her just that little bit more height, making her look casually elegant. But all she saw was a bust she considered too big and thighs with too much muscle. 'If I grow much more I shan't fit into my clothes!'

As Grace wandered away Millie shook her head, closing her eyes for a minute and listening to the sounds of activity in the kitchenette. She could hear Grace whistling some popular tune as she filled the kettle and then the rattle as she got dishes from the cupboard.

Millie sighed softly; they might both know that her time was nearly up but she hated to leave Grace alone. It wasn't the financial aspect that worried Millie; she had worked hard all her life and Grace, now she was doing freelance work, wasn't exactly poor. It was the lack of relatives that worried Millie. She'd learned what it was like to cope without emotional support early in her life and her few close friends were very precious; she didn't want Grace to have to suffer the same loneliness.

Grace came back into the room bearing a tray set with delicate china. 'I know you said you weren't hungry but one of the girls made some scones for elevenses, so I snitched one for you, and I thought you might like just a few raspberries. I know they're your favourites.' She set the tray down and assisted Millie into a more upright position before settling the tray on her lap.

It was a very small meal but Millie only picked at it even so. She smiled apologetically at her granddaughter. 'I'm sorry, darling.'

'Doesn't matter.' Grace set down her own cup and saucer on the side table and lifted the tray, setting it on the floor before seating herself on the bed again. 'It's just...' She shrugged, looking across the sheets at Millie 'Well, while I see you eat I can kid myself a bit longer.'

'Yes, I know.' Millie reached out a hand and clasped the ones resting in Grace's lap. 'I do worry about you, Gracie, what will happen to you when I'm gone. I wish you had a good man to look after you.'

'Aunt Millie, you know I'm not the marrying kind. Who'd want someone who was more at home in a hole in the ground than in a...' she paused, seeking the right venue, 'Night club? Kitchen? Bedroom?' She raised an eyebrow and the tension of the moment was broken as they both giggled. 'You see I don't even know where a man would want me.'

Dan, entering on this ambiguous statement found that he could have answered the sentence without any trouble at all. The scruffy young woman who he had seen occasionally over the last week had been replaced by someone he found he could want in any of those places, and quite fiercely too.

Her casually friendly smile as she greeted him caused a reaction that had his body sitting up and begging. He stepped carefully around Grace, draping his light jacket over his arm and allowing his body a bit of privacy. He'd argue with it latter about its unseemly behaviour.

He nodded to Grace, then spoke to Millie, 'I just popped in to check the drugs with Mary. Is she back yet?' Mary normally did a split shift, going away at two and returning at six to help settle Millie for the evening.

'No, Dan. I said she needn't come back till seven as Grace was going to be here.' She smiled fondly up at the young woman. 'Grace can throw me about the bed, if I have need, almost as well as you can.'

Dan nodded his understanding even while he involuntarily looked more closely at Grace.

'Hey, I'm not a Sumo wrestler you know!' She gently punched her aunt's arm.

Dan had to agree with that. From where he stood Grace had curves in all the right places, none of them superfluous. He found himself involuntarily assessing her figure even while he replied, 'I'll come back later then.'

'Oh, no! Stay and keep us company,' Millie smiled up at him. 'unless you need to get more sleep.'

'No. I've done sleeping for the day. I dinna sleep more than six hours when I'm doing nights.'

Millie looked slightly appalled, 'Don't you get

tired?'

Dan shrugged, 'It goes with the territory, Millie. I'm a free agent; I dinna ha' to do nights. I dinna ha' to work at all if I dinna want to.'

Grace looked him over while he was speaking. She'd naturally been present when he'd first presented himself, but she hadn't really noticed him. She'd been too busy coming to terms with the fact that Millie was coming home to die, to really see anything besides the fact that he was male and a nurse.

Now she observed him more closely while he exchanged a little gentle banter with Millie. His hair appeared to be a soft, red fuzz on his head. He was obviously freshly shaven, the skin that soft pink that came with the application of an astringent lotion. She gently inhaled musk and something else. Mmm nice! The deep blue eyes fixed on Millie were not just assessing, but he was obviously listening to something she was saying and finding it funny. The crows' feet round his eyes crinkled as he smiled.

His accent was odd; sometimes he'd come out with a phrase that was more Coronation Street than Taggart. Weird! She thought there was a soft highland burr too; it revealed it's self in the r's and w's and the odd word. It added a definite sexiness to it.

'Grace.' Millie arrested her wandering thoughts, and they ought to be arrested, thought Grace.

'Yes, Aunt Millie. I'm sorry, I was wool gathering.'

'I said I'm fine, why don't you go and have something to eat with Dan? I'll be OK 'till Mary comes.'

Grace looked affectionately at her relative. She had been the target of her match-making efforts before and, though Millie thought she was being subtle; Grace considered her about as subtle as a chainsaw.

'I don't think so, darling.' She turned her head up

21

to look at Dan and they exchanged a small smile. Evidently he understood Millie too, even in the short space of time he'd known her. 'Dan has better things to do with his time off than listen to me talk about dead people.'

Dan looked back, his face serious but a smile lurking at the back of his eyes. 'I can talk about dead people too. I've passed all my exams!' He raised a quizzical eyebrow.

'Well talk about speaking of hanging in the house of the condemned!' Millie looked at them - a tired but very broad smile on her face.

'Oh! Auntie.' Grace's horrified tones were echoed by Dan's 'Millie, I'm sorry.' Both of the younger people looked embarrassed, but where Dan had a definite red tinge over his cheek bones, Grace went a delicate pink that Dan thought made her look like an adorable cherub.

Millie smiled at them both, 'Don't be sorry my dears, I'd rather talk about it, than go around with a glum face and hushed voices. We all know I'm dying, but I ain't dead yet, and you've both given me a laugh tonight.'

She gripped her granddaughter's hand, 'I love you, Gracie; now go away and talk about dating.'

Grace could feel the heat seeping into her cheeks, 'Auntie Millie!'

Millie, observing the pink tide surging up, laughed again. 'Well I was talking about relative dating at the site, darling.' Her lips twitched, 'I don't quite know what you were thinking of.'

Dan wagged a finger at her, 'You're a wicked owd woman and I could date ye.' He paused, gazed off into the distance as if thinking, then said, 'Mmm! I think it must be Georgian, all those flirting milkmaids and wicked earls!'

Eyes sparkling, Millie grinned back at him. 'I think we'd better stop before she expires from heat exhaustion.' She nodded at Grace sitting with her hands over her, by now, very red cheeks, looking ready to explode as the other two laughed at her.

Dan patted the free hand. 'Content ye, Millie, I'll be going. I ha' to eat so that I can cope with ye this night.'

He swung round; the words popping out of his mouth before he could stop them. 'Would ye like for to join me for a meal, Miss Gordon?'

Millie smiled across at her granddaughter, 'Go away, darling. I'm tired.'

Grace, looking slightly conscious-stricken, stood up, pulling her skirts down over her knees, much to Dan's amusement. 'OK, I know when I'm not wanted.' She leaned over and whispered for her relative's ear only, 'Leave the poor man alone, darling.' before planting a kiss on the soft cheek. Then she turned to pick up her jacket, only to find Dan was holding it out for her to slip her arms into the sleeves.

She shrugged it on while Dan's nostrils twitched and were tantalised by the indefinable scent that was Grace.

Dan turned his attention back to Millie, casting a trained eye over his patient while mentally muttering, 'Down boy.' Millie did look tired, but she looked happy too. 'Are ye needing anything?' he asked softly.

Millie lay back against the banked pillows, shook her head and closed her eyes.

The couple walked out quietly, not speaking until they had closed the house door behind them.

'Don't feel obliged to feed me just because of Aunt Millie's machinations.'

'I dinna do anything I dinna want, Miss Gordon. I should be delighted to be taking ye for a meal if ye'd be wishful.'

Dan stood outside the house, the curl of

anticipation in his stomach coming as a surprise to him, and waited for Grace to speak.

'I don't think so, Mr Campbell.' Grace looked up, and up some more. She hadn't realised just how tall Dan was until that moment. Normally she looked into the faces of most men she met.

Dan felt the disappointment right down to his toes in their sensible size 10 Doc Martens.

'I have some paperwork to deal with and I'm sure you have better things to do during your off duty time than provide meals for middle aged women.'

Grace turned and, walking to the curb, opened and got into a small Mini Cooper. She drove away with a neatness that left Dan standing on the pavement with his mouth slightly open and a feeling that he had just stepped under a cold shower unexpectedly.

'Well lad, that put thee in thy place!' He muttered as he watched the exhaust fumes dispersing in the summer dusk. He glanced up at the window of the house, seeing the curtain stirring gently in the zephyr. He hesitated for a moment and then walked away towards the centre of the town with the idea of finding food and a place to think.

2

DAN PRESENTED HIMSELF AT nine that evening, neat in clean jeans and sweat-shirt. 'Hi! Mary. Sorry I missed you earlier; I was going to do the drugs so you could leave on time for once.'

Mary was five foot one in her stocking feet. She'd graduated three years before and loved the challenge of agency work. She smiled up at her colleague now with an impish grin on her heart-shaped face.

'Oh! I heard all about you being here earlier. Miss Armstrong told me you went for a meal with her niece.'

'Actually I dinna. Miss Gordon had t' paperwork to do.' Dan looked a bit uncomfortable.

'Oh!' Mary pursed her lips over that snippet of information. She thought the woman must be mad; here was this hunk of manhood just waiting to be snapped up and Miss Gordon turns him down to do paperwork. She wished she had the chance!

'On reflection it was probably just as well. I doubt me it would have been really appropriate anyway!'

Mary thought he must be a bit mad too. Miss Gordon wasn't his patient. Still if he didn't fancy her, maybe he could fancy a nurse! She pulled at her short summer dress; being in mufti on this job meant she could show her figure off to its best advantage. After all they had lots in common; she batted her mascara daubed eyelashes, hiding the hungry look from him, but Dan didn't appear to notice. He'd turned away to get the drugs chart out of the file.

Mary gave him another considering look. She had to admit he was the best nurse she'd ever worked with; maybe he was gay. She eyed him speculatively while he was busily getting the drugs out with his back towards her;

it was a shame if he was. It would be, in her youthful opinion, a terrible waste.

'Now, Mary, I think aside from the continuous infusion we need to have some in reserve, the pain is definitely increasing. I've left a message with the doctor's surgery to review and possibly increase the dosage. I also think we need to consider the possibility of constipation if we do that. If the morphine is increased ye'll be needing to monitor her breathing more and perhaps we might think about getting an oxygen tank brought over from the hospital, just in case. The metastases' in her lungs are beginning to bother her a wee bit more too; there's more breathless episodes.'

Mary, dragged back from more amorous thoughts, gave a mental shrug and listened attentively. Whatever she thought about Dan's sexual preferences he was a far more experienced nurse than she was and she could learn a lot just from sharing the nursing with him.

Mary left shortly afterwards; she would have been astonished to learn how accurately Dan had read her expression. He'd been aware that the label of homosexuality would be levelled at him even before he entered the profession; hadn't his father been the first of many to suggest it. He had met most kinds of coquetry, had several invitations from frustrated males and had become adept at avoiding the looks and therefore the involvement. When all else failed he was either incredibly verbally or physically blunt to get the point across.

He dated occasionally but found that service life made it difficult to form long-term relationships. Just when he'd start to think seriously about a girl he'd be moved to a new area and phone calls and letters never seemed to continue long after that; so he'd stopped trying and now kept things very casual.

He came through into the bedroom after closing the door and smiled across at his patient. Millie was resting

26

quietly, her eyes shut and a faint smile on her face. He turned to close the bedroom door and, turning back, found her brown eyes resting on him.

'Hello, Dan, did you have a nice evening?'

Dan walked across and picked up her chart on the pretext of seeing how she was progressing while he thought how to answer.

'I didn't think she'd go out with you.'

Dan looked up, startled at the soft voice. 'I didna think I was sae bad looking as a' that, Millie!'

'Oh, you aren't; it's my Gracie that's got the problems.' Millie sighed. 'She's convinced herself that she's a middle-aged frump and working with pretentious and self promoting males most of the time doesn't exactly give her lots of confidence in herself.'

Dan shed his fleece and folded it carefully, putting it over the back of a chair so that he could deal with Millie more freely. She allowed herself to be lifted up the bed and continued talking as Dan dealt with the night-time routine. 'Archaeology is full of socially challenged people, Dan.'

Dan, who was busy undoing the thick plait of hair that coiled down her back, gave a chuckle. 'And are ye thinking nursing isn't, Millie? Half those in nursing are there because they needed, desperately, to be needed, ye ken. The other half thinks they can solve the problems of the world single-handedly.'

He reached out a long arm for the hairbrush and began to work through the long silky strands, teasing out the few knots that she'd acquired over the day. He started to braid it back up with all the care of a mother as Millie sat patiently in the bed. Finally he pulled out a dark blue ribbon from the drawer of the night stand and fastened the end.

'Do you want a fresh nightie?' He moved over to the small dressing table and brought back a frothy confection, laying it down on the end of the bed. Dan tried to be as impersonal as possible with the female patients he worked with, helping them to maintain as much dignity as possible while conserving their strength for the more important task of getting well.

He fetched a bowl and helped Millie wash her hands and face then turned to the task of giving her back a rub. Dextrously he slipped one item of clothing off and the other on. 'My that's a bonnie dress; it frames a bonnie face too.' Dan smiled down at Millie.

'And there was me telling Gracie you were a perfect gentleman, Dan.'

Dan looked faintly astonished, 'And is it no gentleman-like to tell a lassie she looks pretty!'

'Well not when she can't reciprocate without compromising the gentleman.'

Dan gave her what Millie considered an old-fashioned look and changed the subject.

'Could ye fancy a foot rub?' He settled her back against the pillows and held up a bottle of baby oil.

Millie nodded. 'I'm getting really spoilt. You'll make it harder to let go, Dan.' It was said rather sadly, and Dan looked at her from the foot of the bed where he was placing a towel under her feet. 'Feeling low tonight, Millie? Was it me that upset ye then?'

'No, Boy, I'm just a bit low. It was talking about James last night. I was thinking I'd never get to say sorry, and we did part on bad terms. But I don't know where he'd be now, even if he's alive.' She sighed deeply. 'I would like to tie all the ends up before I die, Dan; we quarrelled so badly before he left and he's rather a loose end, if you see what I mean.'

Dan nodded, pulling up a chair and seating himself before pouring a little oil into his hands and warming it before beginning to massage the soles of her

feet. 'Would it help to tell me what you quarrelled about?'
He concentrated on working the sweet, scented oil into her
feet, allowing her to talk without feeling she was being
watched.

Millie sighed, part in appreciation of Dan's
ministrations and partly because it all seemed so silly now.
'There were so many reasons really, maybe it was a
cultural thing, and maybe we just weren't compatible. I
don't know. The first thing was the hoard. Remember I told
you I found a hoard?

'Mmm!'

'Well it was while I was a land-girl. It was in 1945,
I'd known James about four or five months then. VE day
had been maybe a week before, and the war was just about
over; but you see the rationing didn't stop then, if anything
it got worse. So we still carried on planting things. I rather
liked the planting. I wasn't too fond of the weeding
though!'

Dan changed to the other foot. Millie had small
feet, no bunions or corns and he could feel some of the
tension draining out of her as he worked his thumbs into
her soles and she lost herself in the past.

'Well one day, it must have been June or July I
think, we were mounding up the early potatoes, but I don't
really remember what month it was, anyway I dug the soil
around this plant piling it up. When I knocked the soil off
the spade one lump stayed a lump, if you follow? It was a
soggy summer rather like this one.'

Dan watched Millie as her eyes took on the far
away look. 'I stood on the lump to squash it but it didn't
squash very much and I caught the gleam of metal, so I
picked it up.'

'It was a bit of leather, wrapped around a lump of
metal. I called across to the next row. "*Jen, come and see
what I've got.*"'

'What is it?'

"I dunno."

Jenny dug her spade into the soft black peaty soil and jumped over the row. "I'm six inches taller working on this stuff!" She turned her foot up and examined the large clump of earth stuck like a platform heel to her hobnail boot.

"Oh never mind that. Look at this!" I held out the dirty lump for her inspection.

"Yeuk! I'm not handling that. It's bad enough we have to deal with slugs and worms, I'm not handling someone's old sock!" She glanced around her, "Throw it away, Millie."

But I didn't. I didn't think it was an old sock at all. I knew it might be something interesting. Jenny was still looking around, "And this is summer!" she shivered as a grey cloud obscured the weak sun that was trying to break through and disappeared again. "I wish it would warm up a bit. Then we could go somewhere nice for the afternoon."

Jenny had always had an eye for the boys; for that matter they'd always had an eye for her. I used to just go along to make it all respectable.

"I'm going with Harry to the museum. Are you coming?"

They took us to all sorts of places on our Saturday afternoons off. When it was raining we sometimes went to the museum. It was free and warm, and we could claim that we were doing something educational.

I didn't like playing gooseberry but since the advent of James I'd had company of my own. However, for once I was eager to go to the museum and would like to spend some time there on my own. "Yes, what time are you going to meet him?"

"'Bout two. Get a move on, then, old Sourpuss can't grumble at us having a bit of time off!" Jenny jumped back over her row and began to dig industriously, piling soil against the green potato shoots and shaking the soil off her fork like a terrier shaking a rat.

I turned back to my mound, but not before I'd put the strange lump in my overall pocket for examination later.

We only just got away in time to change. Sourpuss, aka Miss Jean Newton, was indeed sour that day; she had iron grey hair, large black rimmed spectacles and orange lipstick, and she'd didn't have any men knocking on her door.

While Jen was washing in the bathroom I examined the lump. It was coins. I thought I recognised one from some I'd seen in the display cabinets at the museum. I tried to prise them apart but only a couple came away from the lump. I hastily put the whole thing under the corner of the mattress as I heard Jenny coming back down the corridor.

We changed rapidly, taking turns at the fly-spotted mirror to do our hair and use the little bit of make-up we possessed.

"Jen, where did you get that bit of lipstick?"

As I sat on the iron bedstead waiting for her I admired the rich red she was applying with a steady hand. She looked at me slyly, "You really don't want to know, Millie."

"Oh!" I knew she had some friends who dealt in the black market. She came home with extra sugar sometimes and the odd pound of sausages. I didn't like to ask what she'd exchanged for them.

Not looking at her, I smoothed a pair of socks, repaired to the extent that the original colour was all but lost in the darns, with a careful

31

hand. "Jen, we've been friends a long time." I said slowly as I looked at her face in the mirror. She continued patting her waves into place. "I love you lots, Jen. Be careful."

"Yes I know you do, Millie, and no, I haven't done anything silly." She looked back at me, addressing my reflection as she pushed a slide into place among the soft hair. Then nodded at the socks, "You've already put spare toes on the ends of those, love, I think they've about had it."

I nodded, "But the extra thickness will keep my toes warm a bit longer," I pulled them on and then put the hob-nail boots back on. It wasn't elegant but as I'd said, it was warm.

"Did you catch a load of Sourpuss' face when I said we were going to the museum?"

"What was she muttering about anyway?"

"Her Anderson shelter's flooded again. I could have told her it wouldn't be any good in her back garden. She was bound to go below the water table, living down near the river Eden."

"I heard of one man who kept his fish from his fishing trips fresh in his, it had flooded so much." I grinned at her. "I suppose she wanted us to lend a hand digging it out again."

Jenny shrugged, "I can't think why, they're not dropping bombs now."

We left the house and Jenny lit a cigarette and offered one to me as we walked down the street after lunch. We both had cloth jackets and the rather silly hats that were issued to land girls. Jen had a feather in hers that she'd found in the field and dyed a nice green to go with her jacket. Underneath Jenny had got her best skirt and blouse on. I wore slacks and a re-knitted jumper and was glad of its warmth.

I looked her over as we left the lodgings, "Jen, if you'd said you could have had some of my stockings, I've got two spare pairs from James."

32

Jenny looked at me, and then down at her legs, "What gives it away? Have I drawn the line crooked?" She craned her neck back critically examining the line. "I used the patent tool."

I looked at her shapely calves, admiring them and assessing the line drawn on in black pencil with a strange stirrup-shaped tool issued by Max Factor. The line appeared straight against the tan coloured cream she'd applied. "Nooo! It's just that I don't think that shade of blue is you."

Jenny shivered, "Well it's going to rain and I'm cold, Millie."

"Then why didn't you wear slacks the same as me?"

"Because I'm meeting Harry of course!" She sighed in exasperation, "Millie! You have to make the best of yourself, even in these times."

We walked up the street towards the centre of the town, me clicking along in my hobnails and she clacking in her heels. There wasn't much in the shops, except perhaps the Red Cross shop. That had some very venerable items in it. We stopped for a moment to look at the display in its window.

We could see a pair of football boots and a cricket bat, an old fire companion and a pile of books set on a small velvet stool. I pointed, "Oh look, Jenny, there's a couple of Ethel M Dells. I wonder if I've read them." We both studiously avoided looking at the boots; they meant some mother had finally got up the courage to dispose of a dead son's possessions.

Jenny sighed gustily, "You should be thinking of real life romance, Millie, not reading about it in some dusty book." I thought guiltily of the last time I'd been out with James. Maybe it was the thought that someone might have to dispose of our possessions, but life seemed too short not to pack in experience where you found it. We'd all gone to the Palace and James had become quite

33

familiar, with a lot of promiscuous kissing going on in the back row. He'd done more than that on VE day. Unbeknown to Jenny I was experiencing quite a bit of romance.

I could feel myself blushing and ducked my head a bit so that the brim of my hat shaded my face. "Well I'm going in. Are you coming? We've got a bit of time." I glanced at the man's watch on my wrist. "It's only quarter to two."

"Oh alright then." Jenny took two hasty pulls at her cigarette and carefully pinched out the remainder, putting it in her pocket for later. We entered and sniffed air redolent of mothballs and must, with a faint undertone of stewed tea.

The lady in the shop was a member of the Women's Royal Voluntary Service. Her accent was very upper crust but she smiled at us nicely from under her green hat. A lot had changed during the war; she wouldn't have given us the time of day before it; now we were accepted as equals. "Hello, gals, what would you like to buy today?"

I pointed out the books in the window, "I'm not sure if I've read them, can I have a look?"

"Of course you can, my dear." She fetched half a dozen and stacked them on the counter; then went back to her former task of folding sheets. "One of the ladies has just brought these in. Do you think they'll turn sides to middle or shall I put them aside for bandages?" She shook one sheet out and the source of the smell became apparent. We all looked critically at the sheets. They were definitely much worn in the middle but the edges didn't look a lot better, having almost a fringe round the hem

Jen and I shook our heads. The WVS woman shook her head as well. "Yes, that's what I thought. Shame really, we need some decent material. But these were probably on their last legs even before the war." She smiled nicely at me, nodding her head at the books. "Do you want them? They wouldn't have gone in parcels; the boys don't read romance much. I can let you have the lot for a shilling."

I found a shilling in my purse while she tied them together with a piece of string. As we left she was folding the sheets and putting them away in a box, shaking her head over them as she did so.

We carried on towards Tullie House, its door invitingly open. "Hi, Harry." Harry was a tall RAF mechanic from the nearby airbase. He had a beautiful smile that was slightly marred by his crooked teeth, green eyes and the fresh look of a peach topped by black curly hair.

"Hi, yourselves. Jim says he'll be along in a bit, Millie." He turned to Jenny, shaking his black hair off his forehead. "So what shall we look at today? Stuffed birds and bugs, or paintings?"

"Oh I'd like to go into the library." Jenny gave him a wicked grin which Harry returned. "I'll see you in the Roman section then." I said as they headed through the big brown doors of the adult library, past the bust of Robert Burns.

I went outside and round to the museum entrance, passing the sunken shrine in the flower garden. The museum was redolent of lavender floor polish and the strange musty smell of old artefacts. I turned into a room with Roman remains displayed. Altars to Jupiter with their IOP carved at the top and headless bodies on stands. There was a small display cabinet of Roman coins and I wanted to get a closer look at them.

Mr Hogg the curator, a tall, stern looking man, was in his office; but I really hadn't got the nerve to talk to him about my find. I thought they might be Roman coins but I didn't know much about them at the time. Blists Park, where our potato patch was, was near enough to Hadrian's Wall and the Carlisle Castle for the coins to be Roman.

I was scanning the glass cases trying to memorise all the different kinds when James came in. I smelt his Brylcreem and the carbolic soap as he took hold of my hand and I felt the warm palm with its calluses rub against mine.

"Are you looking at coins again?"

I smiled up at him delighted to share my news. "James," I lowered my voice, whispering as I looked around, "I've found some coins while I was digging this morning. I wanted to see if I could identify them."

His response was everything I could have wished for. "Where? Have you got them with you? Let's have a look, darling."

"Not here, I've got them back at my lodgings. I think there's one of those." I pointed out a silver quadrans of, according to the label, Augustus Pius. James was fascinated, "Did you know they used to chop them in four." He indicated the coin, which was a bit triangular. "If they hadn't got enough change. Like those loaves I sometimes see in the shops."

'The next time I saw him I gave the coins to James. He said he'd get them cleaned and dated and tell me what they were, but he never did, and I was so disappointed. That's one of the things we argued about, Dan.'

Dan, dragged back from the glimpse of a past over before he'd been a twinkle in his father's eye, never mind born, shook his head as if coming out of a trance. 'Wow Millie!'

He looked down and found he was nursing her feet in the palms of his hands, having long since ceased to massage them. To his dismay he found they were quite cold. 'I'm sorry, Millie; I was that caught up in the story.'

Millie smiled along the length of the bedclothes at him. 'It's nice to have an audience, but you must be bored silly, Dan.'

36

Dan smiled back, 'Never think it, but let's get ye tucked up for the night and get these feet of yours warm.'

He whipped out the towel and pulled the covers down, then went to warm a wheat-pack in the microwave. Coming back he looked Millie over carefully. 'Is the pain worse, Millie.'

Millie nodded. 'But I hate being so drowsy I can barely think, Dan. I'd rather have a bit of pain and be able to think straight. I don't want to spend my last few weeks in such a haze I don't know anyone.'

'OK. But ye dinna need to think at this time of night.' He paused as the microwave pinged. 'I'll be back on the instant.'

Returning with the small bag which smelt faintly like a loaf mixed with lavender, he carefully placed it near her feet, and tucked the covers in. 'How's that, cosy?'

'Mmm, nice.' Millie wriggled her toes experimentally under the covers.

'Right now I want ye to get some sleep, Millie; I'll ha' another talk with the doctor in the morning. We can do somethin' about the pain without knocking ye out. Trust me on this.' Dan smiled down at her. 'I'll be here all the night, I'll ha' a think about your James and see if there's any way we might be able to track him down. Would you like that?'

Millie nodded. 'Yes, Dan. I really would.'

Dan settled down in the low green nursing chair at the side of the bed, pulling the nursing notes towards him, fishing out a pen from the breast pocket of his white shirt to write up some of the nursing cares. He'd been busy for a few minutes when Millie spoke. 'Dan.'

'Hello, are ye still awake?'

Millie offered a tired smile, 'I'm a bit scared too, Dan.'

Dan stretched out a hand, offering the comfort of human contact, 'Yeah, I know, Millie, we all are when it gets right down to it.'

Millie held his hand looking at him seriously, 'Even you, Dan?' Dan looked at her, his eyes serious and sober 'Och, aye, especially me. I'm a soldier. I've thought I was going to die, even though I was officially non-combatant. I've watched men die, slow and fast. It's a scary business. But think, yons just another adventure, ye can tell me some more of yours tomorrow. I promise ye'll be here and so will I. I want to know what else parted ye and yon beau.' Dan held her hand and eventually saw the old eyelids flutter shut and felt the hand loose its grip on his. He gently tucked it under the covers.

He had seen men die, some fighting every inch of the way so that the whole messy business was deeply distressing for everyone watching as well. He'd seen some die with calm faces and a sort of inner peace. He figured if you put on the uniform you took the risk of being killed. But however it happened it wasn't a very dignified affair. All he could do was stand on the sidelines, cheer them on, and ease the passage.

He got up presently and made himself a drink, pulling his fleece back on as the early hours caused the temperature to drop. He moved around the room quietly and went to stand looking out over the moon drenched, front garden where Grace had stood the afternoon before. Eventually he flopped into a Queen Anne chair that, like the old queen, stood straight backed against the wall.

It was a quiet street in the suburbs of the old town where each house had a pocket-handkerchief lawn and a border of privet hedge. Millie's house was at the end of the row and had a side garden too. There was a patch of turned earth but Dan couldn't see anything planted in it by the light of the fitful moon. He looked at the houses opposite but it seemed that everyone went to bed at a respectable hour around here; the only night life was represented by a couple of prowling cats.

He became aware of the scent of the honeysuckle as it released its heady aroma on the night air and delicately touched a forefinger to the blossom releasing more scent to draw in a lungful, then thought of the young woman who must have brought it and sighed deeply; she really had got a spectacular figure which he and his body had appreciated enormously.

'My Grace brought it this afternoon.' Millie spoke into the silence as he sat with his back sideways to the room

'What, are ye awake again?' Dan swung round looking across at her in the dim night light, ignoring her comments on the flowers.

'I'm a bit thirsty I think.'

'Will ye tak' some tea?' Dan held up his mug.

'That would be nice, Dan.'

'Alright, tea. But nae talking; ye need t'sleep, Millie.'

Millie nodded. Dan went into the kitchen but as he brought the tea back asked, 'Do you like her, Dan?'

Dan didn't pretend not to understand. 'I hardly know her, Millie. And I dinna think she liked me o'er much at all.' He offered a wry grin, 'She certainly gave me the bum's rush this afternoon.'

'She's shy and a bit scared too.'

'Aye, Lass, it's something the whole human race suffers from. We're a' good actors under the surface. Now drink your tea and go back to sleep.'

Millie drank up and handed him the mug, obediently closing her eyes. Dan put the mugs on the side and sat down again next to the bed, the chair sighing slightly under his weight and weariness closing his eyes.

After a minute a warm, soft hand crept into his and squeezed it lightly; without opening his eyes he returned the gentle grip.

'Whist, Millie.' He murmured

A faint chuckle came from the bed and the silence closed in again.

Dan sat thinking, Yes, she was a bonnie thing was Grace Gordon. It was a pity she didn't seem to like him at all. For he thought he might like her a lot, if his body's reaction was anything to go by. It had been a long time since he'd felt the urge to bed a woman, he mused.

He'd learnt the hard way to keep such urges under strict lock and key. It wasn't just the health risks either, though as an army nurse he'd seen plenty of sexually transmitted diseases and even the odd case of AIDS; he was forever, it seemed, preaching safe sex. It was the whole emotional thing he thought. If you couldn't offer to be there for a woman when she needed you, it left you both vulnerable to temptation. So it was better not to get involved.

He sighed again, but the chance would have been nice.

GRACE WASN'T HAVING AN easy night either. She'd lain in bed for a good two hours until she felt she knew both every vein in her eyelids and every crack in the ceiling plaster. She sat up, switching on the overhead light and bunching the pillows up behind her back. The mirror on the wardrobe reflected her face back at her and she thought for the hundredth time that she must move the bed out of its direct line.

She averted her eyes from the image a trifle guiltily. She was having to deal with an unexpected problem. Rumours of the death of her libido had

40

apparently been grossly exaggerated. She shifted in the bed a bit uncomfortably. This would never do! Scrambling out hastily, she felt under the bed for a pair of soft mules.

She'd lied about the paperwork and that was weighing on her conscience. She found the picture of a certain Scotsman's face floating across her inner eye, superimposed on the images of the heads of perfectly innocent Roman coins, surprising. Hadrian clean shaven and sans his laurel leaf was a bit disconcerting to one of her disciplined mind too.

Getting up she pulled on a filmy negligee over her shoulders, to match the ecru coloured, satin nightshirt. It was a hot night she told herself. And she was worrying about Millie. Then she sat down at the desk in the corner gazing at the blinking light of the standby on her computer. She shrugged; who was she kidding? It was that man!

She pushed the books away from the front of the desk and sat staring into space while she tried to understand what her mind was telling her. OK, so he had a good body, and he smelled better than some of the men she'd worked with. His voice was a pleasant growl, its gentleness sending an unexpected shiver down her back when he'd been speaking to Millie. But she'd heard pleasant voices before. John, on site, had a great voice and when in the mood could entertain the whole dig with a song.

Maybe it was the mystique of the caring profession; like doctors and vicars. Weren't you supposed to fall a bit in love with your doctor? She shook her head. He wasn't a doctor, or even her doctor, so that didn't work. Maybe she needed to get out more. Maybe she needed to stop thinking about him.

'You're just sex-starved, Grace Gordon. The poor man would be horrified to think of you lusting after his body.' Grace grinned, and then gave a shudder, 'God

41

forbid the man should even suspect I've been thinking about him like this.

'What's more I'm obviously cracking since I'm talking aloud now!' She pulled the books back towards her. 'It's a shame some of these museums haven't got everything catalogued; it might help to know why that Pontin was there and in such good clean condition. We've got the sixth and the ninth legion, but neither was stationed down south that I can find. Auxiliaries - maybe that's where I need to be looking. Now let's see if I can remember which auxiliaries might have been around here in that time frame, and where they came from.'

She sat pouring over the books for twenty minutes but wasn't any further forward. 'Oh Hell!' She rubbed a hand over her wild curls, making them curl even more wildly. 'I can't concentrate. Will you get out of my head?' She closed her eyes tightly; the image of Dan sat firmly behind her closed eyelids mocking her efforts.

She looked across at the clock. Two o' clock; coming rapidly to a decision Grace stood up and began to dress, pulling on jeans and polo shirt and fastening a stout pair of boots on her feet. She grabbed her old red waterproof as she shot out the door. Ten minutes later she was in her little car headed across the town to the quiet countryside on its perimeter where a hole in the ground represented the latest activity of modern man to understand his ancestors.

The streets were nearly deserted. The odd group of teenagers roaming in the centre of the town had given her a momentary qualm. But this far out nothing much stirred, not even the wind. She parked neatly, taking a torch and a strange piece of metal with a nice wooden handle attached, off the passenger seat, and going towards the metal gate in the boundary fence. The fence was partly to protect the farmer's field in which they had their site, and partly to protect the public and the odd cow or two, from falling in the holes.

Fishing in a pocket of her jeans for the keys to open the padlock she discovered they wouldn't be necessary. It was open and swinging on one of the bars. Tutting to herself at the carelessness of some of the helpers, and vowing she'd have a word with them later that day; she pushed open the gate and walked confidently along the dusty path.

The moon was nearly full tonight; her shadow walked in front of her, playing hide and seek under the trees as she followed the path around the perimeter of the site. Grace sniffed the air. No rain, just dust and the faint tang of the Solway Firth estuary away to her right. She looked up at the sky, making out the constellation of the Plough as it dodged out from behind a cloud.

She approached quietly, her feet scuffing up little puffs as she walked. The moon was causing the clouds to chase their shadows across the open fields to her left and throwing an old World War II pillbox into stark outline, and she paused for a minute listening to scuffles in its shadow and the quiet coughing of a sheep. She didn't head down into the shored up area though; instead, switching off her torch, she stood accustoming her eyes to the darkness. When she was confident that she could see well enough for her purpose she carefully held the rod out in front of her.

She'd used dowsing to locate things before, but it wasn't exactly an orthodox approach. She had a reputation for being able to pinpoint remains, which she owed in part to the dowsing, but in the somewhat sceptical world in which she worked she wasn't going to admit that; however, she saw it as no more of a tool than magnetic survey, geophysics or aerial photography methods.

'Now,' She murmured to herself, 'let's think dead Roman bodies; not live Scottish ones, Grace.'

She slowly began to pace over the ground, her whole attention focused on the area in front of her feet, and her concentration became fixed on the piece of metal. She was walking away from the ladders; which was why she didn't see the man's head rising quietly above the parapet or his eyes watching her; first with puzzlement, then astonishment.

Philip Jardin had served his time for manslaughter, he'd even had the time reduced for good behaviour, but he hadn't given up his job. It was too profitable and he had a client who used him, and others who would take whatever he could steal. Sometimes he even stole to order. He cautiously watched Grace now; he'd heard of dowsing but never seen it before and he thought it would be a great gift for a man in his profession.

He couldn't afford to be seen. He'd seen the young woman before. It took him a few heated moments to recognise Grace. She might be fifteen or so years older but he'd know that hair anywhere and he thought she might just recognise him. If she did she'd know exactly what he was up to. He wasn't a man who liked violence. The accident all those years ago had been just that; an accident. The job and the client were the same though, and he paid well and sometimes, as now, in advance.

Grace suddenly stopped with her back to him and he waited expectantly for her to mark the place. When she continued to stand still he wondered if she'd heard him, or just what had claimed her attention.

She bent over and started to move the rocks at her feet into a little cairn. Philip was only prevented from rubbing his hands together in a frenzy of expectation by the knowledge that he'd fall backwards if he did.

He didn't dare to move as Grace turned around and began to walk back towards him. The moon chose this moment, however, to disappear behind a cloud, and he took the chance to duck down and feel his way down the ladder again, swinging under it and hugging the sides of the pit. He could hear her feet approaching and the sweat popped out on his forehead and began to roll down his face.

Grace was humming quietly to herself as she walked over to the excavation. She looked down as she neared the edge, seeing the various levels and neat Wheeler box grid laid out and the piles of buckets and scrapers over on the far baulks partially covered with a tarp. She stepped back and lowered herself to the ground, swinging her legs over and allowing her boot clad feet to bounce against the back wall like a small child.

She leaned back on her elbows, gazing up at the night sky, watching the stars wheeling overhead amid the racing satellites desperately trying to hide behind clouds, then peeping out again like children in a game of hide and seek. She looked back into the long flat worked area; she liked the dig best when no-one was in it. She could people it with long-dead armies and listen for the faint echo that was left by their passing. She relaxed, laying back and stretching her arms up and her hands behind her head, watching the face of the man in the moon.

Jardin, underneath her, was wondering what on earth she was doing and praying she would stop it and go away very, very, soon. He watched as her legs slowly stopped their quiet drumming and stilled and he shivered in the damp air that heralded the morning dew. He'd got to get out and away before the dawn light revealed his position.

He started a stealthy climb of the short ladder, pausing at ever creak and stray night noise. Eventually his head emerged a mere three feet from where Grace was dozing on the edge. He pulled himself up, all but crawling along the ground to prevent the rustle of clothes from disturbing her as he stood up.

Finally he considered himself far enough away. If it hadn't been for curiosity both of them might have escaped unscathed. He just couldn't resist looking for the spot where Grace had built her cairn. He tripped over it, banging his knee and gave a muffled grunt and Grace, half waking, turned and slid into the pit.

Philip heard her yell and then a lot of very unladylike swearing and concluded that she was relatively unharmed by the four foot fall. He took to his heels as if pursued by a bear even as he thought it, limping and cursing all women under his breath as he headed to the gate.

Grace crawled up the ladder and stood at the top rubbing various parts of her anatomy so recently admired by Dan. She looked down her rather dirty person and laughed, 'Well that was a damn stupid thing to do. Talk about mooning about!'

She also began to limp her way towards the gate. Having gained the entrance she turned and carefully padlocked the gate, watched from nearby bushes by a curious cat who'd abandoned his pursuit of a harvest mouse, much to the mouse's relief. And, from a parked car, by a man with a very sore knee who was hoping not to become the pursued; though he did have a passing resemblance to the mouse around his teeth and jaw line. Grace turned and got into her car and drove away with a slight clashing of gears.

Philip watched. He'd debated going back in but thought the chance of remaining unseen now that the dawn was definitely lightening the sky, to be very slight. He drove away, following Grace at a distance until he saw her turn of into a small street of flats, then he continued driving. Philip thought he might return to the dig that night to find out just what Grace had been dowsing for; and if it was worth stealing.

3.

GRACE ARRIVED AT THE dig at half past eight that same morning finding she was limping slightly as her buttocks, which had stiffened in the intervening hours, objected to the climb down into the excavation. She greeted her fellow workers with an impish grin; she knew she might have to explain the large scratch down her arm and hand, and was only grateful that they couldn't see the even larger bruise on her dignity.

'Hi, John, how's it going?'

'Well the sun is shining and the local school has promised us some sixth formers for the grunt work, and I'm a dad; so I guess it's going good.'

Grace looked at his serious and good looking face, 'How's the kid?'

'Oh! Mother and baby doing well; they come home tomorrow; I've got some new photos on the mobile. Wanna see? They're even more beautiful today!' said the besotted father.

Grace grinned across the pile of earth at him as John fished in an inside pocket. John had grown from a gangling teenager to a strong man. He'd chased girls relentlessly for much of his twenties and early thirties until one had finally caught him a couple of years ago. His Sandra had presented him with a baby the week before and everyone had to look at new photos every day.

Grace admired the small squashed specimen which she didn't think looked any different from yesterday's photos. 'Yep, beautiful.'

John looked at them himself and a silly smile wandered across his face, coming to rest in his eyes. 'Aren't they just!'

'John?' Grace, chasing an errant train of thought, dragged his attention away, 'Can I ask you a personal question?'

John gave her his quiet smile, assessing her face, 'Fire away, but I don't promise to answer.' His lips twitched.

Grace looked at him standing in a pool of sunshine and rain water, a few grey hairs glinting and the grey-green eyes serious now. 'Why didn't you ever hit on me in all the years we've known each other, John?' She felt herself getting warm but held his eyes as she waited for his answer.

John rubbed the back of his neck with a hand, screwing his face into a comical expression, then used the same hand to help her over the puddle so that they both stood on dry ground: a small oasis of tranquillity in the centre of what was about to become a very busy area. ''Well now, that's a curious question coming from you.' He looked her over, 'I could counter with why do you want to know?'

'Oh, it doesn't matter.' Grace started to turn away, but John caught an upper arm, holding her as she would have moved away. He'd seen the embarrassment, but something else too: hurt or maybe fear of the answer.

He looked at her as she turned back to him, looking pointedly at his hand on her arm. 'And that look, my lovely Miss Gordon, is partly why I never hit on you.'

'I'm sorry, John.' Grace found herself blushing slightly.

'I said partly.' He let his hand drop, 'You're a lovely woman, Grace, but I knew you when you where barely a teenager, I couldn't make a move when you were so young, even if I'd been inclined, and by the time I might have, I was too fond of you in another sort of way.'

Grace stood with her mouth slightly open, looking

at him, 'You look like a stranded goldfish, Grace. Close your mouth. You are a gorgeous piece of womanhood, and if I wasn't madly in love with my wife I might even be tempted.' He grinned at her. 'I'd love to know what prompted that question though.' He raised a quizzical eyebrow. 'Somebody finally got past your barriers?'

Grace looked around in a relieved way as she heard the voice of her boss talking. 'I'm sorry, John, that was gauche of me, putting you in that position.'

'You don't believe me.' John's face mirrored his astonishment, 'Well I'll be damned!'

'Quite likely, John. Especially if you spend half the day showing pictures of that infant of yours. What don't you believe, Grace?' The accent was Oxford and the big man who'd just come to a stop beside them looked as if he would be equally at home amidst those gleaming spires; even dressed in cords, a thick jacket, and wellingtons, as he was today. He looked from one face to the other. He rubbed his beard with one hand while placing the other on his hip in what Grace privately called his 'Francis Drake pose'.

Both opened their mouths at once; John beat Grace by a short head, 'She doesn't think she's a beautiful Proserpina, David. That's why she freezes us all off.'

Grace gasped, 'John!' she could feel the heat rising up her body as if she'd just sat down in a hot bath.

David Walker looked her over in an assessing way as if she was a newly discovered artefact that he hadn't quite managed to catalogue yet. Then, totally ignoring her, looked at John. 'Well,' he dragged the word out, 'I would have said more Artemis myself, with just a touch of the three graces, though that's because I'm more partial to the Greeks than the Romans. But she definitely has a certain sort of something, I've always thought so. Ornamental, as well as clever at hunting for our particular prey.'

Grace stood frozen; looking from face to face as the two men, grins spreading across their faces, looked her over from her scarlet face to her green wellingtons. She could have stood in for an Italian flag.

'I,' she finally said, 'am going to start work. I've got a feeling about my body. I think we need to open a new trench.'

'No.' Her boss grinned widely at her, 'Your body definitely doesn't belong in a trench.'

Grace looked ready to thump someone. She turned her back smartly on the roar of laughter from the two male archaeologists and stomped away to organise the workers.

As she was arranging for the digger to scoop off the top layer of grass where she'd built her little cairn earlier that morning, David came over. He still had traces of the smile in his green and sparkling eyes but was wise enough to keep his thoughts to himself. 'So why do you think we need to look here, Grace? It's a good few feet laterally from where we found the femur, and the geophys' didn't indicate much when John went over it.' He tugged an ear and eyed the soil that was being exposed by the ministrations of the small back hoe of the JCB.

'Call it one of my hunches, David.' She looked him over carefully for signs of what she believed must be incipient senility. Nothing else she could think of would explain his comments earlier. He'd always seemed to be totally dedicated to archaeology, with whiskey as a second wife.

'Oh! Like that is it. Fair enough, your hunches have paid off before. But you'd better get the tarps ready; it's promised more rain for this afternoon.' He looked up at a sky from which the sun had disappeared and the clouds where piling like old grey rags. 'Have you got enough diggers and shoring?'

'I don't think I'm going to need shoring.' She

looked down at the four by eight area being exposed. 'And I don't want any extra diggers for the time being. Just in case it's a dud.' She grinned at him, and then waved at the driver to stop. 'I'm going to try step-trenching down to about five feet; we'll see what we've got then.'

David smiled enigmatically down from his six foot. 'Hmm!'

Grace felt herself colouring again and wondered why her face had chosen this week to act as a Belisha beacon.

'OK, I'll leave you to it.' He wandered away in that deceptive way that had new site members thinking he didn't know what was happening, until he caught them out in some crime of omission.

Grace pointed across to the driver and stood watching the JCB bucket chewing into a different part of the earth and piling the resultant spoil; and silently berated herself for asking John what she now thought must have been a really stupid question. It was all that nurse's fault. First he stopped her sleeping, and now he'd interfered with her working relationships. She worked up a good head of steam as the back hoe backed off and she stepped down into the shallow pit, slapped on her hard hat, and began to scrape away the soil.

She'd been scraping for nearly three hours with nothing much to show in the finds tray but the odd bit of medieval pottery, when her trowel hit solid stone and she slowed the pace to a crawl. She shifted from her seated position to her knees on the current 'floor' and reached for a small brush and pan. She had been working for several minutes when she became aware of David's presence. She wasn't in the least surprised to find him looking down into the hole, however, as she tipped the spoil into a small bucket.

She measured the distance back to the top with a professional eye, barely three feet. She leaned back on her heels and took in the exposed corner she had cleared so far. It appeared to be a bit of solid stone. This certainly wasn't what she'd been expecting.

'Got your body then have you?' Grace looking up at his face saw that he was serious, but then she reflected; he was serious when it came to work.

'I don't know what the hell I've got, David.'

David came down and stood next to her looking down at the solid rock; then crouched to examine the hard sandstone slowly emerging from the soft earth.

Grace leaned shoulder to shoulder with him, smelling the familiar clean earthy smell of male sweat and the Old Spice he still favoured for his aftershave.

'I think you're going to have to extend the step a bit. You can't possibly be at bedrock yet no matter what geophys indicates.' He shuffled back in the cramped confines. 'I'll help you shore it up; you're going to have to go a bit wider and deeper here.'

He indicated the area with a sweep of hand and at Grace's nod climbed out, temporarily blocking her light with his bulk as he disappeared from view. Grace blinked as a few clods of earth slipped back down and cascaded on her head. David was right, she needed shoring. She hated it when he was right and she was wrong.

She remained sitting on her heels, gently scraping the soil away and piling it into the bucket until David returned with a couple of the young students. Then she climbed out herself while they set about the task of making the pit safe to work in. She stood sipping water from a bottle and watching the progress with David, who smiled across at her.

'So how is it going then? Still think you're going to find a body?'

'Dunno, David, the soil isn't as impacted as I'd expect for that stone to be at the medieval level. It shouldn't be there, it's too far across for the village midden; and anyway we found that. It might be a well-lid I suppose. There's the Tudor manor, according to the aerial surveys John did, somewhere over on this side of the village.'

She shrugged, pushing back her yellow hard hat. 'He spotted what looked like defences around that side,' she swept a wide arm, 'so this could be either part of the Vicus, the Roman or medieval fortifications, or part of the Manor. They're all piled on top of each other at this point, which makes dating the finds easier here so long as you know what you're finding!' She gazed back across the dig at the areas of the small medieval village they'd exposed a few days before.

'Between the ploughing and the rabbits, the whole area's a mess. Not to mention half the stones have been robbed out to build other things.'

'Yes, John was telling me he thinks he might have found an early Punic profile ditch with a later defensive ditch on top. I don't know if it's worth putting a trench across to confirm that's what it is. It would certainly help to date to second century.' He rubbed his beard and Grace heard the soft rasp. 'It's outside the contractor's area so there's no hurry to excavate; I'm inclined to leave it. We've only got so much time!' He sighed.

David squinted down into the hole where the young men had nearly finished, with a great deal of grunting, in getting several posts into the soil. They appeared to be struggling with the placement of the last but one.

'Hold it lads, let me come down!'

'What you spotted, David?' But Grace spoke to his departing back. She peered over the edge eagerly, trying to see, but the hole was becoming decidedly crowded.

David emitted a muffled yelp and a not so muffled

swear word. 'Go up, give a man room!' He began to scrape away the area where they'd been struggling with the post. Grace, unable to resist, swung her legs over and dropped into the hole with a shower of loose dirt.

'Hoi! It's my hole.'

'Yeah, and you've got something that definitely isn't medieval in it. It maybe a Tudor well-top as you say but I don't think this bit is.' He raised an eyebrow with the look of a school boy finding someone else had got some swap cards he wanted, allowing Grace room to wriggle alongside him and begin to carefully excavate the area.

They worked companionably together for the next half hour until David sat back on his heels and leaned against the wall. With a wave of an aristocratic hand he said. 'Go for it, it looks like a modern tin box to me. God knows how it came to be here.' He snapped merrily on his digital camera, recording as she continued to excavate.

Grace felt her heart drop into her boots. A modern tin box sitting on a possible well-cap wasn't exactly what she'd been hoping for, but it did explain the softness of the earth. She worked down the sides of the rusty and battered box, loosening the remaining grip the earth had on its latest treasure until she could lift it free. She gently released the final edge and wiped away the clinging soil. She and David look at her prize with astonishment. 'Cream Crackers!'

'Well that's what it says on the side.'

Grace shook it slightly and then, at the resultant slight sound from inside, looked across at David with a glow starting in her eyes.

'OK, let's get on top and see if we can have crackers for lunch.' David climbed out first then leaned over the edge and took the box she handed up to him. He set it gently on the ground and reached for his camera, 'Let's get it on record.'

John, who'd been keeping a weather eye on the hole into which his colleagues had disappeared, now came across the ground at what, for him, was a run. As he moved others from the team looked up and started to converge on the pair at the edge of that morning's new pit.

David kept the camera in his hand as Grace wrestled the rusty and slightly bent lid from its bed around the top of the tin with the aid of her heavy Swiss pen knife.

'Careful! You don't want to cut your fingers and spoil exhibit a.'

'And there I thought you loved me, John.' Grace, however, did turn the edge of the knife away a bit as she prised at the metal which, with a squeal from the body of the tin, lost its grip, sending the lid sailing away to land with a plop in a puddle.

'Well it certainly isn't a Roman body.' David drawled as he gazed into the tin. 'It looks like old newspapers.'

He glanced around at the crowd of eager student archaeologists. 'Come on boys and girls back to work. We'll update you as and when. This weather isn't going to last much longer.' The group moved away reluctantly in two's and threes under his quizzical and up-raised eyebrows. 'John, can you do the honours with the tape measure. Grace, with me.' He loped away, scooping up the tin lid in passing, heading towards the large garden shed they were currently using as a document and finds store.

Grace followed in his wake, threading her way round the grid pattern site of other people's diggings, with her precious prize in her hands. She pushed open the door and set the box down on the wooden table.

Kate, a post grad' student, was already occupying the room; she was seated on a hard wooden chair at the corner of the table and looked up at their rather precipitate entrance. She leaned forward, carefully blowing on a detailed drawing she had been making of a pot she was extrapolating from a small red shard of pottery, then looked at the pair of them.

'Hi, Kate, how's it going?' Grace smiled at the serious young woman.

'Fine. W…what have you got for me this t…time?' Kate brushed back the red hair curling against her cheeks and adjusted the large glasses on her freckled nose.

'I'm not sure she's got anything for you, Kate.' David barely glanced at her as he spoke and Grace watched the twenty-three year old shrink at his suddenly abrasive tone.

Grace smiled nicely across, 'Come and see anyway, Kate. Everyone else has had a good look. I found it in my hole and David's laying claim to it. It certainly isn't the rest of the Roman body I expected to find.' She twinkled across at her Boss.

David grunted and, putting on protective vinyl gloves, began gently to extract the paper from the tin. 'Make yourself useful then!' He addressed Kate somewhat testily as he nodded at the neglected camera.

Kate hastily picked it up and began to angle the lens as, barely breathing, David unfolded the crisp newsprint. 'It's the Glasgow Evening Herald.' He started to read the headlines. 'On the Day that Peace Broke Out'. VE day. It doesn't look as if it's even been read!' Turning, he grinned at Grace, 'What we have here, I believe, is the genuine article circa 1945, my dear.'

Grace looked into the box. 'Here Kate, get a photo of the contents so that I can disturb them.' Kate obligingly clicked the button half a dozen times.

'Right David, can I start lifting them out? I think this must be someone's time capsule.' David was fumbling in his top pocket for the pince-nez that he kept there. He glanced across, 'I'm pretty sure you're right there, Grace.

You look at that; I want to look at the paper.'

'If I lay them out, Kate, can you photograph from several angles?'

'Sure. W…wait while I get some gloves on then I can t…turn them over.'

Talking quietly to one another Grace and Kate lifted out the few items that had been nestling under the paper like chicks under a hen.

They were just removing the final item, a Blue Cross Match-book, when David returned his attention to them. 'So what have you got, Grace?'

Grace felt Kate shrinking against her. Really the poor girl is terrified of him, she thought. 'We've got mementos of the 2nd World War, David.'

She swept a hand to encompass the finds. 'Wills Woodbines - one packet of five, price 2d, unopened; one Baby Ruth chewy bar - United States issue, unopened. Hmm,' She looked across at Kate with a grin on her face, 'wonder if it's edible!' Kate pulled a face as Grace continued to enumerate their finds.' One sample bottle of Grants' Whiskey, a dram, unopened. That should interest you, David.' She offered the other girl a smile but got a blank look in return. 'A small pen knife of an unbelievable bluntness, a wad of pencil approximately two inches long, a whistle, your paper, David, and a nearly used ration book with a few sweet coupons left in the back.'

'Ration Book got a name?'

'Well the writing was black ink, but it's now rusty brown, and it's not very clear but I think its 'MacKay'….and possibly 'Ian' but I wouldn't swear to that. It's got a number so we might be able to track it that way.'

David looked over the finds while the two girls stood watching him. Eventually he spared Kate a brief glance and said 'Got all the photos?'

'Yes, sir.'

'Don't call me sir!' He snapped at her and Grace felt the slight tremble that went through Kate's body.

He turned away immediately and started issuing instructions to Grace as to the proper preservation of the find. Then ended up saying, 'I'll log it for you, Grace, if you want me to? Why don't you get back to your hole and see if it is a well-cover, before the rain descends on us.'

Grace nodded and spared Kate a look, catching a surprising one back. Kate was looking at her with something akin to hatred. She shivered. What had she done to upset the girl now!

Grace looked back at David. 'Sure, David, that's fine.' Some imp of mischief prompted her to say. 'After all, you probably remember most of this stuff!'

Kate uttered what Grace later thought of as a gasp of dismay.

David gave her a filthy look, and said somewhat testily, 'I'm not in my dotage yet, Grace. I wasn't born when this lot was around. I didn't even qualify for a ration book.'

Grace left the room to a silence thick enough to deaden a heavy metal band.

'I DON'T KNOW HOW much I've got but this bit appears to be a skull.' Grace gently touched the smooth brown bone she'd just revealed as David stood on the edge looking down at her some five feet below. She had managed to clear the remaining soil and reveal an oval sandstone cap. With a bit of pulling and tugging and digging, and the aid of another student, built like a pocket Atlas, this had lifted to show a definite well shaft in reasonable condition.

'Any water down there?'

'No. Dry as a.....well, as this bone.' Grace smoothed the skull again.

'Can you date the well shaft?'

'Not my area, David. I'd say Roman, at a guess, with this kind of stone and mortar; but I think you'd better come down and have a look yourself.'

'Finish with your skeleton first. I'll get the camera while you work.' David loped away with surprising speed as John wandered over. 'Oh! Great!' He stood looking down into the five or so foot deep pit of the hole and shaft. 'Can I bring the youngsters over?'

'Sure.' Grace rubbed a grubby hand down her old blue jumper. 'Just don't let them knock the sides of the trench. I'm not sure which way he's facing. If he's an east-west alignment, which is what it looks like, then that puts him at a lot younger than the rest of the site. If he was buried here that is.' She grinned up at John, the pleasure of the find reflected in the glow on her face.

She turned back to her task, concentrating on the finicky and delicate task of exposing the human remains as rapidly as possible. She barely registered John's small talk on positioning of bodies and how much bones could reveal about the person; his life, diet, religion and, even, health.

David was quietly clicking away above with the digital as she opened up the area. Just occasionally he would tell her to stop while he took photos from a different angle. She nodded to Kate who'd been summoned to sketch the various areas of soil as they were exposed while the colour was still good in the stratigraphy.

Kate showed a remarkable ability to produce not only scaled drawings, but sketch the past in a way that brought the scene to life. She now moved carefully around the edge of the well, making notes before settling to making a detailed drawing of the position of the skeleton.

Grace stopped as the top of the skull was revealed.

She sat back on her heels and looked up at her boss, sitting on the edge like a kid at a fishing hole, 'I'd ordinarily say it was a Christian burial, which would put it at late third or fourth century, and we're almost sure this is a late second century site, David, aren't we? But something's just not right.' She pointed out some deep cracks and a hole in the skull. 'It could be post mortem crushing from the weight of soil but there isn't that much soil in here. I have a feeling…' Her voice trailed away as she looked back down at the mortal remains.

David scrambled down the steps she'd cut into the side of the earth, he waited for her to climb up the ladder she'd set at the side of the well; then stepped down himself into the four foot circle of stones and moved delicately down until he could get a view of the bones which were curled up in the centre of the well. He positioned himself so that he impacted as little as possible on the earth yet to be removed. He crouched down, examining the skull with as delicate a touch as Grace herself.

'Well, you'll know better when you get it out of the ground.' David nodded at the remaining area at the bottom of the well yet to be uncovered. 'As to the positioning, we know this was just a temporary camp, maybe it was used that way more than once. It's a typical typography for a practice camp.'

'If he's Roman he shouldn't be down this well, David. I wonder if he was thrown down and if it was before or after he died. He seems to be curled up like he'd gone to sleep!' Grace shook her head, 'I think he might have been a murder victim, the body landing naturally on its side.' David nodded again. He eased across and photographed the body from a different angle.

Grace stood back, allowing him to record the details of the levels she'd dug through. Then he smiled at her and prepared to climb up, 'Kate, do you want to come down and make a few notes?' It might have been phrased as a question but both girls knew it was an order. This was

David's site and he said who did what and when.

He climbed out, and then extended a hand to Grace, as Kate walked round the side of the pit and prepared to go down. They moved back to allow her access as John came over with some bottles of water. He handed one to Grace and sat next to David, who'd found himself an up-turned bucket. Grace took off her hat and dropped it on the ground, revealing wild curls plastered to her forehead from the heat of her exertions.

She sat gingerly on the side next to the two men. They all looked down at the skeleton which was slowly being exposed to the light of day for the first time for nearly two millennia and also at the down bent blue hard hat of Kate as she rapidly sketched and measured for the site notebooks.

Grace took a long drink of water then pulled a clip board over with the recording sheets attached. 'So just how did you get your hunch, Grace? I've seen you pull this stunt three times now and I'm blowed if I can figure it out.' Grace raised her head from the form she was filling in and saw the two men watching her. John waited patiently for an answer he didn't think he was about to get.

She offered a cheeky grin. 'Women's intuition, John?'

'Nah, I don't believe in that. You saw something or worked it out from the other info' we've got!' John shook his head.

'You might have seen her do it three times; I reckon I can count six. The first time I thought it was a sheer fluke, but I'll figure it out eventually.' David leaned back, his hands wrapped around one soggy and clay bedaubed knee as he gently rocked back and forth eyeing his young colleague.

Grace moved uneasily under the combined cynosure of their eyes, setting down the clipboard and pulling off her jumper in an effort to hide her face for a second. This had the unfortunate effect of revealing the scrapes she'd acquire the night before.

'Tetanus up to date Grace?' He looked pointedly at the horses in the far field. 'When did you do that?' Grace glanced down at the grazes which were now turning an interesting shade of blue.

'I fell over.'

'Looks nasty; what did you fall over? Are you going to sue?' He joked.

Grace, looking anywhere but at the two men and feeling incredibly guilty, muttered, 'I wouldn't dream of suing you, David. I fell into the dig last night.' She shifted her position again laying the jumper over a convenient spade dug into the ground.

David looked astonished. 'But you were my rep at the meeting yesterday afternoon!'

John wagged a finger, 'Aha! She comes and communes with the spirits of the dead after everyone's left. I was right; it's the goddess Proserpina not Diana the huntress, David.'

Grace took another gulp of water as the two men looked at her. 'I couldn't sleep that's all. So I came to see how you'd got on yesterday afternoon and I...well I lost my footing and fell in.' She moved from defensive to attack. 'Anyway it's a good job I did; you need to keep a better eye on the troops, David. The padlock wasn't fastened.'

David looked annoyed. 'I left last, Grace, and I locked up!'

'Oh!' She looked curiously at him; she didn't quite know what to say. She exchanged a puzzled look with John.

'It wasn't locked, David, honestly. It wasn't even

through the holes; it was just swinging on the gate.'

David shook his head like a bear annoyed by bees. 'I'm positive I fastened it.'

He rubbed both hands over his thick salt and pepper coloured hair and she heard the soft rasp as he pulled his hands down and rumpled his beard. 'I think I'll just check that everything was as it ought to be when we arrived this morning.' He grimaced, 'Where exactly did you fall so that we can discount that?'

Grace clambered to her feet as the two men stood up. David looked down into the hole, 'Stay there, Kate, and finish the drawings.' Kate, after a quick glance up and a small nod, bent her head again to her work.

Grace began to limp across to the main site. John on her left said, 'Land on your fundament did you, Grace?' and gave her a sly grin. Grace, however, was now looking at David as he headed purposefully towards his team, and didn't respond to the teasing.

He bent to his rucksack, pulled out an old bike hooter, and gave a couple of toots as they came up to him. People began to down tools and head in their direction as David moved to the centre of the site. 'I'm a little concerned folks. Grace came back last night and found the gate unfastened. Anyone know anything about it? I'm not going to bawl you out, so own up.' David looked grimly at the group.

The small group looked at each other then across at the big man standing before them. Heads began to shake. The younger element exchanged a few more glances then one of the young teenage men spoke up, 'Most of us were in the pub till closing time, David, then we all went back to the hostel together.'

A few of the older men looked perturbed, 'Why would anyone want to come back? It was a nice night but we'd all put in a hard day.' Doug, the site foreman, spoke for the majority.

'I don't know, Doug, but there's been so much theft from digs lately that I'm a bit concerned. I need you all to go and check your site records and, if you spot any anomalies, get back to me ASAP!'

The crowd dispersed to look at paperwork and compare it with the area they were working. 'David.' Grace looked directly at his face which had a decidedly worried look about it. 'What gives? Just because the gate was unfastened doesn't mean anyone's broken in.'

David looked at the young woman before him.' I want you to tell me what you were doing here last night, Grace.' He spoke quietly but very firmly.

John looked at the pair and began to sidle away. 'No, John. You're the most senior after me and something funny is going on. I've thought so for a few days but I couldn't prove it. Wait while I get the site notes.' He moved away and the pair trailed after him to the side where he'd left his rucksack.

'You see.' He pulled the clipboard out from under some protective plastic and started leafing through the reports. With a long elegant finger he stabbed at several notes pointing them out to the other two. 'Some of the measurements don't match from day to day. I've been checking and Kate does an excellent job.' Grace glanced across to the area she'd been working and wished that Kate could have heard that. David never seemed to offer that young woman any praise to her face.

'The young ones might have been a bit sloppy,' David was continuing, 'but not as sloppy as all that.' He handed the files to John and turned to Grace, 'Nothing's gone missing, except a Pontin,' he flashed a small tight smile at Grace, 'and I see that's returned. You'll have to tell me what your aunt made of it, Grace.' He paused, 'But not just now, tell me how you came to be here last night.'

Grace, taking in the seriousness of the situation, took time to marshal her thoughts. 'It was like I said, David, I couldn't sleep. So I thought I'd just come down and see what progress had been made. I got to the gate and it was unfastened.' She checked his face but David didn't look as though he was going to contradict her again.

She glanced around to ensure she wasn't overheard for the next bit. 'I had a hunch.'

'Wait a minute. What time was this?'

'About three,' She held up a clay and dirt encrusted hand to stem any other comment. 'So I went over the area with a dowsing rod.' John was listening as intently as David now; the two men raised eyebrows but said nothing. She looked at the faces expecting to see disbelief at best, mockery at worst, but they waited impassively for her to continue.

'Anyway, after I was satisfied I'd found what I thought should be there, I went and sat on the edge of the dig.'

'You went and sat on the edge.' David looked over her grubby person with faint disbelief and not so faint astonishment. 'Why in God's name?'

'It was a fine night and I wanted to think a bit!'

'It's the mysterious man, David. It's got her all unsettled!!'

David spared his colleague a withering glance before returning his intent gaze to Grace. 'So you wanted to think.' His face said what he thought of people thinking in the middle of a deserted dig at three in the morning. 'Then what?'

'Well I sat down and then I lay back to look at the stars a bit.' She rounded on John who'd covered a snort with a cough. 'Oh go away if you can't be more helpful!' She turned back to David who, without taking his eyes off her, said. 'Shut up, John!'

John subsided and Grace, who was going rather red, said, 'Look I know it sounds silly, but I've got a lot on my mind at the moment. Anyway I fell asleep.'

'You fell asleep?' Even David couldn't quite repress a smile, despite the gravity of the situation.

'Yeah I fell asleep; and then I must have rolled over, and I fell into the excavations, and if you think the scratch is bad you should see the bruise on my backside.' Grace glared at the men, daring them to laugh at her.

'OK.' David managed to keep a straight face, 'Did you see anyone about? Anything strike you as different or out of place?'

Grace shook her head. 'Nothing David, just the padlock unfastened.'

'OK, Grace. Get back to your skeleton. We'll see what others have got to say at lunchtime. It's nearly one now, break in half and hour.' David put the boards back under their covers and the two men separated to go round all those on sight, checking if anyone else had seen anything unusual when they'd started work that morning.

Grace went back down into her hole and continued to scrape away dirt while her mind was busy speculating. Of course she knew that theft of antiquities was big business. One of the big museums had had to close its doors to the public because half the stuff in the store rooms hadn't been catalogued and the artefacts were being stolen before the staff could do it.

But this was a relatively small dig, not like the high profile millennium dig the city had organised a few years back. What they were finding was just what you'd expect for a practice camp five miles from the main one. A few coins and pot shards from the medieval and Roman periods had turned up.

They hadn't disturbed the Tudor site much; there simply wasn't time and it wasn't an important farmhouse, as far as they knew. They'd put in a trench to confirm its position, triangulating to get the corners, and left it for future archaeology to reveal anything else.

The biggest find had been the human remains and until this morning they were so small as to be almost insignificant. They certainly hadn't warranted much of a write up in the press. So Grace couldn't think of anything a would-be-thief might be after.

She was so absorbed in her thoughts that she barely noticed the first few spots of rain. David's voice alerted her, however. 'You'll never get it out before the rain. Best cover him up and put a tarp over.'

Grace looked up first at David and then at the lowering sky. 'Oh help!' she all but yelped, as she took in the weather pattern. David came down and helped her lightly re-cover the bones with soil. 'Come on. Out you come!' He held out a hand as she clambered over the edge and, working together, they pegged down the tarp over the hole. 'I'd better put a fence round it. Don't want someone falling in again.' His grass green eyes twinkled as he looked at her, 'Go and get you jacket, you'll be soaked.' He shrugged into his own protective rainwear as he said it. Grace scooped up her jumper and left him to mark the site while she fetched her coat from the site office. Before she could leave it, however, others started arriving.

Everyone crowded into the small hut. It filled up rapidly and resembled the black hole of Calcutta, with bodies lining the sides of the walls, and the windows fogging up as the rain began to stream down outside. David brought the chattering meeting to order. 'Right folks! Go and get your lunch and if it's still raining at two make your way to the cataloguing area.'

One of the female students spoke up, 'Couldn't we excavate some more under canvas, David?'

'No, Alice. I said cataloguing and that's what I want done!' David gave her a sharp look. 'John will show you where to go boys and girls.' He nodded at John and the sixth-formers.

He waited while everyone filed out again, holding Grace gently by the arm as she prepared to leave with the rest. 'Just a minute, Grace.'

She gave him an enquiring look. David perched on the side of his desk, looking at her seriously, 'I've contacted the police to do a few patrols during the night, so you'd better not do any midnight walks for a day or two.' He smiled rather grimly. 'I'm probably just being paranoid but…'

Grace smiled back at him. 'That doesn't mean they're not out to get you.'

'Yeah,' he sighed, 'you know archaeology used to be such fun before it got all complicated with politics and culture. Now we've got people claiming that any human remains that we happen to pull out of the mud is their long lost uncle Jimmy and that we're violating their human rights investigating said body.'

'Is that what you think this is all about?'

'God knows! There has been a bit of a stink with the aborigines claiming back their ancestors.' He rubbed his head and shifted on the side of the battered tin desk. 'And I know what you're going to say, and I agree with it. The cases are different; those remains should go back. But you'll never get some people to see other remains differently. It doesn't matter if it's a Palaeolithic 'Lucy', or some hapless Roman; as far as they are concerned all human remains are sacred and we shouldn't touch them, archeologically speaking.'

'That's bunkum, David, there's so much we can learn now from even a bit of a skeleton.'

'I agree, but the current argument says bodies aren't artefacts and should be treated reverently.'

'I've got no argument with that, but we don't

68

exactly sling the bodies around like meat in an abattoir.' Grace paused 'It's difficult to set the upper, or do I mean lower, limit, David. When do you want archaeology to start? Last week, last year, last century? If it doesn't start until there is no written historical evidence of our ancestors then its last week for an Amazon tribe, and it shouldn't start at all for the Romans and Greeks.'

Grace looked at the frustration on his face with a certain amount of sympathy. The whole archaeological process had changed focus since David started; once they had just been happy if they could date things, now that was a relatively minor problem, everyone wanted to know what happened when, but now they speculated on the why too.

'Our little time capsule is archaeology to some people.'

'Yeah I know. And everyone's had a good look so it's bound to leak into the press. I hope that I'm just being paranoid.' He exhaled slowly then turned round as Kate came in pulling her notebook from under her jumper, her hair hanging in rats tails round her face and down her back where her hard hat hadn't protected her. She had a red streak of clay down one cheek as well.

'For God sake, Kate! Can't you take more care? Look at you, you're soaked!' He eyed the notebook she was laying carefully on the big wooden table in the centre of the room. He tossed a towel, which was laying on the desk, across to her and turned back to Grace.

Grace frowned at him. She hadn't realised that David could be so unchivalrous; he'd always spoken to her in a kindly fashion, even when he was being the boss rather than her aunt's great friend.

'Anyway, my dear, how is Millie?' She caught the shadow of the sadness he felt crossing David's face as he spoke softly to her.

'What can I say, David? She's still with us, but I'm not even speculating on how much longer she will be.'

'Yes.' He sighed, 'Well give her my love, and you come and go as you need to, Grace. If you want to spend more time with her you do it.' He held up a hand 'I know we're on a tight time frame here, but once the remains are in the lab you can work at your own pace. And believe me; you can't get these precious weeks back.'

David turned and left abruptly, leaving the door swinging after him. Grace looked across to Kate and found her gazing at the door with an expression on her face which Grace puzzled over for quite a while.

4

She'd left the dig somewhat reluctantly; it wasn't that she didn't want to see Millie, she did, but she wanted to work on the skeleton too. Going through the rain with her umbrella, however, had been like heading through a surfing tunnel; she expected to see fish looming on either side and was somewhat surprised when it was only John who emerged from the solid wall of water, hair dripping and clothes moulding his body.

'Hi.'

'Hi yourself, are you headed into town for lunch?'

'Yeah, I've got this longing for chips and runny egg yolks. The way Sandra makes them. I really miss her. I shall be glad when she gets out of the hospital.'

'You aren't expecting her to cook for you the moment she comes home are you?'

'Hey! I'm just a man.'

'Being a man is not an excuse - it's a confession!' Grace cast him a sidelong glance as he waded along beside her through the stream of red mud currently serving as a path. He grinned back.

'Actually her mum is keeping me well supplied with casseroles and things; but she's a health junky and I long for something greasy and bad for me.'

They reached the gate and John stood back for Grace to exit. 'Are you coming back this afternoon?'

'No.' Grace shrugged, 'I can't do anymore on my bo...' She stopped speaking as she noticed the twinkle in his eye. 'On the skeleton I've unearthed; with all this rain,' she said feeling, her cheeks warm. 'I think I'll go and visit Millie and tell her all about the time capsule.'

'OK, I'll tell David when I see him; I've got some nubile young women to supervise this afternoon.' He winked, pushing sopping hair out of his eyes, and became serious. 'How is Millie? I've not managed to visit since she came home from the hospital; what with Sandra and the baby and everything.'

Grace shook her head. 'Not good, John, she was only given a few weeks and they seem to be going frighteningly fast. It was lucky that David asked for me to work on this dig. I might have been down south, or even abroad, otherwise. I seem to have been away so much these last few years. If I'd been around we might have spotted the cancer sooner.'

'Hey.' John touched an arm lightly, 'Stop it! Millie loved that you travelled and had such a special job. She didn't want you living in her pocket. Knowing Millie I bet she wouldn't have told you even if you'd been here.'

'Yeah, John, my head knows that, but I'm having a bit of trouble with my heart.' She grimaced at him, blinking raindrops and possibly tears away. 'Go and have your lunch and don't worry. I'll be OK.'

She walked across to her car standing at the side of the road and John watched as she got in and drove away. He'd always thought of her as a self-sufficient career woman totally dedicated to archaeology. The new model that was emerging under the stress of these last few weeks was rather different and he wasn't sure he knew how to deal with her. David, coming up the path at this juncture, distracted him from his somewhat soggy reverie.

'What on earth are you doing, man?'

'Just thinking about women, David.'

'Well that's a singularly unprofitable topic; there's no understanding them at all in my experience, and I'm too old to begin trying now. I'll be in the site office all afternoon if you need me.'

GRACE PULLED UP OUTSIDE her door as the downpour changed from torrential to monsoon. She stood just inside the flat, dripping on the carpet and sniffing the air. The place smelt unlived in and damp, but there was another smell tantalising her nostrils. Nope she couldn't recognise it. She turned back, pushing the door closed.

She pushed the half closed umbrella into a drip tray near the door, hung her jacket up, and then trailed through to her small sitting room. It was comfortably furnished with a rattan and bamboo settee and chairs.

In the window alcove there was a small dining table with a top covered in books in various stages of disintegration, some laying open face up and some open face down. It was impossible to see what the table top looked like, for aside from the books two A4 notepads covered in her copper plate script lay amidst the clutter.

She ignored the untidy heap as she passed through into the miniscule kitchenette and grabbed the kettle to fill. As she turned to set it down she thought she heard her front door bang. Startled, she swung round, kettle in hand, and ran towards the door.

The door stood ajar allowing a puddle to form on the cork matting and the umbrella laying half in/half out of the door. Picking up the umbrella Grace pulled the door fully open and looked out, but the street resembled Bangor on a wet weekend, nothing stirred. Feeling rather silly brandishing a kettle and an umbrella she closed the door, replaced the brolly, and wandered back to the kitchen muttering to herself. 'David's got me as paranoid as himself but I could have sworn I'd latched that door!'

She set the kettle to boil and went into the bedroom to change. Here more chaos met her eye. She glanced across at the computer as her eye caught its standby light winking. 'I must be losing it completely; I'm positive I switched that off last night before I went out.' She

73

wandered over, shedding her damp shirt on the way and unhitching her jeans. She flicked the switch on the computer allowing it to shut down, then sat on the office chair to undo her boots and kick them off, standing up to wriggle out of the tight jeans and dropping them and her thick socks, onto the damp top, gathering the lot up as she made for her tiny bathroom.

Standing in bra and thong she looked at herself critically, mentally cataloguing her assets. A 36 bust with no sag, 'But' she muttered 'a C cup would have been better than a D', a nice flat stomach and, she craned round and looked at her bottom; aside from the bruising her butt looked trim and taut and not too bad.

She looked down at the despised thighs and sighed. 'Face it, Grace, you do too much walking and clambouring around to have nice thighs.' Having finished her self-inventory she shrugged at herself in the mirror. 'They were obviously teasing me, and I let them away with it.'

She grabbed the towel off the rail and had a hasty wash, rubbing briskly with the towel before she applied a bit of moisturiser to her face. She examined this analytically too, but where others saw classic lines in an oval face topped by blond tending to sun-bleached curls, she saw untidiness. The eyes that could change from stormy, sea grey to sparkling platinum examined a mouth that had tiny lines from smiling from cupid lips, all in all her face was something she regarded as adequate and not likely to send small children screaming down the street.

With another shrug she abandoned the search for whatever it was John and David had been talking about and covered the disparaged thighs in clean jeans. The bust was covered by a long and heavy red jumper usually stored at the bottom of the closet. She'd hoped not to see thick woollies until next winter and sighed a bit as she put it on. It had been a wet summer so far.

The ensemble successfully, she thought, hid the worst features and Grace, casting an eye over her bedroom, happily closed the door on it. She wasn't a good housekeeper; the dust bunnies under the bed where generally chasing her non-existent cat by the time she got around to hovering.

The kettle had boiled and switched off but she made instant coffee anyway, wandering through with the slightly tepid mug to the sitting room and looking at the jumble of books resting on the table.

Setting the mug down she picked up one of the notepads, and scanned the page. Oh! Yes! The paper on the incidence of syphilis prior to Columbus' return, she must get that finished or the publisher would be sending her impolite letters.

She sighed. There seemed to be so many demands on her time at the moment, it was just as well nobody fancied her, she wouldn't have the time to cook anyone chips and egg, not that she was much good at cooking anything as fancy as that. Her lips twitched, and she pulled a face as she finished off the cool coffee.

She made a dash for the car half an hour later and, climbing in, decided that she really needed to get a haircut as she looked in the mirror to check for traffic. Pulling away she was unaware that her departure was being watched from a car down the street.

'HI, AUNTIE MILLIE. HOW'S your day gone?' Grace entered shaking her head to dispel the rain that had managed to land between car and door. Her hair curled madly around her face as she smiled determinedly at Millie.

Millie looked at her sleepily. 'Not so bad, darling. They've given me some new medicine for the pain and it's making me awful sleepy, but Dan says I'll get used to it in a day or two and that it'll kill the pain but not my brain.'

She smiled tiredly at her granddaughter.

'Do you want me to go?' Grace looked down lovingly at Millie.

'Oh, no, darling, but I might fall asleep on you and I don't think I'll be very good company today.'

'Well that's alright. I can read the paper and sit still for once if you do drop off. I'm a bit tired myself.' She grinned down at Millie, determined not to let this new development make them both miserable, 'Shall I tell you why?'

At Millie's nod she pulled up the green nursing chair and relaxed against its high back. She began to talk about the previous night's adventures with her dowsing rod and the latest finds that morning at the dig.

Millie lay half dozing, half listening. 'It's odd. I've been talking to Dan about the war when I was a land army girl.' She smiled up at Grace. 'I was telling him about James. We spent VE night in a Morrison shelter together.'

'And who might James be, my lovely aunt, and just what is a Morrison shelter?' teased Grace lazily from her seat.

Millie, who had been drifting on a cloud of analgesia, suddenly realised what she'd said. She looked slightly horrified and Grace, mistaking her look of panic, moved closer to the bed. 'What is it, darling, have you got more pain?'

'No it's alright, just a twinge. Carry on with what you were saying, Gracie. Did you say there was a Baby Ruth bar? We used to get those from the GI's - they were very sticky, very sweet and, to a sweet deprived nation, absolutely delicious.' She smiled reminiscently.

Grace, after a few moments of hesitation, sat back in her seat and continued to speak about the dig telling her about the worries David had, and the fact that he knew that she had brought the Pontin for Millie to see. 'He sends his love, and so does John.'

'How's the baby and Sandra? Has she got over her pre-eclampsia OK?'

'They're both doing fine; I have to look at new photos every day. John is so proud of them both it's a wonder he doesn't burst all his buttons off.' Grace found herself growing warm with embarrassment as she thought of what she considered her stupidity in asking him foolish questions that morning.

'You know, darling, I quite thought he and you might…..' Millie stopped.

'Might what, Auntie Millie?'

'Might make a match of it.' Millie had a sparkle in her eye that Grace was glad to see. 'Especially after you met in such a dramatic way.'

'He was twenty to my fifteen, Auntie, and what's more all I did was hold on to him while David sorted out that slime ball Jardin.'

Grace patted the hand lying on the counterpane. 'Our paths might have crossed a time or two since he swapped to archaeology, but he's never seen me in that light.'

'How can you possibly know, Gracie?'

'Oh I have it on the best of authorities - his. He says I was too young to start with then too sister-like for him to hit on me.' Grace, following that bit of conversation to its ultimate conclusion, felt herself blushing.

'What extraordinary conversations you must have with men, darling.'

'And you were all full of maidenly modesty were you?' Grace watched the soft colour steal into her Grandmother's cheeks. 'James?' she said, softly teasing.

Millie smiled back but refused to be drawn.

77

'Would you like a drink, darling?'

'Is that a hint to change the subject or a genuine desire for liquid, Auntie?'

'Both.' Millie looked at her fondly.

'OK. Tea or juice?'

'Tea if you don't mind, love.'

Grace went off to the kitchen and Millie drifted off to sleep, so that Grace coming back with the tray found her breathing so softly that for a minute she just stood, watching, to make sure that Millie was breathing.

She sat down with her cup, her heart beating a rapid drum roll of fear, and sighed. She sat watching the beloved face and wishing she could turn the clock back or that she'd spent more time with her Aunt. Who, for instance, was James? It was obvious Millie didn't want to talk about him, but Grace wished she'd asked more questions when she was younger. There seemed so much she didn't know about Millie's past, and never would know now.

Millie dozed for nearly an hour and the miniature carriage clock on the bedside table said five before she began to stir. Surfacing, Millie open sleepy eyes to see her granddaughter watching her. There were still traces of tears on those dusky cheeks and Millie felt her own filling at the sight of them. 'Don't, darling.'

'I'm sorry, Auntie Millie.' Grace ran a careless hand across her cheek, brushing tears away and reaching for the box of tissues. 'I'm just being selfish. You're all I've had for so long now. I don't remember mum and dad at all and it feels like I'll be losing a part of me, and who I am, when there's no one to talk about them.'

She sighed and blew her nose and then took the old hand that was offered. 'I told John that you wouldn't have got sick if I'd been around.' She scowled at the memory of his answer.

'I'm a foolish old woman, darling, but I wouldn't have told you if you'd been living in the house with me.'

'Yeah that's what John said.' Grace pulled a face.

'He was right; I kept finding excuses for being tired and feeling wretched because I didn't want to admit something serious might be wrong.' continued Millie. 'I've always been a bit of a coward where illness is concerned.'

'If I'd been here I might have noticed sooner. Then I could have nagged you.'

'When has nagging ever worked on me?' Millie offered a very small grin. 'I liked boasting about my niece the archaeologist to the over sixties club. I got an awful lot of vicarious kudos from your globe trotting fame, darling.' She paused for breath. 'And I loved every moment of it. I wouldn't have wanted you to come home and stop doing what you love for me.' A small chuckle followed and Grace did her best to smile too.

Millie paused then said, 'What do you want to know about Polly then, Gracie?' Millie patted the hand of her granddaughter.

'That's the trouble. I don't know.' Grace sighed 'It's just knowing someone who knew them. I know they were both only children, but why did you get me instead of Dad's parents?'

'We're back to the war, darling. The family came from London and the blitz flattened their row of terrace houses. Greg was a baby then, they evacuated him first to Oxford and then near St Bees here in Cumberland so he was saved, and after the war they put him in an orphanage up here. He was nearly sent to Australia once.' Millie smiled 'I remember him telling me the thought of never seeing a building older than two hundred years filled him with horror. He said he wouldn't have met Polly either and that was an even more horrible thought.'

Grace smiled through her drying tears, 'You see it's

comments like that I shall miss.' She leaned forward, 'Did they want me, Millie?'

'Good grief of course they did, child. Whatever put that thought into your head?' Millie tried to sit up more and found herself panting a bit.

'I'm sorry, Auntie, I shouldn't be distressing you.' Grace eased her back on the pillows.

Millie lay back against the bank of lace and linen, her brown eyes serious as she looked at Grace's sad face 'Just because they didn't have you until they'd been married a while doesn't mean you weren't wanted, darling. You were adored by them both. I barely got a look in for the first six months. It took a lot of persuading to let me keep you while they went on holiday. They'd never been abroad and it was a special break. If you'd gone too I'd have lost all my family. And I loved you all very much.'

Millie opened her arms and Grace sat on the bed and was enfolded in the warm and familiar embrace of baby talc and lily of the valley. 'I'm going to miss you, Auntie Millie.' She gave a hard sob and the floodgates opened.

They sat quietly after the first fierce hug, Millie stroking the tight blonde curls and patting Grace's back as she hiccupped her way back to quietness. 'I know you'll grieve, darling, but I've got to go sometime and I'd rather go with all my marbles and still have been able to get around. I'd have hated having to use a Zimmer frame and drooling into my porridge.'

'You hate porridge.' Came the soggy voice from somewhere around her left shoulder.

'Yeah that's why I'd have drooled into it.' Millie eased Grace back. 'Tell me some more about this find of yours and allow us both to be distracted. I've got to entertain Dan this evening.'

Grace pretended to be horrified. 'Entertaining men

80

at you time of life; and in bed too. I'm shocked.'

'He's a lovely man, Gracie; I like listening to his accent and he has these lovely old fashioned notions of what's proper.' Millie grinned tiredly. 'Make another cup of tea darling and repair your face.'

She patted Grace on the cheek and Grace moved and sat on the nursing chair, reaching for her shoulder bag. 'Repair my face. You make me sound like a road with holes in it.'

Millie looked her over as she applied moisturiser and even found a lipstick and used that. 'I used to nurse you in that chair, Grace, you were always a beauty. I nursed your Mum in it too. It was always a comfortable chair, winter or summer. You'd rush in from school with your laces undone and your hair all over and tell me all about your day and I felt so proud of you.'

Grace smiled, 'Oh, boasted about me even then did you?'

'Of course I did.' She watched as Grace stood up and headed for the kitchen.

'I love you, child.' She murmured it as she watched Grace put it all back together and come back with the tea things and a serene face.

Millie seemed to recover some of her old energy as she sat sipping the hot sweet tea. 'So you found a time capsule. It's a bit of an odd place for anyone to put it. In the middle of a Roman dig. Do you think whoever put it there knew the Roman remains where there, or was it pure coincidence?'

'Well we didn't; and we're supposed to know these things. It wasn't until the farmer sold the land for redevelopment and the contractors began to dig that the Samian ware emerged.'

Millie shook her head, then, head cocked on one side, said, 'Help me sit up, darling, and find the atlas. I've

81

had an idea.' Millie grinned impishly.

Grace lifted Millie up the bed, becoming aware of how frighteningly light she was becoming. She hid the shock she felt in a flurry of plumping cushions then turned and went through the connecting door to the sitting room to find the big atlas of Britain.

She stood clenching both fists and her jaw for a minute until she was back in control again. 'I will not upset her again,' she muttered to herself and blinked back more threatened tears. When she was sure she could raise a smile she went back clutching the large floppy atlas like a barrier to her chest.

'Here you go.' Grace laid it on the covers. 'What's this idea?'

'Wait till I get my specs on.' Millie fumbled them on and turned the book open to the Cumbrian page; she peered down and shook her head. 'No, this is no good; see if you can find the ordinance survey maps, they're in the sideboard, in the bottom draw.'

She lay back as Grace left the room. 'I'm sure I'm right,' she murmured.

Grace pulled open the drawers of the old fashioned sideboard, pushing aside photo albums and packets of Kodak prints. Finally she pounced on a stack of thin blue maps fastened together with a rubber band and pulled them out; in doing so she dislodged the photo album and it fell with a soft thump on the carpet. 'Bother!' she gathered it up and went into the other room with the whole pile.

Coming back Grace saw Millie's eyes closed, and almost tiptoed away, but she opened them again. 'I was just resting. Bring it over, darling.' Grace put the pile on the side and sorted through to find the right map.

They unfolded the unwieldy paper and Grace folded it so that the area of the dig was visible.

82

'Look!' Millie carefully traced the contours, 'This is the Solway and your bunker. Yes?'

Grace squinted at the page, 'Yes.'

'Now show me where you found the Metal box.'

'It would be about here. I think.' Grace pointed, 'X marks the spot.'

'Now see that disused railway line. It was part of one they laid in the First World War for the munitions. In both wars they used some of the same bunkers to protect the Solway. I think your 'Mr Mackay' was stationed at the bunker and these lines run very near it.'

'I wonder what he did between the wars.' Millie gazed off into the distance.

'Eh!' said Grace inelegantly.

'Well I wonder if he knew about the disused line.' said Millie somewhat impatiently. 'If he did, he might know about the well you say you found. People round here were still using wells for drinking water; right up to the sixties in the rural parts. But they were marked by the railway for the steam trains as emergency stopping places too.'

'Millie, you're a genius.' Grace beamed at her.

'I wonder if I'm right.' Millie smiled happily at Grace.

They were gathering up the maps when Mary came in, 'It's a terrible night, Miss Gordon.' She nodded across at Grace then turned back to Millie. 'Have you had your supper?'

Millie looked at Mary. 'No we've been busy talking. But I'm not really hungry, Mary. I've had some tea though.'

Mary nodded. 'OK, but you let me know if you want anything. I'll just go and get your six o'clock meds and I'll be back.'

Millie pulled a face as the young nurse left the room. 'Yeuk! Medicine. It's a wonder I don't rattle with all the pills they keep shoving into me.' She leaned over and whispered to Grace, 'I'd palm them but she's a bit too sharp.'

Grace swallowed the chuckle as Mary came back in with a medicine cup with several tablets and capsules.

'I'm going to love you and leave you, Auntie Millie; I'll tell David your ideas about the railway line. I think you might be on to a winner there.' She leaned over and gave Millie a gentle squeeze. 'Behave yourself, Auntie.' She dropped a light kiss on the white forehead and ran a hand down the soft grey hair before she stood up and gathered her belongings. 'I'll see you tomorrow, darling.'

Grace left the room with a smile which faded as she left the flat and got into her car. 'I suppose I'd better eat too.' she muttered as she put the car in gear, flicking on the windscreen wipers as she drove away. With that thought in mind she headed towards the outskirts of the town and the large trading estate.

Thank God these places stayed open late Grace thought as she looked round at the car park half full of cars and big puddles from the recent rain. She pulled a couple of re-usable bags out of the back seat. David had laughed at her the first time he saw them and accused her of doing him out of a job. But judging by the number of plastic bags being ferried towards car boots she didn't think that midden heaps and rubbish tips were likely to go out of fashion so quickly that archaeologists would find themselves with no sites to dig.

The store wasn't actually that busy and Grace wandered along the freezer aisle without having to fight off the massed hoards of Genghis Khan in her efforts to buy yoghurt. She was actually feeling too miserable to be really interested in food but knew she ought to eat. She was standing debating the merits of low fat as against custard style in a dreary sort of way when a pleasant voice that had haunted her dreams the night before, spoke next to her.

'Miss Gordon, how are ye this day?'

Grace looked up; all the misery on her face very plain for even a slow Scot to see, and Dan was far from being slow.

'Grace, is everything alright with Millie?' Dan abandoned formality in concern.

Grace nodded dumbly. She turned away, abandoning the yoghurt to its fate. She just wanted to go home, she decided, and have a good cry in peace. Something of her intentions must have shown on her face. For Dan forsook his empty shopping basket and followed rapidly in her wake.

He was right behind her as the automatic doors closed with a whoosh of warm air into the damp evening sunlight. He came up to her as she was juggling bags and trying to put the key in the car door, unable to see what she was doing for the tears blurring her eyes.

'Nay then, you're not fit to drive, sweetheart. Come on let's get ye somewhere quiet and you can tell me all about it.' He put a gentle arm round her and Grace, much to her surprise, allowed herself to be escorted to a dark blue Jeep Cherokee and to be installed in the front seat and driven away.

Dan didn't say anything while he drove, swinging the big car onto the A19 and heading over the border into Scotland. The only sound in the cab the gentle swish of the tires on the still wet roads and the thunder of a passing Eddie Stobart lorry headed south. Ten minutes later Dan was pulling up at a large motel just off the Gretna Green service station.

'Out ye get, lass; we'll ha' a quick cuppa while ye

settle yourself.'

Grace, who had been wondering if she'd lost her mind in the last five minutes, sat and looked at him in astonishment.

'Ye need not be scairt o' me, lass, I mean ye no harm. But you obviously need a shoulder and mine's handy.' He looked at her quizzically.

Grace looked back, 'I'm perfectly alright, Mr Campbell.'

'Greetin' like a bairn over the dairy products would seem to indicate different, lass.'

Grace looked at his face; he wasn't exactly classically handsome but his blue eyes were kind and what she saw was concern and nothing else.

'Come along, I've the lodging here for the minute, while I serve your aunt. Or we can go over there and sit in the café awhile if you'd feel safer.'

Grace, watching his face, decided that she really didn't have anything to worry about; the man was just offering comfort to a fellow human being. She got out without another word and stood waiting while he locked his car.

He courteously allowed her to enter the reception area first then indicated a pair of heavy fire doors, 'Do ye take the lead lass, its number twenty-two just down the corridor.'

Grace, walking down the corridor past a line of windows that looked out on a green square of lawn surrounded on three sides by similar windows, wondered if grief made you stupid. What was she doing going into a stranger's bedroom without a qualm! Though she had to admit that she secretly felt very safe with Dan.

Dan flipped a card into the lock and opened the door, allowing her to precede him into number twenty-two. She had stayed in similar motels when she'd been on far flung sites and this was the average run of the mill motel bedroom. It was possibly cleaner than some she'd been in. She noted an en suite shower and toilet next to the front door and a small open wardrobe behind the door. Dan's shirts and a couple of jackets were hung in a tidy line on coat hangers inside it.

The room had twin beds neatly made; a lap-top computer case was placed on the end of one, its zip undone so that Grace saw a small cluster of wires poking out. A settee was pushed under the window; a small table at the side had individual portions of tea and coffee on top in a little box. There was a kettle, a stainless steel teapot and some heavy pot mugs stacked next to these, and a small cardboard box on the floor.

Dan indicated the seat. 'Rest a minute, lass, while I make us a drink.' He opened the box to reveal his own supplies. 'I canna be doing with these little bits o' packets.' He proceeded to make a strong pot of tea and pour it out without saying anything else. He held up the milk and sugar in turn and prepared her cup.

'Noo then, how can I be helping ye? Is it that it's finally hitting ye, lass? I thought me that ye were being ower calm this last week.'

Grace nodded, the lump in her throat was back with a vengeance and she didn't think she could speak. She took a sip of the strong brew. She set the mug down and pulled out a tissue, blowing her nose vigorously and swallowing hard. 'I'm sorry, Mr Campbell; I seem to be making rather a fool of myself.'

'Nay pay it no mind, lass. It's not easy saying goodbye in stages and never sure when the last time will be.'

Grace sniffed and felt the tears pooling again. 'Oh! Damn! I've cried all over Aunt Millie already today.'

'Aye weel and now ye can cry all ower me.' Dan pulled her into his arms as the damn broke again. He stroked her back with a large and capable hand, feeling her chest rising as she struggled for control. Grace sobbed brokenly for several minutes and Dan allowed her to sniff her way back to calm, patting her and pulling a handkerchief from his pocket when the storm seemed to be easing. 'Better, lass?' He offered the large snowy white linen for her to dry her eyes.

Grace turned a rather blotched face up from the shoulder she had just soaked. 'Yes, better. You're right; it was seeing her today looking so tired, and knowing that it's not really fair of me to want her to linger if she's in pain. But I'm going to miss her so much; she's all I've got by way of family and I don't know what I'm going to do when she's gone.' The last was said in almost a wail.

'Weel, first ye'll greet, then ye'll get mad, then ye'll get sad. And then ye'll come to terms with it. Not all at once; it'll tak' time lass and then ye'll go on wi' your own life and she'll be there in your memory, as a fragrant thought ye can draw on when ye feel alone.' Dan allowed Grace to sit up, but kept an arm round her while she wiped her eyes and blew her nose again.

'Thank you, Dan, you're a nice man. You were right, I did need a shoulder. I feel as though I've been struggling for weeks to keep everything calm for Millie and not let her see I'm worrying about her.'

Dan nodded, 'Drink your tea. What was the final straw then?'

'I think it was realising that she was needing more pain relief and eating just about nothing.'

Dan nodded again. 'And'

'I was talking to her about the dig; and she's always been there to listen and offer ideas. She's always so enthusiastic about my work.' Grace paused to wipe away a trickle down her cheek. 'We'd get out the maps and discuss the area. We haven't done that this time; she'd been too ill and wasn't even sure where the site was, which is really strange. She'd always known before where I was and what I was doing.' Dan rubbed a red wool covered shoulder as she sniffed. 'She came up with a possible solution to a problem I had today, and I'm going to miss that. I know I can talk to the others on site, but it's not the same.'

'Of course it's not, lass.'

Dan's careful blue eyes watched and assessed as she drank her tea and set the mug down on the floor. She leaned back against the settee, and he found that his hand was being tickled by curls turned strawberry blonde by the rays of the late setting sun stealing through the window. He felt the quiver of enjoyment in his stomach stirring, and silently rebuked himself. This was neither the time, nor place, to be thinking those thoughts.

Grace, unselfconsciously resting the back of her head on his arm, sighed quietly and Dan gently massaged the shoulder, feeling the bones fragile under his hand. She closed her eyes which felt sore and gritty.

'You're right; I will come to terms with it. I suppose you're used to relatives falling to pieces all over you?' She opened her eyes, rolling her head along his arm to look at the face close to hers. She, too, was becoming aware of the small part of her brain which had been waving its hands to try to attract her attention and tell her how much she was enjoying this small, intimate time. She turned her head away again at the intensity of the blue eyes looking into hers. His face looked sad she thought.

'It's happened before, lass. But I was speaking from personal experience this time. My faither died last year of the cancer and I still get mad at him for leaving me when there was so much more I wanted to ask him; and sad that I hanna his company to share.' Dan spoke soothingly, but he was feeling less than soothed himself. He was very

89

aware of the soft body relaxed against him in the aftermath of the storm. The scent that was Grace, mingling with the cut grass from the open window, reminded him of long ago summers when life was easier.

He allowed himself to indulge for just a few minutes more before saying. 'Up ye get; do ye go and wash your face and mak' yourself even more beautiful and desirable. Then I'll drive ye back to pick up your car before they lock it in the car park for the night.' He smiled down at the face so close to his own. He was surprised to find how tempted he was to kiss her and moved carefully, easing her away and standing up himself to tidy away the mugs, and temptation, in as easy a way as he could.

Grace felt cold as he left her sitting on the settee and, irrationally, she felt deserted as well. 'Well I'll wash certainly, but beautiful and desirable is beyond my powers.' She joked to cover her feelings as she stood up.

'Beautiful I said and beautiful I meant!' Dan said firmly; looking down at her from his extra six inches with eyes that said a great deal more clearly what his lips had just declared. 'I doubt it's the grief addling your mind!' he said abruptly.

Grace gave him a startled look. She went to the bathroom door and stood looking around and smelling the indefinable scent that she'd been enveloped in five minutes before. Dan appeared behind her as she peered at the neat array of bottles on the sink top. 'You'll be needing your bag.' He held her leather shoulder bag out and started turning away. Grace laid a hand on his arm, stopping him.

'Thank you, Dan. You are being kind, especially when I wasn't very polite yesterday.'

Dan looked at the face before him. He could feel the warmth of that small hand soaking through his shirt sleeve. 'Weel, I said ye could trust me, but don't push, Grace. I'm only fifty percent gentle the rest is aye man; and kind is just no what I'm feeling towards ye. Entertaining

90

women as beautiful as ye in my bedroom is, I find, stretching me a trifle more than I had imagined. I find I want to kiss ye verra, verra badly.'

Grace, after an astonished pause, let go of his arm and shut the door abruptly in his face.

When she emerged he was sitting on the settee leafing through a journal. He stood up at her entrance and after the briefest of glances walked towards her and the door.

'Dan. I'm sorry;' she paused, 'I'm sorry if I said something to make you think… I wasn't being provocative, honestly. I really do appreciate your help.' She stopped speaking as he came abreast of her.

Dan stopped, looking down into her rather anxious face. 'Nae then it's my fault. I shouldna ha' said anything. No matter if it's true ye are both beautiful and desirable. It wasna' you that was provoking.' He looked hungrily at her serious face, coming to a decision; then took both her arms gently, and lowered his head.

Grace hadn't been kissed very often; mostly she'd avoided the experience after the few groping attempts in her teenage years, when equally unsure boys had attempted to kiss her. She normally worried about why they were kissing her and if she matched up to their ideal.

Dan watched her eyes go from the dull slate grey of misery to the colour of clouds with the moon behind them as he lowered his mouth to hers; their lips touched, first slowly and gently, then firmly. He settled down to the job in a manner that said he was obviously savouring her as if there was nothing more important on his agenda than pleasuring them both.

Every idea Grace had had about kissing flew out the window with the first touch. Her initial reaction of being enveloped in warm black velvet was replaced by that of hot desire, like warm honey in her mouth, making her long for something; but she wasn't sure what that something was.

He moved and brought her closer so that Grace was enveloped in an aroma she was beginning to associate with both comfort and something else. A mix of aftershave and spicy soap, and something indefinable that was Dan, assailed her senses along with a faint stir of lust. She sighed deeply as he moved off her mouth and went for a little tour of exploration across her face before coming back to settle on her lips again. Only lifting his to mutter, 'Aye I ken't it would be like this.'

He teased her lips with his tongue and groaned slightly when she allowed him entry. He eased back as they both came up for air, then pulled her close so that her head rested on his shoulder. 'This is no' just ethical, ye are in nae condition to be having a man makin' moves on ye.' He stopped to nuzzle against her hair, and Grace felt the warmth of his body close to hers; apparently she wasn't the only one to have a stir of lust. 'But sweet mercy ye are a lovely morsel, sweetheart.' He stepped back 'I think we'd better get out of here.'

Grace, standing a little bemused, found herself being hustled out the door and along the corridor. She didn't know quite what to think. One minute the man was all politeness, the next he'd been kissing her senseless. Her libido, however, knew exactly what to make of it, and wasn't too pleased to have the encounter stopped. She felt like a small child being dragged away from the supermarket by an irate mother. She wanted to protest in a loud voice that she wanted some more.

'What just happened there, Dan?' They stood outside his car door.

Dan looked silently at her for a minute, assessing her. 'I'm sure ye ken as well as I do what happened, Grace. And if we'd stayed i' that room for much longer, more than that would ha' happened. I'll no' compromise ye, lass, not when you're so vulnerable.'

Dan opened her door and waited for her to climb in. As she seated herself he cleared his throat, speaking softly. 'But lass,' He paused to be sure he had her attention as she fastened her seat belt, and as she lifted her head and looked at him, continued, 'When you're more settled I would verra much like to see ye in a personal capacity and get to know ye a bit better.'

He walked round the car and climbed in, fastening his seat belt and engaging the gears with a sure touch, then drove along a back road that missed most of the A19 and brought them out at Gretna Green before turning towards Carlisle again.

Grace sat quietly beside him turning over in her mind the past hour. Finally she spoke as they arrived back at the shopping precinct. 'I think I should verra much like to see you too, I've never been compromised before.' She rolled the r's and smiled as he gave her a quick glance, before pulling up in a space near her car.

He killed the engine and turned sideways in his seat. 'Good, lass, maybe we might go for that meal when ye ha' some free time and I'm no' so tired that my heid is swimming and my control is all but gone.'

'Oh! I rather like you a bit uncontrolled.' she gave him a shy grin.

Dan smiled back. 'Away with ye, lass, now ye are being provocative.'

Grace nodded. 'Yes, Dan, and I'd rather you didn't wait too long for me to settle either. I'm not a lass, I'm a woman.'

After a thoughtful look Dan got out and came round to open her door, helping her down the steep step as if she was royalty needing a hand, she thought. He kept the hand as he walked her past three other cars to hers. 'In that case, lass,' he bent his head and savoured another long, slow kiss, 'I'll pick ye up tomorrow and we'll find out a bit more about each other shall we?'

'Yes, Dan.' Grace found she was just a wee bit breathless as he handed her into her car. 'I can finish whenever I want to, but when do you wake up?'

'I'll meet ye in the cathedral grounds about one thirty.'

'Fine, Dan.' She paused, looking at his twinkling blue eyes, 'Thank you.'

'It really wasna any trouble; quite the reverse.' he slurred the r' making his speech consciously more Scottish and smiled down at her, slamming the door and watching as she drove sedately out of the car park. Then he turned towards the doors and went inside to do a little hasty shopping for his night-time meal.

5

PHILIP JARDIN WAS DOING his best not to become compromised either; however, he desperately wanted to know what had been discovered that day. He was good at his job and could have joined any legitimate archaeological research facility for almost as much money as he earned stealing artefacts to order, if he'd bothered to get the qualifications. His overwhelming curiosity had always been an asset up to the present, but the night before had been one of his closer shaves.

His thin face had scowled back at him from the rain washed window as he'd waited for his mobile phone to be answered that afternoon, showing that that had been the only close shave he'd had that day. Scrambling around the dig half the night without a result had left him tired and sour.

He had used one of his favourite ploys, posing as a journalist to glean information about the dig. Both times the telephone had been answered by a site member; the first one had claimed he had to talk to the boss. He really didn't want to talk to David Walker, and he was certain those oxford tones had answered him the next time. He remembered Professor Walker as well as he was sure the professor remembered him.

Now on the third attempt he was ringing the hostel where he knew most of the site members were staying. He knew David Walker had a house somewhere in the area so he didn't think the man would be there, but he might get a more junior person to talk. He drummed his fingers on the table in the small bed and breakfast room and muttered. 'Com'on, com'on' in a litany of impatience. Then picked up a pen and tapped that against the cheap pad of Basildon Bond on his knee.

Finally a female voice answered. 'H...how can I

h...help?'

'Hi, I'm doing a piece for the local paper about the Roman dig, I wondered if you could tell me how you're getting on out there. For instance have you found anything of local interest?' He tried to make his voice sound professional and yet enthusiastic; somewhat hampered by the Geordie accent he'd never completely lost.

'I'm sorry I can't give that i...information over the phone. You'll have to c...contact the press office or ring the Professor in the morning. I'm sure he'll be h...happy to help you.' The voice was a little hesitant.

'Oh I don't want to trouble him. I just want to keep the public interested. Surely you can tell me what you are finding out there.' He found his palms sweating as he waited. He thought he recognised the voice, he was almost sure he'd got the same bloody student as the first time. 'Damn!' he muttered under his breath.

'I don't think so. C...can I pass a m...message on Mr. ... er! W...what did you say your name was?'

'I'm sorry, you're breaking up. I'll ring back.' Philip Jardin switched off the little machine and shuddered. The new breed of student was far more cautious. When he'd first begun his somewhat dubious career, he hadn't even had to bribe them, and someone always talked. Now most of them were actively suspicious of strangers. He didn't know what the world was coming to when youngsters didn't trust the older generation. Then he grinned, revealing slightly bucked teeth; however, there was always one.

He sat back and looked at his watch. It was only eight, far too light to go wandering about the dig yet. He'd have to wait and suffer another sleepless night. 'I'm getting too bloody old for this game.' He muttered.

He flipped open the mobile and keyed in another number.

'Hi, boss.' He cocked his head, listening

'Yeah it still looks interesting, but I've not had a really good look at the finds yet.' He flushed, his face going brick red as he swallowed annoyance. 'I know you're not paying me to sit around, boss. I'll go and have another look tonight, but the shed was securely locked last night and someone came roaming around the dig before I could pick the lock.'

He scratched his chin while he listened to the voice on the end of the phone. 'Honestly, boss! There was a girl there after midnight.'

He shook his head and made a face at the phone. 'How should I know, she was just wandering about. OK, boss, I'll be careful.' He sighed. 'Boss, you know it was an accident, I don't fancy another spell in prison myself.'

He shook his head 'No boss, I know you don't approve of violence.'

He listened some more, absently clicking a ballpoint as the voice made another suggestion. 'I've tried that, boss, no-one is talking. I think they must have found something big.' He shook his head, exasperated. 'I have telephoned! I tell you no-one is talking; my inside contact doesn't know anything much either.' He sighed. 'OK, boss, I'll phone tomorrow, hopefully I'll have better news then.'

He scowled at the phone and threw it on the bed. He rubbed his hands over his face and up through his sparse grey hair. 'God! What I'd give for a decent night's sleep.' He looked longingly at the bed then shrugged; and after another glance at his watch, dug out a battered and much thumbed copy of 'The Complete Works of Tacitus.' 'Might as well see if the great man has anything to say.'

THE STUDENT WHO ANSWERED was left standing holding the hostel phone, looking at it a bit blankly. Doug came through a hall cluttered with wellington boots and bicycles leaning drunkenly against the wall; and looked at Kate standing amidst it like a small fairy, her hair flaming in the light from the open door. 'What's up, Kate? Pizza Parlour hang up on you?'

'I don't know, Doug; it was a sort of odd phone c…call. I'm sure it was the same guy who rang this m…morning asking for info about the dig. Said he was a journalist. I told him he'd have to s…speak to the P…prof' but he rang back again tonight, and then we were cut off.' She shook her red curls back and blinked long pale lashes at Doug, 'Only,' she hesitated a minute, 'he said he was b…breaking up but I could still hear him clearly, and it didn't feel right.'

'Well David did say to report anything odd.'

'When did he say that?'

'Mid-morning.'

'Oh!' Kate, smiled, 'I must have been b…busy. I missed it; I was in the site office m…most of the day.'

'Well you know now; you'd best ring him up.'

'Couldn't you d…do it for me, D…Doug?' she all but pleaded. 'He doesn't like m…me.'

'Don't be daft, David likes everyone. You wouldn't have been asked back to a dig if he didn't like you. He can pick his own teams these days.' Doug, an interested observer, watched the freckles melt into her cheeks as she blushed rosily. 'He doesn't bite. Go on ring him up; he'll be less than pleased if you leave it and it's important.'

Doug sauntered away at a shout from one of the rooms, and Kate stood uncertainly in the hall. She'd had a massive crush on David Walker since her first dig four years ago when she'd managed to get a placement with him. She'd heard so much about him all her life, and finally meeting him had lived up to all her girlhood fantasies.

She wasn't a fool; she knew the man was thirty years her senior and she'd done her best to accept that he wasn't interested. This summer though he'd almost seemed to resent her presence, being very abrupt with her.

She'd dated other students but found their conversation very insipid after David's. She didn't think he liked her much despite Doug's comments. She thought he was shrewd enough to use people if they were good at their jobs, regardless of his personal feelings however, and because she needed to work for him she made sure she was good.

She paused and took several deep breaths before punching in his phone number; then stood rehearsing in her mind what she had to tell him.

'Hi P…professor. I've just had an odd p…phone c…call.'

'Well call the police, girl, not me.' David shouted testily into her ear.

'No, Si… Professor,'

'For God sake girl, call me David.'

'David, er!' She felt herself blushing again and not for the first time cursed her fair skin. 'It wasn't that kind of p…phone c…call.' She began to relate the contents of the two phone calls she'd had that day.

David listened so quietly she wondered if he'd heard her. 'Si'…Pr'… David, can you hear me.'

'Of course I can, I'm not deaf. I'm coming over to the hostel.' He hung up on her and Kate was left holding a phone again, its dial tone turning to a continuous purr as she stood there. Doug, on his way back down the hall, gave her an odd look. 'Haven't you phoned yet?'

'Yes Of course I have. He's c…coming over.'

Doug grunted, 'Hope he brings some beer.' He went into the communal sitting room cum dining room,

99

and Kate heard him joking to someone in there that, 'the old man was slumming tonight.'

Kate stood in the hall for a minute or two longer after she'd replaced the receiver; she certainly didn't think her bit of news warranted a visit, slumming or not, and now she was worried that she'd exaggerated something that was of little importance, in the hopes of seeing David Walker again that day.

David Walker was wondering if she'd exaggerated things too. However, he admitted to himself that he'd been glad of the excuse to be with not just the team, but Kate as well. He had felt an instant attraction to that young woman when she'd arrived on her first dig, all eagerness and ideals. The intervening years had only strengthened the attraction.

He had no business even looking her way and he had decided that after this dig, no matter how good she was, he couldn't afford to have her on his team. She wasn't a student anymore, it was true, but she was thirty years younger than he was, and she disturbed his peace of mind too much.

He detoured via an off licence knowing his team's penchant for beer, and prepared to listen to Kate tell her tale again among the safety of numbers. It was probably nothing, but all these little nothings seemed to be adding up to a great big something. He wasn't sure what yet, but something.

Kate was sitting at the big wooden table in the dining hall, slightly apart from the rest of the team when he arrived. They'd been lucky to get this place, he thought, as he came in the communal hut. It had been a part of one of the old RAF bases and the MOD allowed the few remaining Nissan huts, normally used by outward bound teams, to be rented by the University for 'Site Digs' on or near this end of the Wall.

He made his way to where he could hear the

babble of voices coming out of a door and entered the large dining room on the wave of noise. Two students were playing a game of draughts in one corner, sitting on two chairs with a third between them supporting the board. The room was redolent of instant coffee and the stew which had apparently been the evening meal.

Several students sat on the arms and seat of a settee, whose rough pelt covering gave the impression of a hungry and toothless lion gumming them, as they sat watching another couple playing chess from the dubious comfort of two equally sagging armchairs. David dumped the box of beer cans he was carrying at the end of the long table covered with old fashioned oilcloth and, taking a can from the box, went to sit down, swinging his leg over the bench seat. He chose a seat midway between the team and Kate, almost opposite a big bowl of red apples.

The students gravitated to the table, and the beer cans, as he said, 'So tell me again, Kate.' People swung their legs over the benches and the chattering stilled as they all settled down and listened to what their boss had to say.

He watched the colour rise in Kate's cheeks and couldn't decide whether to be annoyed with her or himself. He usually ended up being annoyed with her as a cover for the fact that his mind and body liked her company far too much for his own comfort.

'It's like I told you, D..d...avid, 'she stuttered over his name, 'When I w...was in the site office this m...morning a man rang up s...saying he was a journalist and asking about the p...progress of the d...dig.'

'And?' David watched her expressive face and wondered what he saw in her. She wasn't exactly beautiful; pretty in an Anglo-Saxon, red-headed way, he decided, and those brown eyes could melt a man's resolve if he dared to look too deeply in them. He glanced round the room to make sure no one had observed him.

Kate was speaking; she'd managed to almost

101

jettison the stutter but he could tell she was still nervous by the way she gripped the mug in her hands. Hell! What was he going to do about her?

'Well I told him he'd have to t…talk to you or the press office at the uni'. Then this evening he rang the h…hostel.' She nodded her head, 'I'm s…sure it was the s…same man this evening, and he asked the same questions. He seemed ….' She paused searching for a word. 'Shifty.' she nodded again 'Yes, shifty; as if he didn't want to t…talk to you personally D…David, just wanted the information.'

'OK that's clear so far. Anyone else had any mysterious phone calls?' He popped the tab on the can and took a drink, observing his team closely. Kate felt as though she was glowing like an electric fire as everyone looked at her. Was he secretly poking fun at her? 'Doug said you told us to r…report anything odd.' She said defensively.

'And quite right too, my dear.' David tried to soften his growl as the others laughed. He knew they all laughed a bit at Kate for being so shy and keeping herself to herself, and he was guiltily aware that he'd contributed to the problem by not stopping the sly comments. The trouble was, he thought, he was too scared of giving away his own feelings to say too much at all.

One of the other students spoke up; she was the very antithesis of Kate, being tall and thin, her skin a dusky apricot and with a personality apparently as wide open and guileless as the Australian outback from which she originally hailed. 'I got the same kind of phone call about four o' clock, Kate. What did your voice sound like?' she blew a bubble with the gum she was currently revolving about her wide mouth as she waited for Kate's answer, big brown eyes fixed shrewdly on the older girl's face.

Kate shrugged, 'I'm not very good at voices, it was just a m…male voice,' She frowned in concentration. 'Tenor

I think,' she thought about it a bit more. 'Not as deep as John's v...voice, and an accent.'

'Yeah, now you mention it there was an accent, I'm not very good at your pommy accents,' Alice grinned as an apple was hurled down the table by one of the men. She fielded it neatly, shuffling her gum aside to sink her very white teeth into its flesh. 'More like David's than John's, but you're right; deeper than David's' she spoke through the apple and David gave her a repressive look from under his brows then smoothed his beard down, covering his mouth and face.

He looked round the group; 'Well it doesn't get us much further. It could have been a genuine inquiry, in which case the bloke will ring again tomorrow. Then again it might be someone fishing to see what we've got.' He paused and sipped beer. 'I think we'd all better maintain a masterly silence unless we know exactly who we're talking to.'

'I've checked over the 'finds' and Kate's notes and, while there appear to be a few places where there is a difference in depth, that could be accounted for by extra scraping for photos and sketching. ' He nodded at Kate, 'Nothing wrong with that Kate, but let's be vigilant girls and boys. Make sure of everything when you clear up your loose at the end of the day.'

'Now.' He sat back, 'Who'd like to give me a game of chess before I go home and rest my old bones for the night? You lot might be able to party half the night and play all day but I can't.'

GRACE WAS ALSO AWAKE. She wasn't quite sure of anything anymore; it seemed her well ordered life was disintegrating around her. She'd been able to rely on what she thought of as the predictable attitudes of David and

John, only to have them confound her that morning.

The only stable and predictable thing in her life at the moment was her archaeology. She sat propped in the bed hugging Mr Gladly, her bear, and thinking about the events of the day. She smoothed the bare patches on the bear's tummy.

Dan had been kind and understanding. He'd been mostly undemanding too, except for those last few minutes. And that appeared to be the most unpredictable thing of all. Men didn't make passes at her. She knew what she looked like and she was 'OK'. But between David and John that morning, and Dan that evening, she was feeling a bit confused about her self-image.

She tried to push the whole incident away and fixed her mind on the previous conversation with Millie. Could the well have been used by the railways? That would explain the relatively soft soil in the hole and the choice of venue for the deposit. The man couldn't have foreseen Lord Beeching's sweeping changes to the railway system and the fact that that well would be abandoned so soon after the war to be buried in a cow field, could he? He must have thought it was a good place which would be easily accessible in the future.

She visualised the site as she'd seen it that morning and matched it to Millie's ordinance survey map. Suddenly Grace sat up; she'd had to search for that map in the cupboard. Millie had been too sick to look at maps and plot the site. 'I wonder how she knew there was a well there, Mr Gladly.' She patted his head and put him down in the chair next to the bed where he normally sat, leaning over to pick up and cradle a mug of tea between her hands. She sat sipping the tea, a slightly dreamy expression on her face; so that it was perhaps as well that her audience was only a very old bear.

She surfaced from this dream world half an hour later; what quirk of the mind had brought the phrase to the surface she didn't care to speculate, but she got off the bed and went to boot up her computer muttering. 'Marston, no; Morden, no; Morrison hmm! I think that was the name.'

She switched on the internet and started hunting for Morrison shelters. 'Good grief, it had enough nuts and bolts didn't it!' She looked at the large metal cage displayed on the screen with a jaundiced eye. 'I'm not sure I would have wanted to crawl into that thing; I'd feel like an animal at the zoo. Still if bombs are dropping on your head it was probably safer than being outside.' She continued to study the kinds of bomb shelters, becoming fascinated by some of the more esoteric detail.

She pulled down the information onto hard copy and went back to the bed, sitting on its side while she read over the pages. 'Well! Well! Could accommodate a double bed underneath, and be suitable for use as a table during the day. Big table that. Aunt Millie I'm so proud of you.' She gave a chuckle and then tapped the papers on her hand. 'Now do I tell her I've guessed her secret?' She got up and wandered into the kitchen to make a fresh cup of tea while she thought about it.

Aunt Millie had changed the subject as soon as she'd inadvertently mentioned the shelter and the mysterious James. Was it even right to be checking up on her now? Grace frowned in concentration. She might ask David in the morning. She trusted his judgement, or at least she had, she amended.

She shuffled the papers into a neat pile and went to get ready for bed. It had been a long day and tomorrow promised to be equally as long. And, she told herself, you will not think about a certain Scotsman, he's not offering anything but a pleasant flirtation as a means of distracting you from your worries, Grace.

She couldn't do anything about her dreams, however. She told herself virtuously that the subconscious was uncontrollable and had nothing to do with her. She smiled happily as she climbed into bed and snuggled down, willing herself to go to sleep.

DAN ARRIVED PROMPTLY AT Millie's that evening. He was tired. He'd only had one day off since taking the case, and the Motel had been noisy that day so that his sleep was constantly interrupted. In the finish he'd abandoned the attempt to get any more rest and had got up.

Grace's distress and the romantic interlude with her had taken more self-control than she had been aware of. He wasn't normally so lacking in self-discipline and found it rather unsettling that she had unknowingly reduced his knees to the consistency of mush. Along, he thought disgustingly, with his head. He knew better than to get involved with patients or their relatives, no matter what they smelt like or how much of a delightful armful they were. He must be tired.

He never slept while on duty. Not only was it dangerous for the patient but it was actually illegal. He wondered how he was going to stay awake that night on less than four hours sleep. He'd bought some high caffeine drinks with the idea they might help, but was a bit doubtful of their efficacy.

However, when he saw Millie he realised that staying awake wasn't going to be a problem. She was going to require his nursing care. 'How are you finding yourself tonight, Millie?'

Millie looked across the room. 'I'm not finding myself at all, Dan.' She paused for breath, 'In fact I don't feel like me at all. I feel as though I'm floating several feet above me.'

'Take your time and tell me what ails ye then and we'll see what can be done.'

As he headed towards the bed he gathered up the

sphygnomometer in passing. 'I'll just do a set of obs' while ye talk.'

Millie obediently held out an arm so that he could take her blood pressure. 'I don't know why you're bothering to do that, Dan; after all it's not as if you can do anything about it.'

'Weel, that's not entirely true, Millie. It could just be that your oxygen is a bit low and that's why you're feeling strange.'

He strapped the cuff and placed the stethoscope, listening carefully for the changes that signalled the different pressures. 'That's a bit low too. Ha' ye had much to drink this day?'

'Not really. I'm feeling a bit sick if the truth is told.'

Dan was busy fitting a small clip to her finger. 'Did ye no' tell Mary, she has a wee tablet that could ha' cured that for ye.'

'I didn't want to fuss. I know I'm dying, Dan, I didn't think there was much you could do about it.'

'Hmm.'

Dan moved away, 'I'm going to make some coffee for us both; that will keep me awake and give ye a wee caffeine boost. That'll help the blood pressure a wee bit. I'll get the little pill; it'll take away the sickness. It's the increased analgesia Millie, it can make ye feel nauseous, I had a chat wi' the doctor yester en' and he charted it for just this situation, he's put it PRN so you can ha' it when ye need it.'

Millie raised a small smile, 'What's PRN, is it a long complicated name for this pill?'

'Och sorry, Millie. It just means whenever necessary. Then I'm going to gie ye a bitty blow o' Oxygen. Yours is a bit low and your brain is feeling fuzzy in consequence. Ye'll feel much better, no' just on the instant ye understand, but gie it half an hour and ye'll see.'

He went about his preparations on soft feet, not bustling but accomplishing the work quickly and efficiently. Millie found herself with a nasal cannula hissing oxygen quietly into her lungs and a cup of coffee sitting on the side ready to drink as soon as she had taken Dan's 'wee tablet '.

'Right then; has the floating feeling gone a bit?' He stood back while she sipped the water and washed down the pill.

Millie nodded and handed back the glass, 'How odd.' She fingered the cannula.

'It's no just flattering to ye, but it will help, Millie. Now bide a while wi' yer eyes closed. I'll be right beside ye.'

He sat down in the nursing chair with his own mug of coffee steaming gently on the bedside table, 'Hold my hand, lass.'

Millie felt the large warm hand holding hers as she lay back against the banked pillows. She listened to the quiet hiss of the oxygen and the ticking of the clock, and tried to relax. 'I'm scared, Dan.'

'Aye, Millie, I ken that.' He offered no false hope; just his presence as he gently rubbed his thumb over her palm.

Millie lay quietly and gradually felt herself calming. She cautiously opened her eyes to find Dan watching her. 'No' floating on the ceiling quite sae much?'

'No, Dan.'

'Good. Now for the second part of the cure, drink your coffee, lass and I'll gie ye a little wash and mak' ye more comfortable. I ha' some news for ye.'

He waited for her to drink most of the coffee and then went about the task of washing her face and

108

smoothing the bed clothes in a companionable silence, conscious of Millie's eyes resting on him trustingly.

Eventually she broke the silence. 'Will I know, Dan?'

'Ye might, then again ye might just float softly away in your sleep.' He didn't pretend not to understand. 'Would you be wanting the minister then?'

'I'll ask Mary tomorrow if she'll arrange a visit.' She paused, 'Will that be soon enough?'

'Aye, lass. That'll be soon enough.'

He sat next to her again noting her breathing which was easier and that there was faint colour in her cheeks. He smiled down at her. 'I ha' twa bits o' good news for ye; at least I think they're good. Yon lass of yours has agreed to ha' a meal wi' me the morrow.'

'What Gracie? Oh! Dan, I'm so pleased.' She beamed at him and Dan, seeing that smile, mentally noted that the anti-nausea was effective at that dose apparently. Millie was obviously feeling a bit better. Her brow wrinkled, 'When did you see her, Dan? She was with me most of the afternoon.'

'I met her doing her shopping, Millie; she was telling me you'd solved her current archaeological problem.'

Millie looked surprised for a minute. 'No, I only offered an idea, I'm sure they'd have got round to it eventually.'

She shifted slightly on the pillows. 'It was only that they'd found a time capsule from VE day. Which is odd because you and I had been talking about that. Grace found it on top of an old well shaft, in a biscuit tin and she was wondering if the person who put it there knew about the well. I know the army used the railway line near her site, in the war, for munitions dumps. And the railway used the natural wells.'

109

'Oh aye! That's interesting! And how did ye come to ken that, Millie?'

'Well,' He watched the faint pink deepen a bit. 'James and I used to bike out along there when he could get the petrol. It's not far and there were some nice bits of Roman wall incorporated in the side of the old church. James loved Roman stuff as much as me. So we'd go looking for bits of pot and things if it was fine at the weekends.'

Dan leaned over and altered the flow rate, 'I'll just take you down to two litres now. Ye look much better.' It was more a statement than a question, but Millie nodded.

'What was your other bit of news?'

'Weel I'm no promising, but I e-mailed an old army buddy in the American forces and he has a contact among the pension's people.' He grinned, 'Ye have to follow the money, Millie, we Scots ken aboot that sort of thing' He mocked himself gently and tapped the side of his nose. 'We might be able to trace a certain James Belsham, formally American Air Force, given a little time.'

'Oh! Dan!' Millie went quite pale again. 'How can I thank you?'

'Ye'd better save your thanks, Millie; my friend might not be able to track him down even so.' He paused a minute. 'He may not want to see ye, Millie.' he warned. 'Even if we do find him he might be marrit and not wanting any ghosts from his past.'

Millie nodded her understanding. 'He was a bit hot tempered, but he usually got over it quickly enough. It was just that last time, we argued past bearing.'

Dan monitoring her breathing and pulse noted the slight hitch. 'Dinna stress yer sen, Millie.'

'No, it's alright.' She gave a lop-sided smile, 'It all started with me wanting one of the brand new swimsuits.' Dan raised a mobile eyebrow but held his peace. 'James was going over to Paris, something to do with Project Green.' She waved a hand in dismissal of this historical detail. 'Anyway he'd told me about the summer fashions over there. Not that they were a lot better off than we British were, but he was describing how some man had invented a new two piece swimsuit that was going to be available the next spring and I said would he get one for me.'

Dan offered a sip of water. 'Thanks.' Millie handed the glass back, 'Well James thought it was not at all nice for a respectable girl to wear. He said I wasn't going on show like other GI brides. This came as a shock to me as he'd not asked me to marry him then!' Millie grinned and Dan could see exactly why her James had wanted to marry her.

'So?' he prompted.

'We argued a bit about that, but I could see he was really upset by it so I let the subject drop.' She looked sad and rested back against the pillows a minute, panting.

'Hush, Millie; ye dinna ha to talk'

She closed her eyes but started speaking again, 'When I found out the swimsuits were supposed to be smaller than the atom and I heard all about the Atom Bomb I wouldn't have wanted one anyway, Dan. Then he had to go away again.' She frowned, 'No, I think it was Project White not Green,' She waved a hand in dismissal of an irrelevancy from her point of view. 'Anyway he was away for several weeks and didn't come to see me until after the Atom Bomb was dropped. We argued dreadfully about that.' She stopped, breathing in little gasps.

Dan looked at the clock, he'd give her another twenty minutes then he'd try to get her to settle to sleep for a while. It wasn't that he wasn't interested but he was conscious that she had had a bad day. However, she obviously needed to get this of her chest.

'The Atom Bomb, that was a terrible waste of life.'

'Well that's what I said, Dan. I said it was wrong to kill innocent people without giving them a chance. And he said that civilians in Britain had been dying for five years. James said that it would save more lives in the long run.' She was getting agitated and Dan held her hand, soothing her.

'He said that soldiers out in the east were dying every day and the bomb had stopped the killing. That there wouldn't be any futile engagements with men dying to take bits of land they'd only have to give back when we won the war.' She sighed.

'But I could only think of the children and babies who'd died. I suspected I might be pregnant by then but I hadn't quite worked up the courage to tell him about it. But I kept thinking, 'what if it had been my child who was to be sacrificed', and I wouldn't forgive his hard-heartedness.' She patted Dan's hand, 'It was too late to stop it and he was partly right, a lot of civilians all over the world had died. That was the last time I saw him.'

'He was a serviceman, Millie, and I should imagine what he'd seen wouldn't exactly endear the enemy to him.'

'He went away again after that time, I know he was ferrying P38's for Air Transport Command, and he'd barely land in the USA before they'd put him on a plane and send him back to England to fly another one back. Harry told Jen and she told me.' She sighed deeply. 'I would like to tell him I'm sorry, Dan.'

'I'll do my best for ye Millie. Ye should rest a while now though.'

He dimmed the main light and came and sat down again. 'I like your Grace, Millie, and if he's like her then he'll want to see ye. Sleep now; I'll be here when ye wake.'

Millie closed her eyes, settling on the pillow trustingly. Dan sat watching her until he was sure she was asleep. He got up and went across to the window, pushing the catch and standing near the resultant opening. He breathed deeply and then walked back to sit next to the hospital bed, occasionally monitoring the oxygen and comparing it to the readout from the small machine clipped to Millie's forefinger.

He was a little worried; he'd dealt with terminal cases several times before. However, he had committed the unpardonable sin of becoming attached to Millie and knew that he'd pay an emotional toll for that. It wasn't that that was worrying him, however, but the sudden downwards turn that she was apparently taking.

Both the doctor and he had thought that Millie might survive the month of August at least, which meant another four weeks. Her condition when he'd arrived the previous night was telling a different story. It sometimes happened this way he knew. The mind might still be fighting but the body was too exhausted to keep on with the struggle.

His buddy might be too late getting that information at this rate. He sighed, thinking about Grace the previous evening. 'It's going to go hard wi' ye lass; I wonder if ye'll let me be there for ye when ye fall.'

Around five he got up and wandered to the window again, fighting off the slightly surreal feeling that came with being overtired and worried. He stood next to the slight gap to feel the cool air on his face, noticing for the first time that it was raining yet again. Really it had been a terrible summer so far; too many days of rain or dull grey cloud.

Coming back to the bed with yet another cup of coffee he saw that Millie's eye were open and watching him. 'Alright, lass?'

'Yes Dan, I just feel a bit restless. I'm rather tired of looking at these four walls, but I haven't got the energy to do anything else,' she frowned, 'and that's perilously close to whining.' She shook her head in self disgust.

Dan gave her a considering look. Then he moved the nursing chair next to the window's low sill and came back to the bed. 'How about if we do this?' He disconnected the cannula and pulled back the covers. 'I don't want you to be off the O_2 too long, but a few minutes won't hurt ye.' While he spoke he moved her gently to the edge of the bed and swung a shawl around her shoulders.

'Now, I do my he-man stuff.' He swung her up and walked across the room, settling her in the chair so she could look out the window and then going back to fetch a blanket from the small linen trolley behind the door.

'There's damn all to see, Millie, except the rain and the street.' He settled the blanket around her legs and tucked it firmly round her waist.

Millie, somewhat breathless from the speed of his actions rather than lack of oxygen, gave a low laugh. 'Oh! How nice. Can you open the window a bit more, Dan?'

'Dinna tak' cold lass!' He edged round her and pushed the window wider so that the draft blew on her face, then adjusted her shawl round her shoulders. Millie held out a hand over the sill and felt the rain landing on her palm. 'Oh, Dan, I didn't think I'd feel rain again.' She sniffed, 'Sorry, I know it's silly.'

'Nae then, lass, you're entitled to feel what ye want.' He crouched down in front of her, offering a clean tissue. 'Tell me when ye want to go back to bed.'

He slithered down the wall and leaned back against it looking into the room, his head resting against the side of the chair. 'I was thinking about yon story ye told me about the Atom Bomb and remembering other battles I've been involved in.' He pulled his knees up and wrapped his arms around them, settling comfortably on the carpet.

'Death's a strange experience, Millie; it's frightening and mystical and rather wonderful, and none of us want to face it head on.' He paused to shift and settle again, 'I mind when I was out in Serbia there were these wee Yugoslav bairns; they hung around the unit begging for sweeties and what they really needed was a square meal and a bit of peace. Ye could see the fear on their faces when the shelling started. They knew what death was all about alright, and they were scared,' he shrugged, the frustration ripe in his voice, 'and there was naught I could do for them either.'

Millie brought a hand down and gently stoked the head, feeling the hair soft and yet slightly springy under her hand. Like red deer pelt she thought absently.

Dan smiled slightly but didn't look at her. 'Ye asked me the other night why I left the army. It's true my time was up but truth to tell I was glad to be out of the Army; there is still a lot of need out there, but I kent I couldn't take much more of the killing and maiming. It seems ye only ha' so much stomach for it and then ye ha' to get out while ye can still the nightmares, or they started to eat ye up inside.'

Millie sighed gently.

'I get nightmares, Millie. It's one of the reasons I do nights; I don't dream sae much during the day.' He looked up at her 'I dream about a young woman sometimes, I treated her in Afghanistan. My buddy wanted to marry her, she'd been circumcised, Millie.' He shuddered, looking back at the far wall of the room 'God, it made me sick t' ma' stomach, and it took guts to come and see a male nurse. They burnt her to death; her male relatives, when they found out she'd been seeing an American serviceman, Millie, and we couldn't do a bloody thing to them.'

Millie continued to stroke the head, offering back the comfort of touch she herself had received from Dan. She cupped his face and looked directly at him as she spoke 'You are needed, Dan, and you are helping me. At least I get to say good bye and I've enjoyed my life to the full. It hasn't been shortened by anyone.'

Dan reached up and took her hand, 'Aye weel,' He sighed. 'Ye dinna want to hear my troubles.'

They sat together in companionable silence, until Millie said, 'The dawns coming up, Dan.'

'Will I pop you back in bed, Millie?'

Millie sighed. 'I think you'd better, Dan, I'm starting to float a bit again and my fingers are tingling.'

Dan lifted her and carried her across the room. 'Let's get some oxygen into ye and that'll go away. Would ye like a wheat bag for your feet, and a drink?'

He tucked her under the covers, settling her against the pillows and attaching her to the oxygen tubing again.

'Yes to both, Dan, thanks, and then I think I could sleep again.' She smiled tiredly up at him, catching his hand as he would have turned away. 'Thank you for sharing with me, Dan. It makes me feel as though I'm needed and this time is important too; I'm not just waiting for death.'

Dan nodded. 'Aye Millie, I know, and I dinna regret it, but it seems awful selfish o' me a' the same.'

He disappeared into the kitchen and returned to tend to his patient. As he sat beside her while she drifted into the deep sleep of exhaustion he reflected that maybe he too needed someone to be needed by, and maybe that someone was Grace. He thought of her the previous afternoon and the sweetness of her; she might be a bit shy but she was right, she wasn't a girl, she was a woman. He smiled to himself; he'd willingly go without a little sleep to be in her company that afternoon; maybe they could hold each other up when the fall came.

6

AT EIGHT THIRTY THAT morning the dig looked like an
upturned anthill. People scurried about the place setting
up equipment and, every so often, casting hasty looks
upwards at a sky heavily laden with sodden clouds.

David was surly and John was tetchy; and it made
Grace feel quite guilty because she actually felt quite
bright, despite the weather and her concerns over Millie.
She knew she'd been dreaming and the few wisps she'd
tried to grasp before she fully woke tantalised her with
both their happy feel, and what she could remember of the
slightly erotic content.

David stood with John and Grace in the area where
they'd excavated over the past two weeks, looking at the
foundations of the small Tudor manner. 'I think I'd like this
section done in 1:10 rather than 1:20.' He waved a couple of
surveyor's arrows in his hand as he indicated the area.
'Then if you can get the dumpy level we can plot the
relevant features in relation to Grace's well.' He nodded off
in the direction of the previous day's dig.

John nodded tiredly and David cast him an
impatient look, 'What the hell ails you this morning?'

'First night at home with the baby and boy! can
that little fella yell!'

'Well man, we all have our crosses to bear and you
wanted a kid.' David stomped away. Grace and John
exchanged a glance. 'What's wrong with me? I'd like to
know what's wrong with him. He's lost all his native charm
this summer.'

Grace shook her head. 'I don't know, John; maybe
he's worrying about the possible break-in yesterday.'

John shouted at Doug as he hurried past, 'Hi Doug,
can you spare Grace a couple of lads to skim while Kate

does her drawings?'

Doug stopped in full run and came back. 'Yeah. I got one trained and one half trained, that do you?'

'Yeah that'll do fine.' John nodded his thanks. 'Hey Doug, when do you get over the sleep deprivation bit?'

Doug grinned a bit evilly; his son had been born the previous Christmas. 'Feeling knackered, John? Don't worry; the first twenty years are the worst. Like David said to me, 'He'll be playing with the Pleistocene before you know it'.'

Grace laughed both at the joke and at the horrified expression on John's face. 'Never mind John, tell Sandra I'll try to get out to your house to see her over the weekend.'

David came over, muttering to himself. He looked at the cheerful group, 'Come on, I don't pay you to lounge around.' Even his hair seemed to be bristling this morning. 'John, use the theodolite to get the angles as well will you, and look sharp; it's going to bucket down soon.' He stomped away again.

Grace followed his passage towards the site shed with a curious eye. She looked at the puzzled and slightly resentful look on the men's faces and decided she'd just go and have a word with David. He was becoming difficult to live with and she wanted to know why. She'd known the man twenty years or more and he was usually the soul of geniality.

She found him sitting at the table, his hands folded in front of him, and a serious scowl on his face as he glared down at the wooden boards. She came in, shutting the door and sitting down opposite him at the table.

'David, what's wrong?' The question was put gently. 'It's not like you to snap at us. I know you're worried about this break-in, but we're all doing our best and everyone is very security conscious these days. You're like a bear with a sore head.' He scowled at her then looked

118

back at the table. 'Can I help at all?'

David raised a face full of misery. 'Grace, don't push, love.' He hesitated. 'I...I...' He stopped again. He cleared his throat, 'I'll go and apologise in a minute or two. I am worried, and these phone calls are an added worry.'

'What phone calls?'

David gave her a blank look, 'Of course; you weren't there last night. I had a caller yesterday afternoon who rang off as soon as he heard my voice. Alice claims someone rang the office but wouldn't talk, and apparently some man rang, trying to wheedle information about the dig out of Kate last night. I don't want my team in danger.'

Grace saw the colour on his rather rugged cheeks grow deeper as she watched. She suddenly put together a series of disconnected events over the past few weeks and said, 'Oh! David.'

He looked at her, ''Oh David' what?'

'You're in love with Kate. It's her you're scared for.'

'Don't be stupid; I'm naturally concerned for all the team. Kate's a member of that team; she's a young post grad' student working for me.'

'Yeah, and that's your problem isn't it.'

'Grace ...' He growled, as he scowled at her.

'Don't worry, David, I won't talk. I don't like gossip about me, so I'm not going to spread any about you, you know that.'

'There's nothing to gossip about.'

'Do you want it to stay that way?' Grace half smiled at him.

David looked suddenly defeated. 'Oh God! Grace, what the hell am I supposed to do? She's too young for me, even if she wasn't in my care. I can't roll back the years even if I wanted too.' He rubbed his hands over his face;

his emerald eyes had lost all their customary sparkle and Grace realised he looked his age for once. 'I'm looking for excuses to spend time in her company, but when I find them I snap at the poor girl until she can't speak without stuttering.'

'Have you spoken to her about this?'

'Don't be bloody stupid! I don't want anyone screaming sexual harassment at me. You maybe wouldn't remember that stupid student when you were a youngster on your first dig for me.'

'Oh yes I do; even I could read those signals. She was stupid. She should have known better than make a play for you; she was a little gold digger, we could all see what she was up too. Kate is different David.'

David shook his head, the door rattled and the object of their discussion sidled in. Kate looked from one face to the other. David looked thunderous and Grace looked sympathetic. 'I'll ...I'll come back.' She turned to go and Grace stood up. She thought she'd just tied down the look of yesterday, the girl was jealous of her.

'It's OK, Kate, David and I where just talking. I want time off this afternoon,' she grinned, 'for a date.'

Two voices echoed 'You do? A date!' They both looked at her as if she was a rare specimen at the zoo.

It was hardly flattering, Grace thought, when people were so surprised that she should be going on a date. She turned back to David looking him squarely in the eyes. 'I should do a little exploratory dig if I were you, David; I've got one of my hunches. I think you just might find what you're looking for. Use a trowel not a pickaxe; you might find it just under the surface.' She flicked her eyes towards Kate then back to his, smiling slightly at his faint nod of understanding, and then walked out of the door, aware that two pairs of eyes were following her.

Grace closed the door gently and stood with her

back to it, surveying the busy scene before her. Doug was organising his troops, sending little groups to various sections to dig or scrape or sieve. The main interest for this dig may have been a possible Roman fort, but that didn't mean you could just ignore the other archaeological finds that turned up just because they weren't your speciality. They might be someone else's speciality.

She walked across the site, skipping between baulks and noticing that Doug had got one group removing some of them to reveal the full glory of a row of medieval cobbles and several post hole markings. Exchanging greetings as she went she headed for her well and her body.

The tarps were being removed by a couple of burly students and the young Australian girl. Grace nodded, producing a reasonable facsimile of her drawl 'G'day, Alice.' She nodded at the others, 'Are you enjoying our British summer?'

'I might as well have stayed home; it's like our blooming winter.' She brightened, 'But working on Roman remains is cool.' She blew a bubble with her gum. 'Can I help you today, Grace?'

'Sure, but you know you aren't allowed to touch the human remains don't you?'

'Yeah. But I can fill in the reports for you as you clear the loose, and I can clean off artefacts. Right?'

Grace looked across to where the site manager was working. 'Has Doug said it's OK?'

The girl nodded.

'OK, Let's climb in the hole then and we'll see how thing go.'

The two of them removed the unwieldy well cap and propped it on its side against the last step of the excavation. Grace gazed down into the depths and looked round for the small wooden ladder.

'I could have sworn I left that ladder in place yesterday.' She stood looking down in puzzlement for a minute, then turned abruptly away. 'Don't any of you go down yet. I need to speak to Doug and John first.'

Making her way hastily back across the site she hailed John.

'John, can I have a word?'

John sauntered over from where he was putting up equipment. 'What's up?'

Lowering her voice slightly she said, 'Wait a minute, I want to talk to Doug as well.' They walked over to him as he finished issuing a stream of instructions.

'Hello you two. People will start to talk you know if you keep getting together for little chats.' He raised an ironical eyebrow then looked more closely at Grace, taking in the grim expression on her face.

'What's wrong, Grace?'

'Did either of you shift my ladder or go down into the well after I left yesterday?'

'Nah.'

'Nope.' the answers were accompanied by puzzled shakes of the head.

'Well someone's been down there. I haven't had a good look round yet but David and I covered the skeleton up and now it's clear again. And what's more my ladder's gone!'

John looked worried. 'I think we'd better go and disturb David.' He didn't look very happy at the prospect. Grace thought of the pair she'd left in the site shed and shuddered at the thought of Doug walking in on a scene such as she'd enacted the previous day with Dan.

'No, it's OK, I'll go. You two do a quick tour and see if anything else is out of place.'

122

She headed purposefully towards the shed. As she arrived at the door she caught out of the side of her eye the Australian girl, Alice, standing on the top of the step excavation watching her. Alice turned and walked away; going towards Doug, and Grace shrugged and, rattling the door in a very marked manner, entered the shed.

WHEN GRACE HAD LEFT the room, David and Kate had looked at each other. Both looked as if they wanted to stealthily withdraw without attracting attention to themselves - like a pair of very shy deer ready to hightail it out of there.

Finally, as Kate started to turn, David spoke. 'Hang on a minute, Kate, I need a word.'

Kate looked slightly stricken. 'Is there s…something wrong?'

'No. Not that I'm aware of.' David stood up and came round the table. As he advanced Kate retreated, so that they appeared to be engaged in some complicated dance. 'Blast it stand still girl; I won't hurt you!' He growled.

Kate slithered to a stop with her back to the door as if she was about to flee the premises. David stopped a foot away. 'I hope to God you're right, Grace.' He muttered.

'Is it a…about this new exploratory that G…grace wants you to do?'

'In a manner of speaking.' David reached out and took her hands which were now firmly clasped in front of her. He pulled them away from her body and stood holding them gently and waited for the trembles he could feel going through her to stop slightly. When this didn't look likely to happen he said, 'Kate, look at me.'

When she raised scared eyes to his he looked her full in the face. He coughed then, his stomach doing a jig which was throwing his heart into his throat, spoke again. 'Kate, I'm becoming very fond of you.'

Kate looked startled. 'Doug, he said you could h…hand pick your team, he said you wouldn't have a…anyone you didn't l...like.'

'I didn't say I liked you.' He felt the warmth stealing into his cheeks.

Kate tried to pull her hands free. He watched the tears gathering behind her glasses swamping the deep brown eyes. 'Oh! Bugger it! Never mind. You'd better get to work.' He let go of her hands and turned his back.

Kate after a horrified look turned round to the door. Grace entered at this unpropitious moment. She looked the pair of them over. Kate looked as though she was about to burst into tears and David looked as if he was about to explode as he swung back at her untimely entrance.

While she had a sneaking sympathy for the course of true love, she couldn't spare the time just then to sort it out.

'David, I'm sorry to interrupt but I need to know if you went back to my excavation yesterday.'

David did his best to pull himself together. He didn't know who he was madder at, himself for listening to Grace, Grace herself for meddling, or Kate for the way she'd just responded. Nobody, he reflected, liked to make a fool of themselves.

'No, Grace, why the hell should I go into your damn hole when the rain was pouring down and I'd helped you cover the damn thing up in the first place.'

Grace ignored his snarl, 'Someone has uncovered the skeleton. Since we left yesterday afternoon.'

David became the professor before their eyes, his body snapping to attention and his face settling into calm lines. 'Explain exactly, Grace, and then we'll go and ask around.'

'John and Doug are asking already.'

David nodded his understanding.

'It's like I say, David. We covered everything; now the ladder's missing and the skeleton is visible.'

David looked through her in an absent way for a minute, assessing the situation. He suddenly became aware that Kate was still there. 'You,' he pointed at her, 'fetch all the notes and sketches from yesterday; Grace, come with me.'

He strode out and the two girls hurried to obey and follow him.

John was standing at the top of the step excavations talking to Doug as they all drew near. 'Anyone know anything, John?'

'Nope, nobody knows nufin'.'

David turned to Kate and Grace, 'Kate, go down and check your drawings see if it's just been exposed, or if anything else has been revealed.' He watched as John passed Kate his hard hat and she climbed down to the top of the well. Doug passed her down a short ladder which she placed and then carefully climbed down.

'Now, Grace. We covered everything up. Let's see if we can spot where the tarp was shifted.' He turned round at the gathering crowd. 'We're short enough of time without you all gaping, get back to you own areas. I'll sound the hooter when I want your attention.' He shooed them away and then addressed Doug and John, 'All this mystery has got me rattled, Doug, John, you'll have to make allowances.' The two men nodded their understanding. Doug moved off, herding the small teams before him.

John smiled somewhat grimly, 'Yeah well, it's

beginning to get me rattled too and I'm not the project manager. Thank God!'

Grace was looking more than worried. She was looking angry. She began to pace the outer edge of her excavation, with David close behind. 'Here! This is where whoever it was climbed under; you can see there are two sets of peg holes at this place.' She pointed then stood up and looked at the students busily working around the site. As far as she could see everyone had either got boots or Wellingtons on. David was very safety conscious.

'Look, David,' she kept her voice low, 'that's a trainer footprint, you can see the marks; I've got a pair like that, so I recognise that brand. But these aren't mine; they're too small and, anyway, I don't wear them on site. Everyone obeys the safety rules round here regarding footwear.'

David stood looking down. 'They'd better obey the rules.' he said absently. He too looked across at the diligent workers. 'Grace, could we do a plaster cast do you think? I don't know how much use it would be.' He frowned.

'Are we going to the police, David?'

'Oh yes. This is becoming too serious to ignore. You'd better not work down there until I've checked with them.'

'Kate.' David went down the side of the excavation and looked into the well.

'Yes, sir.' Kate turned a white face upwards.

David grimaced at her form of address, 'Come up and tell me what you see.'

David offered a hand down to Kate as she climbed back up, her jeans distinctly grubby and her sketchpad in her hand. He retained her hand as she explained what she'd seen. 'Nothing much has been d…disturbed, D…David. Someone has been down who s…shouldn't have, because you and Kate are both c…careful where you

126

put your f…feet, and there are some f…footprints over the area being t…troweled; where whoever it was cleared the s…skeleton again.'

David nodded his understanding; no archaeologist would trample on the actual area being excavated if they could avoid it. Kate tried to keep her face impassive, even while she tugged gently to remove her hand from David's.

'I can't s…see anywhere that has had artefacts removed; there aren't any h…holes that s…shouldn't be there. It matches up with my drawings though I'd have to d…damp, to be s…sure of the colouring on the s…surface of the bottom.'

'OK Kate, thank you.' The tone was warm; Kate shot him a stunned glance, finally gaining possession of her own hand again. David, aware of his audience, said nothing more. Grace, a patient onlooker and listener, wondered what the two had said to one another. Whatever it was didn't seem to have cleared the air very much.

'I'll go back to the office and make some phone calls, Grace, while you do that little job for me.' He nodded at the place where they'd found the footprints.

Grace nodded her agreement.

'Kate, come back to the office with me, the police may want to speak to you too.'

He turned to John, 'Can you take charge for a bit, John. See if you can have a word with the farmer if you think it's worth putting a trench in over in that corner. We have to keep going, find what we can, before the contractors claim their land.' He nodded to a distant area of the field.

The four of them scattered to their various jobs.

David opened the door of the office and ushered Kate through. Part of his mind had been re-running the scene in the office before Grace had returned; he thought he could see were he had gone wrong with Kate. He wanted to sort things out so that he could concentrate on this new problem at the site.

'Have a seat, Kate, while I make this phone call.'

Kate went round the wooden table and sat in her accustomed place. She was watching David from under her eyelashes, rather in the manner of a rabbit watching a fox. David was aware of her scrutiny but decided that he must phone the police first. When that was done he turned to the young woman sitting so silently, the table a secure barrier between them.

'Right, I think I said something to upset you before Grace came in and that wasn't my intention.' He sat down opposite, waiting for her to lift her deep brown eyes to his face.

'I need to deal with this crisis but I also need to get a few things clear with you too, Kate, so that I can concentrate properly. I want you to answer some questions as honestly as you can.' He paused, thinking, 'Well as honestly as you dare anyway. Let me assure you that I won't be sacking you if you get the answers wrong.'

Kate looked startled.

He stretched out a hand, taking one of hers across the table.' Do you like me, Kate?'

She opened her mouth and closed it again, looking down at their clasped hands. 'Let me clarify that. Do you like me as a man? Not as your boss or the prof'; but as me, David.'

'Y…yes.' She looked shyly up at him.

'Good, we progress. Because I'm fond of you, my dear, which is were we went wrong before, not like, fond.' He watched the colour start to glow in her cheeks. 'In fact I might be a bit more than fond of you.' He could feel his own cheeks growing warm as she continued to stare at him, and thanked a merciful heaven that had prompted him to grow a beard many years ago.

128

'Next question, do you class me as an old fogey?'

She shook her head, making the red-gold curls bounce about her cheeks. 'Oh no, D...David! You're not o...old.'

David possessed himself of her other hand. 'OK.' He took a deep breath, 'Final question. Will you come out for a meal with me today?'

Kate's face lit up and her red hair seemed to flame with sudden animation as she shook it back and looked him full in the face. David watched the transformation and let out the breath he didn't know he'd been holding, in a whoosh. 'Is that a 'Yes'?'

Kate nodded her head vigorously, and then gently pulled a hand away to push her glasses back up her nose. He thought she looked adorable. Her other hand, which had been lying quiescent, now turned over and gripped his. 'So long as I'm not too young for you?'

David grinned. 'We'll work something out between us.'

GRACE PASSED THE OUTSIDE of the east window of the cathedral, admiring its jewel colours, and rounded the corner towards the main door. She saw Dan leaning idly against the warm stone pillars, his head glowing red in the sunshine. He'd come dressed in casual blue slacks and a denim jacket, his white t-shirt dazzling as it peeked out between the lapels. A pair of sturdy boots covered up his size tens yet he still contrived to look smart and, yes she thought, handsome.

She gave a small sigh of relief; she hadn't been quite sure what to wear. For a start the weather was so changeable; then he hadn't said what they would be doing. Was it just to be a meal or would they be spending the afternoon together. She hastily checked her person.

129

Unexceptional; jeans, a white blouse, a light, fire-engine red jacket and her favourite pair of low heeled boots. Yes that was casual enough.

She came to a halt beside him.

'Hi, Dan.'

'Hi.' He smiled his slow smile as he looked at her, thinking she looked as pretty as a picture standing there in the sunshine. 'I like yon restaurant,' he nodded his head towards the refectory, 'but we can go anywhere ye'd like.'

'Oh, here will be fine.' Grace turned with him and he put a hand under her elbow to lead her down the steps and into the cool interior. They both did their best to ignore the frisson of sensation at the contact. The place was nearly empty; only a pair of elderly ladies in sensible tweeds and heavy brogues could be seen dining next to one of the low windows.

'Do you tak' a seat and I'll get a menu.' He walked casually over to the long counter, coming back with a couple of thick cards while Grace went and settled at table next to a pillar. The refectory had a low vaulted ceiling which Dan's head nearly brushed as he made his way towards her.

He slid into a chair opposite and handed her a card remarking, 'Their hot-pot is good, but ye might want something a bit cooler. I was thinking it would be cold again this day.'

Grace smiled at him as he sat opposite her, the light striking his face and causing those brilliant blue eyes to twinkle across at her; she saw that he had faint blue shadows under them though, 'To tell the truth I'm starving. Hot-pot sounds great.'

'Good, what would ye be wanting to drink?'

'A large pot of coffee?' She raised an eyebrow. 'You must be tired, Dan.'

130

'Regretting this?'

'Oh! No, but you do look tired.'

'Thanks, I've the twa nights off noo ta regain ma strength.' He said dryly 'Ye'r sae gud for ma ego.'

Grace lightly touched his hand, 'Sorry.'

He looked across; a gleam in his eyes reminding Grace of a rather intelligent wolf. 'Weel, if a' should ha' a wee nap ye can always wake me up, a' would think it rather delightful t' wake up agin thee, lass.' He watched the faint wash of colour cover her cheeks. 'And even better to sleep beside thee.'

'That's a very provocative thing to say, are you trying to seduce me?'

'Is it working?' Dan grinned.

She was saved from having to answer by the arrival of the waitress to take their orders. 'I thought this was self-service, Dan.'

'Aye, but she can see we've better things to do nor that.'

'Can ye bring coffee lass, before the meal?'

'Certainly, sir.'

They sat quietly absorbing the atmosphere, 'I haven't been in here for a while. It's really gone up market from the small café they used to have.'

'Aye? I found it when I moved to this area; I'm hunting a house so that I can walk yon Wall at my ain pace. It's something a' promised ma' sen a' would do when a' left the army.'

'So why are you working, Dan?'

'A havena found the place yet and a mun eat and not spend ma capital!' He grinned, 'Though t' be honest, I havena quite got into the way o' bein' retired yet and I like

131

ma' work.'

Dan sat back to allow a large pot of coffee to be placed on the table and, when the waitress had again departed, changed to a safer subject, perhaps.

'So, Millie was telling me all about your time capsule.' He held up a hand as Grace set down the pot and reached for the milk. 'I'll tak' it black, thanks.'

'Yeah, it's only a small tin but interesting for all that. We've asked one of the historians at the university if he can track down the man whose name is on the ration book. Of course we don't know if he made the capsule,' She smiled at the waitress as she approached with their meals. 'Thank you.' The young woman trotted away and she looked at Dan, 'But it's worth a try.'

She nodded as he offered her the salt. 'The thing that's puzzling me is how Aunt Millie knew there was a disused railway line there, much less a possible well.'

Dan gave her a quizzical look, 'How do ye mean, lass?'

'Well we'd not looked at the maps but she seemed to know that area,' She cocked her head, looking at him; 'I suppose it's because she's lived here most of her life.'

Dan wondered just how much he ought to say. Millie had asked him to talk to Grace, but he wasn't sure how she'd react to him knowing so much about her.

'Another thing,' Grace continued, 'she was involved with some man. She mentioned his name yesterday evening.'

Dan kept his thoughts to himself as he silently questioned her, his head on one side.

She sipped some coffee. 'Someone called James. You know, Dan, I'm so pleased about that. I've always felt guilty because I know she didn't marry because she had to look after my mum; and then when my parents were killed she looked after me.' She grinned impishly across the plates at him. 'I've always worried that she'd missed out because of me. Now it seems she didn't. That's so ...' She waved her fork. 'Cool, as Alice would say.' She grinned, and ate with relish. She looked down at her plate. 'This is really good.'

Dan found he was being infected by her lighter spirits. 'Aye it is good.' And he meant more than the meal. He sipped coffee and looked at her over the rim. 'So what have you done today?'

Grace looked serious and he was sorry he'd asked as the light in her eyes dimmed, turning her eyes to pewter. 'We've wasted a great deal of precious time talking to policemen instead of working on the dig.' She set her cup down and picked up the coffee pot, holding it out, 'More?'

'Aye,' He proffered his cup. 'I thought ye had told Millie the coroner had confirmed that your skeleton could be excavated.'

'Oh it's not my skeleton. Well it is my skeleton but ...' Grace laughed. 'Let me start again.'

'Aye and take it slow, forebye. I've only had fower hours sleep.'

Grace grinned at him. 'Someone, some unauthorised person, has been digging up my skeleton. I'm pretty sure they haven't removed any artefacts. We checked against the careful notes everyone keeps. But it's more than annoying that they've been on the dig; it's the way they've destroyed evidence that's so criminal. Once you've dug something out you can't put the soil back in exactly same place, so that evidence is gone for good except, for detailed records. And obviously,' she drank coffee, 'they aren't going to leave us any records.'

Dan nodded his understanding. 'It'll be a criminal offence then, aye.'

'Aye.' Grace smiled at him.

'Do you ha' any ideas who might be doing it?'

'Well, there are one or two things that have us a bit puzzled but David, my boss.' she said, at his look, 'David thinks someone on the team might be involved, but he isn't saying much or why.' She grinned again. 'He's not quite firing on all cylinders yet, the poor man is involved with romance for the first time that I know of, and it's knocked him sideways.'

'Oh! Aye, weel he has ma sympathy. I'm a bit that road ma ain self.' Dan looked her straight in the face so that she couldn't pretend not to understand his meaning.

He watched her blushing, thinking how the sun was making her hair like a small halo round her head. He longed to touch; but took a grip on both his emotions and his coffee cup instead, emptying it and setting it down.

They settled to the business of eating, Grace finding that appetite was the best sauce, as she realised she hadn't eaten since lunch the day before, and that had only been a sandwich. She set her knife and fork down with a sigh of satisfaction, looking up to see Dan watching her.

'Do ye want anything else?' She thought he looked serious suddenly and she wondered at the expression which flitted across his face

Grace looked at him a little uncertainly, 'No, no thanks.' She hoped he wasn't regretting their time together.

'I'll away and pay then.' He rose on the words and Grace gathered her shoulder bag and stood up, waiting for him to return. She admired his tall figure as he strode back towards her. Yes, she thought, I can see the soldier in you.

Dan came to a halt beside her; smiling and stretching out a gentle hand and just brushing the curls back. 'Will ye tak a walk wi' me?'

Grace sighed quietly with relief and held out a

hand. Dan clasped it and she felt his warm, slightly rough, palm meet hers. The tension they both felt ebbing slightly with the contact.

'Where would you like to go?'

'I've no idea; it's your town, Grace.'

They walked out the door of the restaurant and stood looking at the edifice of the Cathedral while Grace pondered the question. 'Do you want to stay in town or would you mind going a little further afield?'

'To tell the truth, lass, I dinna care so long as I can ha' a bit o' time wi' ye.' Dan's lips twitched. 'A'm afraid the effect of little sleep and a hot cooked meal are ha'in a rather drastic effect on me.' He smiled down at her, 'But a' dinna want to part company yet either.'

Grace looked him over. 'OK, here's what we'll do. We'll go and get my car and I'll drive us while you have a nap; then when we get somewhere, we can have a walk?'

He nodded and they began to stroll along the road towards the castle and its conveniently placed car park. As they left they were unaware that they'd nearly given a small insignificant man a heart attack by their sudden appearance at that particular moment.

'A' keep meaning to visit that place, but I never seem to get round to it.' Dan nodded at the ancient pile as the castle dominated their horizon.

'I'll give you a tour if you want. Not today though.' Grace looked at him cautiously. She had spoken impulsively; the thought of another day spent in his company filled her with a quiet delight but she wasn't sure how Dan felt about that. It seemed a bit forward now she came to think about it.

'Aye, that would be brawly.'

Grace raised an eyebrow and looked at him.

Dan smiled and shook his head, 'It would be great.

A'm apt t' get broader the more tired a' get. Sorry.'

'It's OK, I rather like it.' Grace gently squeezed his hand and had the pressure returned. 'Here we are.' She unlocked the car and, getting in, leant over to undo the passenger side. 'No central locking.'

Dan got in and Grace became aware of just how small her car was as they both became enclosed in the small space. 'Push your seat back, Dan and relax for a bit.'

Dan took her at her word, stretching out his long legs and laying his head back on the rest. 'It's no just the right thing to ask a girl for a meal and then fall asleep on her. That's why a' said to tak' a walk, a canna just fall asleep when a'm on ma feet.' He rolled his head to the side and watched as she competently put the car in gear and drove them out of the car park and on to the main road.

Grace spared him a quick glance. 'Go to sleep, Dan. Then we can both enjoy ourselves.'

Dan laughed, a slow low chuckle, 'Weel I ken what ye mean, lass, but ye could ha' put it better.' He watched her frowning, then a small smile passed over her lips.

'Aye, lad, a' could.' She gently mocked and reached out a hand to his, patting it before putting hers back on the wheel.

Dan lay back feeling the sleep dragging at his eyelids and breathing in the scent that was Grace, something soft and sweet with just a hint of spice, he thought. She was humming quietly to herself; he couldn't quite place the tune, as she drove them out of the town and along a back road. He gave in to the overwhelming need to sleep and, warmed by the sun coming through the window, relaxed and fell into the arms of Morpheus.

Grace cast him the odd covert glance as she drove. He lay, his hands folded in his lap, breathing quietly. She headed towards the direction of the dig. Not that she was going there but she was heading for the Solway Firth. It had been a bit of a wasted day, as she'd said to Dan, at least as far as work was concerned. The weather might have improved but that was all.

The morning had been spent, first waiting for the police to arrive, and then answering their innumerable questions. They had finally allowed her back into the well to carry on her excavations. David and Kate had been working with her. She'd caught the odd smile that they exchanged occasionally, but she had held her peace. As she'd remarked, she didn't like gossip and there were plenty of others within hearing who might pass comments.

There were some artefacts with the skeleton: there'd been a broken mortar and a thick heavy pestle made out of a fine marble. Neither item had been large but they had been buried next to the body's right hand. There was a small stone which might be a statue, much defaced; David was going to try to identify it when they'd cleaned it up some more. Her theory of the body having been thrown down the well seemed to have as much water as the well did.

There were some unidentifiable small lumps which David had also taken away, locking them in his car. She had finally got the skeleton out, and boxed, with much relief; just before lunch. Her next task would be to examine it in more detail at the lab. The trouble was there was so much more to do on the site and they couldn't afford to lose time.

She had been making her way steadily down narrow back roads towards the edge of the water; now she drew up and put the car into park. Dan didn't stir as she quietly switched off the engine and leaned back against her own seat. She looked at the man resting in the passenger seat, wondering what exactly she was getting into.

With his eyes closed and his face in repose his face presented quite a stern profile. She liked the square chin and the long straight nose. Her eyes rested on his lips for a

137

minute or two. She had enjoyed being kissed the day before, and that was a first. She had also found her body coming alive and she wasn't quite sure how to deal with that sensation either.

She looked at the short fuzz of hair and her lips twitched, remembering the feel of it under her hands. Then she grinned, of course that's what it reminded her of, Mr Gladly's tummy. Well that was hardly romantic; she wondered how he'd feel if she told him he made her feel safe and fuzzy because he reminded her of her teddy. Well maybe not she thought, as the core of her stirred at the memory of the way he'd held her.

Even while she looked his eyes flicked open, revealing their brilliant blue to gleam quizzically at her. Suddenly she didn't feel quite so safe; she watched as he smiled a slow and generous smile that revealed his nice white teeth and crinkled his eyes. He had awakened in the warmth of the quiet car, enveloped in the scent that was Grace, and wishing he could be enveloped in her body too. When he'd opened his eyes to find her watching him he'd seen a little of that longing reflected back at him in her eyes.

'So where are we then, lass?'

Grace turned with relief to the scenery; 'This is a little stretch of coast not far from the dig on the Solway Firth. I used to come here when I was young and wander along the edge of the water trying to imagine what it must have been like for the Roman soldiers stationed here.'

She looked back at him to find him watching her intently; hastily she looked away, her left hand holding the wheel as she looked out the front windscreen. 'Can you imagine being stationed in a foreign country where no-one speaks the language and the weather and scenery are all wrong?'

Dan gave a low chuckle 'Oh! Aye, verra easily.'

Grace laughed, 'I was forgetting. Of course you can, Dan.'

Dan took the hand that gripped the wheel and held it in a warm clasp. 'You're not that old yet, are ye, Grace?' Her body was volubly protesting that she was very young when it came to matters of the flesh. The double-edged question had her moving awkwardly in her seat.

He caressed the palm of her hand with his thumb, causing her pulse to skip. 'I miss home even here.' He said, looking across the stretch of water to the lowlands beyond. 'I was brought up in Fort William with Ben Nevis to our backs. I love the hills and even though Cumberland has a few it's not like the highlands. I've been around the world a bit and nothing compares to my ain land.'

He sat up a bit and Grace became aware of how small her car really was as she caught the aroma of his aftershave and the clean smell of fresh linen. It was like sharing a broom cupboard. Dan brought her hand to his mouth and kissed it softly on the palm, watching her over their joined hands, 'Shall we go for a walk then, lass? You can show me where you came so long ago.' He gently mocked her even while his eyes were telling her different things.

Grace nodded, unable to break eye contact.

'Aye lass, tis dangerous for both of us; isn't it?' He gently let go and turned to get out of the car, coming round to her side as she locked up, and took her hand again.

They set off along the side of the sandy, slightly muddy, bank following the estuary as it ebbed away towards the Irish Sea. Dan swung their joined hands as they crunched along the shoreline. He looked at the estuary and they heard its hiss and pull as it moved stealthily away from them, advancing even while it seemed to be retreating.

He glanced down at Grace as they strolled along,

wondering how it was that she had managed to advance so far into his thoughts that he'd dreamed of her that morning. A delicious dream that he felt he had no right to, but had enjoyed the lingering wisps of, enormously.

He sniffed the slightly brackish smell of the mud mingling with the fresh pasture land on the other side of the road, looking down at Grace as she wandered beside him, and catching a faint whiff of her scent.

'I canna quite place it,' he remarked.

'Can't place what?'

'I can't place your scent. It's been tantalising me for the past half hour.'

Grace grinned, 'Actually you're honoured. I normally forget to put any on.'

Dan stopped, causing her to stop too; she turned towards him in some surprise, feeling a frisson of intrigue at his intent look. 'Hmm.' Dan looked her over, 'I am indeed honoured, lass; for ye could ha' your pick and here ye are walking out wi' me.'

Grace stood looking at him, 'I'm pretty ordinary really, Dan. I've got a feeling it's you that's been able to pick and choose.'

Dan pulled her a bit closer. 'I'm sorry, lass, a' wasna going too, but I must kiss ye,' He brushed back her curls and looked deeply into the silver eyes watching him.

'Don't be sorry, Dan.'

Dan brushed her lips with his and then settled them firmly on hers. The call of the sea birds faded and the sea ceased to run noisily at the side of them as they were both caught up and stunned by the storm of passion that raced through their bodies. Dan tasted the sweetness of her and craved more and yet more. He pulled back, and then just held her, quivering a little. He was rather amazed to realise that she was quivering too.

140

'Och, lass, I dinna mean to scare ye.'

Grace shook her head. 'I'm not exactly scared, Dan. To tell you the truth I'm not quite sure what I am. I've not found myself in this situation before.' She smiled shyly up at him.

'Aye, I kent that and I meant to go a bit slower.' Dan looked down ruefully at her upturned face. 'I think we'd better go and find some company before either of us regrets anything. I'll tell ye to your face I want to bed ye, and we aren't at that stage yet are we, lass?' He raised a quizzical eyebrow. He watched the colour surge into Grace's cheeks. 'Your auntie said ye were shy, but I think its more inexperience, lass. Ye've never been wi' a man ha' ye?'

Grace refused to look away, stubborn pride kept her eyes locked on his. She shook her head.

'Aye that's what I thought.'

He pulled her close and kissed her firmly. 'Weel, maybe I'll get lucky, but we need to ken each other a bit better first, lass.' He took her hand and led her back towards her car without another word being spoken.

He waited patiently while Grace unlocked the car and climbed in, leaning over to pull up the lock on his side. They settled into their seats and fastened their belts. 'Ye're nae insulted are ye, lass?'

Grace shook her head. 'I'd rather you were honest with me, Dan. I told you I wasn't a girl.'

'Aye but ye're no just a woman yet either are ye?' He took her hand as it rested on the wheel and placed a soft kiss in her palm. 'Will ye see me again, after today?'

Grace brought their joined hands to her lips, placing a soft kiss on his knuckles and looking at him over them. 'Yes.'

Dan sighed deeply and smiled back at her. No

more was said, but the silence was comfortable as Grace drove them back to the outskirts of town. She spoke as they drove passed the trading estate. 'Do you mind if we visit Millie, Dan?'

'Nae that's fine.' He smiled across, looking at her profile as she drove competently along the road. 'I'm gae fond o' your auntie.'

They pulled up outside the house a few minutes later and Dan possessed himself of her hand as they walked up the garden path. 'What ha' ye there then?' She'd gathered up a brown bag from the back seat before locking the car. He nodded at the bag and looked at her quizzically.

'It's wrapping paper,' she giggled, a very girlish noise that had Dan grinning, 'Can't you hear it, it goes wrap, wrap.'

'That's a terrible joke!'

Grace laughed at him, the tension of the previous hour leaving her face. 'It's one of David's jokes. They're always terrible. He used to have me in fits as a little girl.'

She unlocked the front door and went inside. Dan followed, then leant forward and kissed her on her nose as she turned to shut it. He put a finger on her lips as she would have spoken, 'Just to keep me going aye.'

She nodded and they went into the front room where Millie sat in bed, the oxygen hissing gently and the radio playing quietly. She appeared to be asleep, but when they would have made to go out again she opened her eyes and smiled softly across the room at them.

'Hello, you two. I was just dozing.' She held out a hand and Grace went over and sat on the side of the bed, proffering a cheek for a kiss from the pale lips, and brushing back the silvery hair.

'Hello yourself, darling, how is it today?' Grace hid the shock she felt at the sight of the oxygen tubing and smiled down at Millie.

Dan, coming soft footed to the bed, smiled at the pair of them. 'Will I make us some tea?'

The two women nodded and he went into the kitchen. He was kicking himself; he hadn't thought to warn Grace about the oxygen and had caught her faint indrawn breath of shock and the stiffening of her body. He prepared the tea, calling himself several kinds of a fool while he did so.

When he came back in they were examining some small items of clothing spread out on the bed in front of them. 'I promised I'd deliver Aunt Millie's present to a friend who's just had a baby.' Grace held up a small bonnet in pale blue for Dan's inspection. He looked at her face, softened as it was by some secret thought. She smoothed the small hat and placed it next to a pair of bootees.

'Are you sure you wouldn't rather wait for them to come and visit? I know Sandra isn't up to much yet, but I'm sure John will bring her as soon as she's fit enough.'

Grace was looking down at the clothes, folding them neatly. Dan and Millie exchanged a glance then Millie shook her head. 'The way babies grow they won't fit if you keep them here. You take them tomorrow, darling, and bring me a picture back.'

Grace sighed, 'OK'

Dan came forward with the tea things and set it on the table while he helped Millie to sit up. Then he sat in the nursing chair and poured out the tea. Grace, meanwhile, had risen and removed her jacket, throwing it on the end of the bed. It wasn't meant to be provocative, Dan could see that, but he did admire her figure while she turned her attention towards Millie, answering some question about the excavations.

PHILIP JARDIN FELT HE'D had rather a wasted night as far as his job was concerned too. He was also feeling a bit badgered, not to mention foxed, the later by virtue of a bottle of scotch which sat half empty on the table. The first phone call had come at eleven o clock, rousing him from the first decent sleep he'd managed that week. He wasn't amused.

'Why the hell did you have to wake me! Couldn't it have waited until I'd had my sleep out?'

The voice on the end of the line wasn't sympathetic. 'Why the hell did you have to leave so many signs of your visit - a blind man could spot them?'

He looked at the phone as if the caller was talking in a foreign language. 'Signs, I didn't leave any signs.'

'You don't call removing the ladder, forgetting to cover the body up again, and trampling around on the wet earth enough signs? Why didn't you just leave a placard saying, 'I was 'ere'?'

'That wasn't me, I covered that blasted skeleton again, and why the hell should I take the ladder out?'

'Don't lie to cover your butt, I know you. We've had the police here all morning asking questions and making it far too hot. The Professor took away a box of things this lunch time, stashed them in his car. How did you miss them? I think you'd better stay away for a few days until things settle down. I'll meet you at the usual place at four.' The phone went dead in Jardin's hand and he swore viciously at the empty receiver before throwing the mobile down the bed, where it slithered over the silky duvet cover and dropped to the floor with a soft thud.

Jardin felt as though he'd been playing with a kitten that had roared in his ear. He thought he was being debonair or suave and that's what had attracted the girl but it seemed not, the lecture had raked against his nerves as if he'd been clawed by a lion.

Half an hour later the phone rang again. And kept on ringing. He pulled his head from under the pillow where he'd only just managed to doze off and looked blearily at the bottom of the bed from where the insistent buzz was coming from. His hair had not just receded, but like the tide, gone out completely; leaving a few reddish-grey strands like abandoned seaweed straggling over a strange pink rock.

He grunted and crawled out, revealing himself in rather tatty striped pyjamas. He looked around the floor, eventually locating the phone nestling under the corner of bed, and raucously proclaiming its eleventh call for attention. 'What the hell do you want now?'

The voice at the other end was icily polite.

'Huh! Sorry, boss.'

'Yeah I went and had another look last night.' He cocked his head, standing in the middle of the room, his pyjamas sagging round his thin waist like a badly folded deckchair, and scratched his bottom as he listened.

'Yeah I heard the police had been called in, but it wasn't me, you know me better than that, I ain't careless these days, boss.'

He hitched the trouser bottoms up and sat slowly down on the bed so that the corner dipped and sagged and his body slithered floor-wards dangerously. 'OK, boss, I hear you. Do you want to know what I found or not?' He shuffled back on the bed, rubbing his free hand over his face.

The murmured answer left him shivering.

'Just asking,' he said, sulkily. 'Anyway there was a skeleton, it was half excavated but it didn't look as if there were any grave goods around. I tell y' boss it was creepy in

145

that well, first time I've had the creeps on a site.' He shivered in retrospect.

'Well my contact says they haven't found any coins, just lots of pottery shards and the usual stuff in the midden.' He continued, 'She did say David Walker had taken some things and put them in his car instead of locking them in the site shed, but she didn't get a look at what they were.'

'I dunno, boss,' He shook his head in denial as his boss spoke at length on the phone. 'He knows my face, boss. I don't want to go back to prison.'

Finally he said. 'OK, boss, but the price just went up.'

He sat holding the phone after his caller rang off, looking out of the window at the sunshine, and thinking. Eventually he moved, mechanically gathering his shaving tackle and a clean towel and heading for the bathroom along the corridor.

Returning, clean shaven and with a towel wrapped around his skinny hips, he encountered his landlady. She believed he worked nights as a postal worker and was good about keeping the place quiet for him. He gave her a half smile. 'Sorry. I didn't know you were about Mrs P.'

She eyed his naked chest with ill concealed distaste; she didn't find a scrawny chest covered in grey hair like an old threadbare carpet very attractive, and her expression said so. 'Please wear a dressing gown in future, Mr Jardin; we don't want to distress the other guests.' She waddled away and he made a face at his door as he entered his room. He was thinking of moving to a different B and B anyway and if he did this job he could have one of those en-suite affairs.

He dressed carefully, for him, combing his hair from one side of his head to the other so that it covered his pink pate in an unhappy trail, to the detriment of his

146

dignity and the encouragement of small boys to throw things at him. He put both his phone and his notebook in his pocket, picked up Tacitus, and left for his first meeting of the day. He checked his watch; it was nearly half one. Just enough time to have something to eat beforehand.

He made his way towards the centre of the town and was strolling down the path as it cut through the side of the cathedral grounds, enjoying the first really fine afternoon for a while and feeling the sun warming his bones, when Grace and Dan appeared like a couple of really nasty genii, from the restaurant doorway. He dodged across to the cathedral itself and entered the main door in a flurry of raincoat and fear; the young guide on duty eyed him as if he was a flasher, but resisted the temptation to ask him if he was.

Philip could feel the cold sweat sticking to his back in the cool and quiet atmosphere. He never came in here; last time he had, he'd been locked up for five years, and he thought God might have a grudge against him, so he avoided what he termed, 'His turf'.

He sidled across the main transept and quickly turned up the far aisle. He stood looking at the faded pictures of saints on the wooden panels, his back half turned to the end of the aisle, allowing his eyes to adjust to the gloom and watching carefully to see who might come in.

He only started to breathe more easily when, after five minutes, no one else had entered the cathedral. He walked up the aisle and sat down with his back to the wall on a seat cunningly set over a radiator. 'I'm getting too bloody old for this caper. This one last job and I quit.' He murmured to himself, pulling a rather grey handkerchief from a trouser pocket and wiping his brow.

Eventually he went outside, looking up and down the path and moving with more haste than grace. He left the sacred precincts, heading for the nearest chippy and the obscurity of the New Lanes in the town centre.

DAVID AND KATE WERE also preparing to eat. David had declared a half holiday. 'It's a Friday folks; tidy your loose and go home and see your wives, mistresses and/or loved ones.' He nodded at a couple of the older men and they laughed. 'The site will be closed until Monday while the police do whatever they have to do. We all need to recharge our batteries.'

While everyone was gathering their property together, John wandered over. 'Are they any nearer, David?'

David shook his head and spoke softly. Nevertheless he was overheard by two girls. 'I don't like it, John, but these thieves can be a bit rough. I'm going to be here tomorrow and we're going to leave a few tempting bits around to try to flush out our prowler. The sooner this whole thing is cleared up the happier I'll be. But for now we'll leave the police in charge.'

He picked up his coat and strode out of the office, following in the wake of his team. John walked beside him. 'I hear our girl has got herself a date. How about that?'

David didn't look around though he was aware that Kate was only a few steps behind him. 'We're all entitled to a private life, John, let's keep it that way.' He changed the subject as they approached the gate. 'I'm going to visit Millie tomorrow, got any messages?'

'Just give her my love. Sandra's longing to visit, but the doctors have ordered her to stay indoors for a few days more. The infection on top of the caesarean has pretty much exhausted the poor girl.' He looked serious, his face stilling. 'I love her to bits, David; nearly losing her that way has scared the hell out of me. She stays home till the doctors give her the OK.'

148

David grunted in sympathy. 'Say hi from me. I'll be over to view my godson next week.' He slapped John on the back and watched him walk away. Was that what it was like he thought? Was Grace right; was he in love with Kate? The mystery phone call had niggled and festered overnight until he realised he was as scared as John claimed to have been.

David waited a minute until he was sure that he and Kate were alone. 'I'm not ashamed of you, Kate; you don't have to walk behind me like a slave.' He looked at her somewhat enigmatically as she answered him.

'I'm not ashamed of you either, David. But I don't want to c...cause gossip and s...speculation.'

David offered a hand. 'We'll cause that no matter how circumspect we are, Kate. People are going to talk and I don't know if I'm doing the right thing by you, girl.'

Kate accepted the hand. 'I'm r...responsible for my c...choices too, D...David.' She walked with him towards their cars. David looked at the cars in a slightly perplexed way for a minute then rubbed his neck, grinning at her. 'I'm not good at this clandestine stuff, Kate. What do we do now?'

Kate was equally puzzled. They stood looking at the two cars, and then David said. 'Drive home, Kate. I'll follow and then we'll see about having a meal and a talk.' He was unaccustomed to feeling so unsure of himself; he looked at her uncertainly, 'Is that OK?'

Kate nodded, gently squeezing his hand.

'I'll talk to you in ten minutes.'

The small convoy set off and headed towards the hostel. Kate parked neatly outside and climbed out, locking the car and waiting for David to pull up. She crossed hastily to his big green Rover and slid into the front seat. David manoeuvred the big car around the slightly muddy patch of earth outside the main doors and was driving away, even while she was fastening her seatbelt, like a bank robber making a getaway.

PHILIP JARDIN TOO HAD been involved in several getaways in his somewhat chequered career. He would have dearly liked to have made one now. His bookie was an acerbic man in his sixties who had been in the game long enough to smell bullshit when he saw it, and Philip Jardin was about to try to shovel some his way.

'You know I'll pay, I always do. I've got a job on, it should clear what I owe and leave us both happy.' He had no intention of paying if he could help it; he would rather put his money on a horse and try to double it than pay and be clear of debt. He had plans for his future that didn't include paying off bookies; and his boss wanted this job finished by Thursday.

'Yeah! Like I've not heard that before!' The bookie sat behind a big leather topped desk. A big bald man, tapping his extremely white teeth with a pencil while he considered the scrawny man before him.

'So when are you going to come into this sum of money that's going to make us both so happy.' The sarcasm passed over Jardin's head.

'End of next week. Straight I will.'

The bookie considered him as straight as a corkscrew but let the phrase pass. 'So you're going to come into ten thou' next week; what you going to do, rob a bank?'

'You know I don't rob banks.' Jardin tried to look affronted but only succeeded in looking like a rather harassed rat accused of taking the cheese.

'Hmm!' The bookie continued to lounge and tap his teeth, much to Jardin's annoyance. He'd been called into the back office and left to stand on the rather nice Turkish rug in front of the desk. He hadn't been offered a seat and he was feeling tired; what's more his feet hurt.

'Look, I've always paid up before.' He tried a winning smile. It wouldn't have won a donkey derby in the bookie's estimation.

'OK, bugger off! I'll see you next Friday and you'd better have the cash, or Little Dennis will be paying you a visit. Capisc'.'

Jardin nodded. He intended to be long gone by then. He cast a sideways look at Little Dennis, who would have stood six foot five in his socks, if he'd ever worn any inside his leather biker boots. Dennis smiled a gap toothed smile and gently stroked his own slightly bent nose. 'I like visiting.' His voice was deep, as it rumbled from his barrel chest, encased as it was in tight silk shirt and black jacket. Jardin shivered a bit.

'OK Mr Barker, I'll see you next Friday.'

'Yeah! You'd better.' The threat was implicit.

Jardin left hastily and Frank Barker grinned rather evilly at his departing back. As the door closed behind him he said, 'Keep an eye on him, Dennis.' Dennis left on surprisingly light feet.

Jardin left the building and stood wiping his brow with the grimy handkerchief. He set off in the general direction of the town hall; he had another meeting and didn't think this was going to be any pleasanter. He did, however, feel more virtuous. He was good at his job and had a certain perverted pride in the fact that he could slip onto a site and back out without anyone noticing him. So to be accused of leaving a trail caught him on the raw.

He leaned against the steps of the town hall, watching the passing foot traffic and thinking longingly of a cup of tea, as he saw some tourists seating themselves at an outside café.

151

He flicked his mobile and spoke, 'I might have something in your line … little Egyptian mummy doll. Yeah, I'll be down there next week.' He rang off after a few more pleasantries then he straightened up as a young woman approached. She didn't offer to shake hands; she just jerked her head at him and kept walking.

Jardin hurried to catch up, and then keep pace with her.

'Why did you have to ring the hostel? Don't you trust me?' Her long legs strode along the pavement and he panted as he walked beside her.

'Oi! Slow down, I ain't as young as I was.'

She eased the pace slightly, 'Well?'

Jardin looked her over, 'I don't get it, what's in this for you? You tell me you don't want any of the cash, but you'll help me steal whatever's worth having.'

'It's none of your business. Now why the phone calls?'

'I'm not used to a partner; I like working alone.' He spoke nothing but the truth, even if his voice did have a slight whine in it, 'If you're alone you don't have to divide up the cash and you don't need to worry about anyone ratting on you.'

She'd quickened her pace as he spoke and he grabbed an arm, pulling her to a stop. 'Slow down for God's sake! Why can't we sit and talk.'

'Do you seriously think I want to be seen talking to you?' The eyebrows rose and a nasty smile crossed her face. It crossed rapidly and departed as if wiped by a sponge, to leave her staring down at him.

She turned to walk on, 'If you want my help then you'd better be more careful. There was nothing I could do to hide the evidence of your visit this morning. You don't want a visit from the police; I know where you live too and

I might just say something accidentally.'

He stopped in the middle of the footpath, much to the annoyance of a mother with a push chair who all but ran into him. 'Idiot!'

He didn't reply to the insult as she weaved around him and continued her erratic passage through the milling throng on the pavement. Her child held out a small toy sword to cut a swathe through the crowds like Boadicea in a chariot; it giggled happily as it passed out of his life. He rather wished the young women in front of him would also pass out of his life too.

'Don't you threaten me. I don't need your help; I'm doing you the favour letting you help me.' He all but shouted the words as the girl continued to walk away.

She came back rapidly, 'OK tell the world, why don't you?' She took his arm 'Walk and talk.'

Jardin stood his ground, 'I'm going home, unless there's something you want to tell me. I've got plans and they don't involve snooty foreign females.'

She sighed in an exaggerated manner, 'OK, OK, don't go near the dig over the weekend, they're setting a trap. The police were in with the Professor most of the morning plotting your downfall. Right!'

He nodded. She turned away, and then turned back, 'I'll be in touch.'

Dennis, an interested observer of these noisy confidences, shrugged as they parted. He mentally flipped a coin and followed the girl at a safe distance. If she was helping that weasel Jardin, then he wanted to know who she was, and what she was helping him to do.

He followed her round the marketplace and down to Bitts Park car park, observed as she got into the back of a car with several other young people and watched as they drove away. Oh well! Life was full of gambles, that one had come in evens and he'd lost the bet.

DAVID WAS DRIVING AND hoping that his gamble was going to pay off too. He was betting against the house with the odds stacked against him. Kate was so young or, conversely he thought, he was so old. She still had her career, her life, before her. He didn't want to ruin that, but he did want her.

Kate sat quietly beside him for several minutes until she said suddenly 'W…where are we going, D…David?'

David glanced across at her then returned his attention to the road. 'Changed your mind, Kate?'

'No David, just c…curiosity.'

'I thought we'd find a nice quiet pub; we're not exactly dressed for haute cuisine dining. I don't know a lot about you, Kate,' he cast another sideways look, 'and you don't know a lot about me.'

The drive was short and David drew up round the back of a picture postcard pub. 'Will this be OK?'

'Yes, it's very p…pretty. I don't really know much about this area, I was b…brought up down S…Salisbury way.' Kate offered the information with a tiny smile.

'Good, then we have something in common already. I'm a southerner too.' He got out, coming round to help her out of the car. 'Do you want to eat out here? The sun is still shining, despite all the gloomy prognostications of our British weathermen.'

Kate nodded.

They headed towards a wooden table with benches either side, and a somewhat gaudy umbrella apparently growing from its middle. Kate slithered along the bench and David stepped over the end and sat down beside her. He handed her one big menu and picked up

154

another for himself.

They settled down to read. Kate, after a glance at the prices wondered what she ought to order. She didn't know what eminent professors earned, and the young men she went out with occasionally wouldn't expect her to order rare steak at twelve pounds a time. David shifted in his seat turning to her, 'What do you fancy?'

She shook her head, 'I've no idea, David, it all s...sounds delicious. You order for me, I'll eat anything but s...spaghetti and tripe.'

'Aha! Two things we have in common. I hate tripe, especially the written kind.' He grinned and nodded at the young waitress who was hovering over by the doorway to the pub entrance.

She came and stood by the table and David leaned back and spoke to her. 'We'll have steak and chips.' He turned back to Kate, 'How do you like yours.'

'Oh, well done p...please.'

'Right, two steaks, one medium rare, one well done and all the trimmings. What will you drink?'

Kate pointed at the house red on the menu. 'Is that sweet?'

'Oh no, miss.' The waitress had a soft, border accent.

'Then that will be f...fine.'

David nodded his agreement and the waitress departed with their orders. He leaned sideways on the table. He looked at Kate; the sun was rioting among her hair shooting sparks of gold and flame about her face. Her brown eyes, behind their large frames, assessed him just as seriously and carefully; he thought she looked like a very appealing owl.

He smiled a slow smile. She watched it creep up and enter his eyes so that they twinkled like a pair of emeralds. She found herself responding, an answering smile dawning on her face so that the deep brown glowed at him.

'You really are rather pretty when you stop worrying and relax.'

He reached for her hand as it lay quietly in her lap, 'I'm not very good with women, Kate, I usually end up saying or doing the wrong thing and they feel insulted and go away.' He frowned at her, the smile dying and a serious look settling on his face. 'I don't think I want you to go away. Can you bear with me, and tell me when I go wrong?'

Kate looked back equally seriously, 'I d...don't think I want you to go a...away either, D...David. But I'm not very g...good with men; it's the s...s...stutter you know. It annoys them.'

David looked at her, 'But you don't always stutter, Kate, do you?'

'No.' It was said a little uncertainly.

'So I'll help you not to stutter, and you'll help me to mind my manners. Is that a deal?'

Kate nodded shyly.

David leaned in, 'We'll seal it with a kiss.' and gave her a small salute on the downy cheek.

Kate was surprised as the soft beard briefly made contact with her cheek and she caught a whiff of David's aftershave. She looked at him, feeling a new tension in his body as it rested on the bench next to hers.

David was surprised at his own feelings. What had been meant as a small gesture had startled him. The soft cheek had been so inviting and the delicate scent so delectable as he'd brushed against her, he wanted to repeat the action, to see if he got the same shiver of electric the next time. But he wasn't sure he dared. He didn't want to frighten her away.

He settled back, releasing her hand and putting a little distance between them as the wine arrived. He thought they'd better talk about neutral things for a while. He poured out and clinked glasses with her.

'So, what do you think is going on at the site? Have you got any theories as to why anyone should be snooping around?' He paused. 'I've got a notion myself that it's a fishing expedition to see what we turn up.'

Kate looked uncertainly at him for a moment; did he really want her opinion, and if she offered it, would he shoot her down in flames, dare she speak the truth? She grabbed her courage as it threatened to slip away like mist in the sunshine, and it was almost as negligible she thought. 'I think you're right, we haven't f...found anything s...spectacular yet, interesting but not s...saleable.'

'Hmm! Yes,' David unable to resist, despite his very new resolution, took the hand next to him and held it firmly, feeling the faint tremble going through it. 'Are you scared of me, Kate?'

'No... yes..., a bit.' She stumbled over the answer.

'That makes us equal then and we have another thing in common, for I'm a bit scared of you.'

'You?' Kate looked at him in amazement.

'Oh! Yes. Just because I'm fifty-two doesn't mean I'm full of confidence. Does it help to know that?'

Kate looked him over carefully; he didn't appear to be just trying to placate her, he actually looked a bit uncertain. 'Yes, David. It really does.'

She gave him a proper smile for the first time and David's heart bounced once and began to beat a more rapid tattoo. He felt as though he'd got a rubber ball bouncing around inside his chest, threatening to block his

157

throat. He couldn't speak, so they sat quietly just holding hands until the meal arrived. Then David reluctantly released her and they both settled down to eating, keeping the conversation to the commonplace as they tentatively explored each others' background.

'So you live with your mother normally do you?'

'Yes. We've got a little cottage just outside S…Salisbury and she keeps my room for me. It's been nice to have a b…base while I've been at uni'. I suppose she'll be h…happy for me to keep it as long as I want.

'And your father?' The question was put delicately.

Kate looked frightened for a minute and David puzzled over her expression even while she answered him. 'Mum d…divorced him when I was about four. I know he's s…still has a bit of contact with her but I d…don't.' She glanced across at him, then fixed her eyes on her plate again. 'W…what about you?'

'Oh, mum and dad still living, and independent with it. They live outside Cambridge in the family home. It's a great barrack of a place but they won't shift to something smaller.' David shrugged, 'I suppose while they're active they don't need to.

After the meal was finished and they were sipping coffee David, who'd been mulling a thought over, said. 'I want to take the finds home that Grace got out today. However,' he paused, looking squarely at Kate, 'I don't want you to feel that you will be on duty or that I'm luring you back to my 'den of iniquity'. Do you feel comfortable with that or would you rather I took you back to the hostel?' He waited patiently for her to come to a decision.

Kate looked at the glinting green eyes trained on her face. 'I'd like to c…come back with you; I'd actually quite l…like to see what we've got. Have you any idea what they m…might be?'

'Not a clue. It's like Christmas Day, unwrapping all

158

those knobbly bundles, isn't it?'

'Well my bundles tended to be b…books or p…pencils so they weren't that knobbly; but I know what you m…mean.' She stood up as he did 'I'll just go, er…'

David grinned, 'Yeah, I've got to just go er … too; I'll see you at the car in a minute.'

As they set off towards his house David was lecturing himself sternly. 'Keep your hands to yourself; she's young, she's shy, she needs space to get to know you better.'

Kate knew it wasn't far away from the site to his house. She also knew that, except at the end of digs when he threw a party, he guarded his privacy. She recognised that to invite her back to his home was something offered to few people. She too was delivering a silent lecture. 'Don't blow this, Kate. You might love him but he's not sure; he thinks you're too young and when he finds out the truth …' She stopped the thought, shuddering slightly so that David, glancing at her, wondered if he was really doing the right thing taking her back with him.

She stifled the urge to touch. She wanted to touch his beard and see if it really had felt as soft as she thought; to just be held for a minute and, she thought, holding hands was never going to be enough.

The house when they arrived was set back off the estuary, looking across to the Scottish shoreline. It wasn't that large, Kate thought it might have been an old farmhouse at some time but it appeared to have been renovated so its outer bucolic charm was matched by modern conveniences inside.

They entered a room which shouted farm office, the odd bit of tack on a chair next to the door, and the smell of leather and cigarette smoke mingling with the slight smell of old books. They settled down at a big mahogany desk from which David quickly removed piles of papers. He pulled a newspaper from a stack next to his chair. They were all folded back to the Times crossword Kate saw and, much to her awe, filled in, in ink. With a quick flick he spread several sheets over the desk top. 'My cleaning lady has definite views about using this table for cleaning finds,' he grinned at her, 'and you definitely don't want to hear them.'

He hauled the cardboard box off the floor and began to lift out the mud and clay encrusted objects, and with the delicate dentist's tools that were part of their trade, they began to tease away the debris of years. By the time they both realised what the time was, it was nearly eight o clock and they had both been bent over their work for several hours.

'I think it's time I fed you, young lady.' It was the first thing David had said for a long time. He smiled across the desk at his assistant as she pushed her glasses back up her nose in the now familiar gesture. 'Come along; let's see what I've got in the fridge.' He walked round the desk and held out a hand; then just stood looking down at her.

'What's w…wrong, David?' Kate was alarmed by his arrested expression.

David reached out an unsteady finger and brushed her cheek. 'Something that was said last night. It doesn't fit.'

'I t…told you the t…truth, D…David, honestly.'

David was amazed to see the tears gathering in her eyes. 'Not you, darling, someone else.'

While Kate was grappling with the 'darling' she found herself held against a warm chest covered in a blue flannel shirt; David tipped her chin up, "And yes, I did say 'darling', I think you could very well be my darling. I've rarely spent a more contented day, despite all the fuss this morning. I've been wanting to hold you for four long years, Kate.' He made the simple statement while he watched her

160

face. 'I know it's too soon to know if this is just chemistry but, my God, girl, it's good to finally do it.'

Kate uttered a sigh, 'I've w…wanted to be held, David.' She looked up at the face close to her own and put her hands gently on his shoulders.

A stunned look crossed his face. Then, proving that he really had earned his professorship by his quick grasp of the subject in hand, he kissed her fiercely and very thoroughly.

GRACE WAS SITTING HOLDING Millie's hand; they'd drunk tea and the two young people, at least, had eaten biscuits. Grace had talked about the excavation and her work and Dan had been fascinated. His ideas of archaeology were based on the tales of Indiana Jones; what she was talking about sounded far more detailed and technical.

Now, however, she'd fallen silent and so had Millie, Dan wondered if he should go away and give them both a bit of privacy. He stirred in his chair by the bed and Millie looked at him, 'Dan, do you think you could lift me up a bit?'

'Aye, o' course, Millie.' He suited the action to the word, raising her and resettling her on the pillows.

'I had the minister this morning, Grace; I asked Mary if she'd ask him to call. He's a lovely young man.'

Grace frowned; 'I would have asked him if you'd said, Aunt Millie.'

'Yes I know, darling, but I've been doing a lot of thinking and I wanted to see him,' she hesitated, 'while there was still time.'

Dan watched the colour leach from the calm face of Grace; it was her only outwardly visible sign of shock.

'Anyway,' Millie continued, 'we had a nice talk; he's a sensible young boy and he gave me some advice, so I need to talk to you now.'

'Is it about the funeral, Aunt Millie? I thought you'd talked about that already.'

'No, darling. Well yes, I have talked about the funeral but I need to talk about something different.' She stopped, breathing rather fast.

Dan, watching carefully, quietly turned up the flow of oxygen a little. 'Will I be leaving ye in private?' He moved to the foot of the bed.

'No, Dan, you and I have talked a lot this last week and I'm not saying anything you can't hear.'

'Aye,' He looked into her eyes, reading the fear and the need there. 'Weel tak it steady, lass. Ye dinna need ta' fear I'll gab about it.'

Millie smiled at him and then nodded at the album laying on the bedside table. 'I'm glad you brought that through yesterday, Gracie. I want to talk to you about some of the photos.'

Grace, looking puzzled, began to lift it down, resting it on her knee. 'We've looked at the photos before, Auntie.'

'Yes, darling, the ones of your parents and your father's parents and mine and you as a child but I want you to look at some of the earlier ones. You'll find them in the little pocket at the back.'

Looking rather mystified, Grace opened the big leather bound album and looked in the back cover, 'You mean this bit?'

'Yes, darling.' Millie watched as she pulled open the flap.

'I thought this was where you stored the negatives.' She pulled out several packets which did indeed prove to be negatives. However, there was a small brown envelope which, when opened, had a handful of black and white photos inside.

'We didn't have many photos taken during the war. It's not like now, you snap away all day on that digital, Gracie, and put it on the computer, and have hundreds of photos. Then we mostly had to have them posed.'

She lifted the photos out of Grace's hand; lifting the top one and handing it back. 'This is your grandfather, darling.' She held out a black and white image of an American serviceman. 'I always wanted to tell you, but once you start living a lie it's so difficult to know when to stop.'

'But …' Grace looked confused.

Millie smiled at Dan through a haze of tears; he came round the bed from his position at the foot and took her other hand. She looked up at him gratefully, then turned back to face Grace. 'Let me tell it my way and then you can ask questions if you want, darling.'

Grace nodded, sitting still and silent on the side of the bed. 'You guessed some of it last night. I had a boyfriend; well he was more than that. VE day we both got a little tipsy. Oh not so that we didn't know what we were doing, but what with everyone celebrating in the streets and being so happy well ….' She blushed, a faint colour washing her cheeks. 'Well we made love. It was lovemaking, Gracie. I won't have you thinking it was something sordid.'

Millie smiled softly at her granddaughter. 'We'd been in love for months and when the opportunity arose we both took advantage of it. It was very special and we made your mum that night. Only then we quarrelled and he didn't know about Polly when he left.'

She gripped Grace's hand tightly, 'I couldn't admit

163

Polly was mine. It's not like it is now, Gracie, and people talked of course. I went away down south before I began to show, and I stayed away for three years, and when I came back she was a toddler and they couldn't prove anything. I said she was my cousin's child. So Polly grew up calling me Auntie and then so did you and, just once, before I die,' the old eyes pleaded 'I'd like to be called grandma. Can you forgive me, darling?'

Grace leaned forward 'I love you, grandma'; I'm so pleased you didn't miss out on loving someone.' She put both arms round Millie's shoulders, holding her gently while her grandmother quietly cried in her arms.

Dan had stealthily withdrawn his hand when Grace had hugged Mille; now he stood with his back to them looking out of the window at the soft evening sunshine. He could hear them softly talking, but not the words, until Grace called. 'Dan, come and meet my Granddad, James Belsham. Grandma tells me I look just like him. I have his eyes and his hair.'

'Aye, weel noo, that's no bad thing, he was a handsome man wasn't he.' He held the photo, looking at Grace.

'Now how can I answer that? If I say yes I'm vain, and if I say no I've insulted Granddad.' Grace grinned at Millie.

Millie smiled tiredly back. Noticing this Dan said, 'Would you like a wee nap, Millie? We won't go away; we'll just sit here quiet like. Would you like me to tell Grace some of your stories about James?'

Millie nodded at him, 'You mustn't mind, Gracie. Dan's been so good to me; listening and helping me get enough courage to tell you. I trusted him with my secrets.' She patted her granddaughter's hand, giving her a pleading look.

'Don't be silly, darling. Dan is a good man and I

164

trust him too.' Grace gave Dan a look that had his insides melting and swirling. He remembered saying it was dangerous for both of them, but now he wasn't quite sure where the danger was coming from, he'd thought he meant their physical attraction, now he wasn't so sure.

8

MONDAY MORNING SAW EVERYONE returning to the site with renewed enthusiasm which, unfortunately, was about to be wasted. David and his myrmidons had laid their trap over the weekend only to catch a stray badger going about his lawful occasions and a party of hedgehogs on a foraging expedition.

The police had departed the previous evening considering the project a waste of manpower. While David didn't agree, there was very little he could do about it. He assembled his team. He cast a glance over their hard hats and visi-vests and spared a cursory glance to survey the foot wear on offer for his inspection. They all seemed properly equipped.

'Right, this is what's happened, boys and girls. You know that Grace found her excavation disturbed on Friday morning.' He noted the nods. 'The police have checked out all the local parties who might have an interest, and I've asked around at the uni' for anyone wanting to buy what isn't for sale and, truth to tell, we're no further forward than we were on Friday.'

He looked around the group, noting disappointment and varying degrees of interest; what he was looking for was a look, something to indicate hidden knowledge and he thought he caught it on two different faces, one singularly strained. But it still didn't add up properly, not on two faces.

'We can't do any more for now, but I want you all to be vigilant, make sure you keep accurate finds records. Anything you think might have value for collectors you bring to the site office straight away. Don't put it in the trays, and folks.' He paused, 'Don't talk about your finds, not even to each other.'

There was a quiet gasp. 'Don't you trust us, Prof'?'

'Yeah I trust you, but you all talk too much!' It was said grimly, and the look that accompanied it spoke volumes.

'Now let's get to work. We've only got ten days left to finish this site, and there's still plenty to see and find.'

The small group dispersed, Doug chivvying them towards their various holes. Grace stood looking at David and John as the others moved slowly away. 'So what aren't you telling us, David?'

David looked around to make sure everyone was beginning work. He lowered his voice a bit. 'Do you remember Philip Jardin?'

'How the hell could we forget Jardin?' John spoke loudly and bitterly. 'If it wasn't for that guy my best mate might have been with me now. I hate his guts; if he's at the back of this I'd like to break his neck for him. Five bloody years, that's all he paid for Max's life!'

'You need to learn to speak your mind, John.' David raised an ironical eyebrow. 'Don't hold back will you?'

'Sorry, David.' John, looking slightly ashamed, lowered his voice.

'Yes, well what I was about to say was, the coppers have spotted him in the area and they think it might be him that's sniffing around our site. What's more it fits his MO pretty well.' David smiled rather tiredly, 'However, they also think that someone is keeping him informed of our progress!'

'Oh! Bloody hell!' John rubbed a hand up over his hair. 'But we know this team, David, there's only a few students' that are new.' He looked dubiously at David then around the site, seeing several speculative looks being thrown their way by the team. He wondered absently if any of them had heard his outburst then dismissed it. 'Surely none of them…'

'I don't know, John. I hope to God they're wrong but…' He too looked around the site at the industry going on. 'All we can do is be on our guard.' He shrugged, turning to Grace who had been a silent spectator of their exchange.

'Grace, I saw Millie Saturday, while you were out shopping.'

Grace nodded, 'Yes, she said.'

'I'm sorry, dear, she's failing fast; do you want to be with her rather than here. You know you can go if you want to.'

'I appreciate the offer, David, and I'll probably go after lunch. You're right she's slipping away so fast, between Friday and last night the change was…' Grace found she couldn't speak; she just looked at David, her mouth working. She gained a bit of control. 'Don't offer me sympathy. I'll never get through the day if you do.' She turned and left them, abruptly walking across the site to her well.

The men watched her for a minute, exchanging looks, 'If Sandra wants to show off the new baby, John, she'd better make it quick.' David looked grim.

John nodded. 'I'll wrap them up and take them in the car this evening.'

They turned away to start work when they were stopped abruptly by the ear-splitting scream that Grace had just produced. They turned back and shot across the site at a run. Heads were turning and people were beginning to converge on Grace but David, reaching Grace first, halted the tide. He glanced down into the well, and then held up a capable hand that had everyone sliding to a stop. 'Everyone stay where you are.'

He looked again into the hole she'd so diligently excavated the previous week, removing from it the body of a Roman. Now the hole had another body, one considerably fresher but, he could see, just as dead. John, coming up, peered into the hole and David heard his sharp intake of breath.

'John, I think you'd better call the police.' He raised his voice 'Everyone else go to the site office and wait outside it until I come.' He looked back at John, lowering his voice again, 'And, John,' he looked meaningfully at his second, 'watch what you say, boy.' As John started back the way he'd come David called after him, 'John.' John halted, looking back. 'John, Kate's in the office. Send her out will you.' He put an arm around Grace and held her shivering body next to his. 'OK love, we'll sort it out.'

'Oh! God! David is that…?'

'Yes, I'm very much afraid that's Philip Jardin.'

DAN WAS LYING LOOKING at the ceiling; the noise coming from outside the door was akin to someone dragging a small mountain along the corridor, in chains. He shook his head; he didn't want to move but if this noise was going to go on he'd have to find other accommodation fairly quickly.

He put his hands behind his head and sighed, making the sheets pull taut over his chest. Not, he reflected, that he'd have a job for much longer anyway. Millie was failing rapidly now. He'd reluctantly taken his two nights off over the weekend and hadn't been in the least bit surprised to see how much she'd changed in those forty-eight hours.

He climbed out of bed, glancing at the clock on his way past. Damn! He'd barely made four hours sleep. He scrubbed his hands over his face and pulled off the t-shirt and boxers he wore to sleep in, heading towards the bathroom and a shower. He really didn't want to be awake.

Maybe he could contact Grace. He hadn't seen her

to speak to since Friday evening when they'd parted at his car. He stood under the shower allowing the hot water to wake him up. He didn't think she'd go out with him again just at the moment; Millie would demand all her attention, and rightly so. But, dammit, he did want to see her.

He wandered back into the bedroom and began to pull open drawers and to dress. First a meal and then he'd go across to Millie's, Mary would be gone at two anyway, unless Millie had got any worse, so he wouldn't be standing on toes. And, he thought, Grace would definitely be visiting.

GRACE DIDN'T THINK SHE could be awake; she must, she thought, be trapped in some form of nightmare - one where people asked her questions through the wrong end of an ear trumpet. Kate and David had walked her back to the site office, supporting her on either side as if she was going to the scaffold.

She'd been aware of their quiet exchanges as they'd shouldered her passed the team outside and taken her almost bodily into the room. She was also aware that Kate was shaking almost as much as she was; David had got the pair of them seated at the table and made tea in thick white mugs, liberally laced with whiskey from a flask in his back pocket. He and John had taken their Glenfiddich neat.

David had called Doug in from outside and now David, John, and Doug, stood just inside the door awaiting the police. 'Doug, I want you to get the whole team together in as few cars as you can and travel, in convoy; and I mean that, they must stick together, and take them back to the hostel.' He touched the younger man on the shoulder. 'No-one must leave for any reason and, Doug, don't let them use a phone either.' Doug nodded dumbly, the shock clear in his usually cheery eyes. 'The police will want to interview everyone, but I don't want the team on this site. Do you understand?'

Doug shook his head. 'I don't understand anything, David, but I'll do what you say.' He looked across at the two mute girls sitting huddled together at the table. 'Do you want me to take …?' He nodded across at the girls.

David shook his head, 'They'll want to interview Grace here, and Kate can act as support for her.' He cast an eye across at Kate, 'I hope!'

Doug departed, rapidly putting everyone into four cars of the senior staff and driving away, watched by David and John, 'Well this'll finish this dig off. We've been here before, John. By the time the crime scene is released our time will be up and there'll be more dirty washing on view than a Monday at the washhouse.' It was said rather bitterly, David rubbed his hand over his hair. Then looked at the girls again.

He went round the table, and placed a comforting hand on Grace's shoulder. 'They'll want your statement, Grace; then I suggest one of us takes you to Millie's if you don't want to drive.'

Grace looked over her shoulder at him; he could see she was making an enormous effort to regain some calm. 'Sorry I screamed, David; dead bodies are my stock in trade, I'm just not used to them being so fresh. There's no mistake is there?'

'No, dear, he was very dead.'

He transferred the hand to Kate, 'OK, Kate? You don't mind staying, for a bit?'

Kate shook her head, 'No, David.' He saw she was pasty white and all her freckles stood out vividly on her cheek bones; all her vitality seemed to have drained into her hair. He wanted to hold her and tell her not to worry, it would be alright, but he felt their relationship was too new and fragile to publicise with such open displays. He contented himself with gently squeezing her shoulder.

THE POLICE WERE A bit surprised, and at first considerably more than annoyed, to find that most of the witnesses had been summarily removed from the crime scene. But, when they discovered David's actions they were less annoyed; it was going to be a lot easier to interview people at the hostel, seven miles away indoors, than have to stand around outside trying to do it.

'So, Miss Gordon, you went to the excavation that you've been dealing with and pulled back the tarp and saw the body?'

The detective was a man of about her own age, dressed in a neat, single-breasted navy blue serge suit. He spoke with a country accent, but he had shrewd eyes that looked at the site office and the set up for the finds with approval. He observed the girl in front of him with a certain amount of compassion but didn't let that colour his thirst for knowledge.

He and his subordinate had arrived nearly an hour after the body had been found and Grace had had time to calm down, but she was still shaken by the odd shiver of shock. The Police had cordoned off the area, their blue lights whirling and flashing over the scene like some mad carnival, as they had surrounded the site. Now white clad constables where spread out, methodically searching the area for some *raison de etre* of why a man's life should have been taken.

In the office the two men now sat trying to establish the chain of events that had led up to the incident. The older man sat quietly at the site desk with his back to the table. After a glance across at him, Grace ignored him because the man in front of her, sitting in the seat normally occupied by Kate, had done so; but she was nevertheless aware that he was writing down what she said.

'Did you go into the hole? Touch the body?'

'No, no. I never even thought to check if he was dead, I just screamed and David came running.' Grace shook her head; 'Anyway,' she said slowly, 'the ladder wasn't there.' She frowned. 'It should have been, I didn't take it out.' She shook her head; the inspector could see she was clearly puzzled.

The Detective sat back, placing the cap back on the fountain pen with which he'd been absently doodling while he listened, and glanced down at the file in front of him. 'So to sum up: there's been trouble on the site, Professor Walker talked to everyone this morning and then you went to your work, only to find the body in the well. You didn't touch it and nor did anyone else afterwards. Would that be accurate?'

Grace nodded her head.

'And you recognised the dead man as being Philip Jardin? Would you like to explain how you knew him?' The question was shot silkily at her.

Grace opened and shut her mouth, then managed to speak, 'It would be about fifteen years ago, Detective McInnis; I was working on a site in Carlisle as a student. The man, Mr Jardin, was caught trying to steal from the site and he killed,' she paused, shut her mouth and then, opening it, said, 'someone. He's aged, but I recognised him still.'

'Ah! Right.' He glanced down at the open file again. 'And who was in charge of that site at the time?'

Grace looked at him, answering reluctantly. 'Professor Walker was temporarily in charge; he had a stake in the funding and had come to see how things were getting on.'

'I believe that the excavations there were never completed?'

173

Grace shook her head.

'No doubt it cost the professor a lot of money having to abandon his work there?'

Suddenly grasping the tenor of the questions Grace looked horrified. 'Yes, but David would never…'

'Well someone did, Miss Gordon, and the professor has got a motive.'

Grace lost the little colour she had regained. 'That's a foul thing to say!'

They sat looking at each other for a moment before the detective spoke 'Now, Miss Gordon, as a matter of routine I need you to account for your movements since yesterday evening.'

Grace looked at him for a stunned moment. 'I was at home most of the evening working on my computer. I can't produce an alibi Detective Inspector, I didn't know I was going to need one'

'You said most of the evening?'

'I spent until seven with my grandmother. Then I did a little shopping and went home.'

'No doubt your grandmother will verify that. I think that will be all for now, Miss Gordon.' His face remained impassive as she looked at him with horror and hatred equally mixed. 'We'll speak to you again if necessary. Can you ask John …' he paused, glancing down, 'Williams to come in please?'

Grace stood up, 'Can I go?'

'That depends where you wish to go, Miss Gordon.'

Grace cleared a suddenly clogged throat. 'My grandmother is very ill and confined to bed.' She swallowed, 'If I'm not needed here I'd like to spend my time with her.'

Detective McInnis looked at her steadily for a moment. 'Yes, that should be alright. Please give the address to the constable outside.'

'I'd rather you didn't disturb her.'

'That's understandable; we'll be as discrete as we can.' He eyed her face, 'Now if you could …' He nodded at the door and Grace, taking the hint, went out.

She would have spoken to John but the constable foiled her attempts by asking who the Detective Inspector wanted next.

'He wants John, Mr Williams.' She shot a warning glance at John then walked away towards where David, and Kate, could be seen glumly watching the swarm of forensics and constables walking all over the site with their size twelves. 'David this is horrible. He's looking for motives and he all but accused you of murdering Jardin, so they obviously don't think it was an accident.'

'I never did think it was, love, not with his head in such a …' He stopped, 'well never mind.' He closed his lips on whatever thought he might have uttered.

'I think I'll go to Millie's. They' she indicated with her head the closed door of the site office, 'know where I'm going to be.' She didn't make a move, however, because she thought Kate looked as if she was about to faint.

'Come and sit with me for a bit, Kate.' She took the younger girl by the shoulders and led her to a couple of battered chairs placed near the office doors where members of the staff where wont to rest their weary limbs and talk tactics with David.

The two girls sat down and Kate rubbed a hand under her nose. 'It's h…horrible, Grace, and it was all so b…beautiful this m…morning.'

Grace gave her a curious look as the younger girl looked hungrily across at David standing leaning against the corner of the shed. 'I wish I'd never come on this dig.'

175

'I thought you and David …' she said delicately, watching as the red stormed back into Kate's cheeks. 'I'm not prying, Kate.'

'No you d…don't. I was so j…jealous of you too.' She raised the faintest glimmer of a smile.

Grace reached out and patted a shoulder. 'There's never been a need. David's a good man, and I've known him since I was sevenish. I could never think of him that way.'

'You're s…so l…lucky, to have had him in your life. I w…wish...' Whatever she wished she wasn't going to share, however. David came over to them, resting a hand lightly on Kate's shoulder in a gesture of comfort. She put her hand up on his and held it tightly for a minute, looking up at him with an expression that had Grace hastily looking away towards the busy police.

'Have they finished with you, Grace?' David looked across at his young friend.

'For now, David.'

'Do you want one of us to take you to Millie's?'

'No, I'll be alright now.' Grace continued to watch the minions of the law at their busy work. She heard David speaking very quietly to Kate but she carefully tuned it out.

In the office John was wishing they'd finished with him as well; unfortunately they'd only just started.

The preliminaries appeared to be over, however. 'Now, Mr Williams, I understand you were speaking to the Professor when the body was discovered, is that correct?'

John nodded.

'Did you recognise the deceased?'

'Not immediately; one doesn't expect to see the familiar in an unexpected corpse, Inspector.'

'And having recognised him what were your

176

subsequent actions?'

'David asked me to come here and phone the coppers and send Kate out to him.'

'Ah yes; that would be Kate Hamilton?'

John gave a brief nod.

'And then what did you do?'

'I helped Doug organise the team and kept them quiet until David had decided the best course of action.'

'So you didn't go into the well at any time?'

John raised an eyebrow. 'No, I did not! But if you're looking for traces, I've been on, in, and around that well for the past few days, since Grace opened it up; so you'll find my boot prints all over it.'

'Just so. Now perhaps you can tell me, as a matter of routine you understand, what you've been doing for the last twenty-four hours?'

John sat still for a few seconds; he felt as if he'd been sucker punched.

'Mr Williams?'

'Yes, Inspector, I heard you.' John looked him steadily in the eyes. 'Yesterday was Sunday; I spent the day with my new son and his mother. She and the baby didn't leave the house at all; we had the relatives round to lunch, and tea. After tea I went with my father and father-in-law to the local for a pint to wet the baby's head. I was back in the house around nine. After that we were on our own until this morning.'

'And this morning. What time did you leave for work?'

'Baby woke about six and I left at seven. It's a twenty minute drive to the site here.' He could see the pit looming, but there was nothing he could do to avoid it.

177

'And what did you do between half seven and half eight.'

John looked him squarely in the face. 'I slept in the car in the car-park, Inspector. It's a very new baby and while Sandra can grab the odd hour in the day, I can't. I'm exhausted at the moment, half an hour's peace seemed like a gift from the gods.' His mouth twitched, 'But of course the gods always exact a price don't they?'

'Hmm. I wouldn't know about that sir, I'm a catholic myself.' Inspector McInnis coughed. 'Right then sir, moving on. How did you feel about the deceased, sir?'

John was, as he said, tired. He was tired of the cagey questions too. 'I hated his guts, Inspector. I'm not sorry he's dead. He cheated my best friend out of his life and the five years he served for that life will never be long enough.' He looked squarely back at the Inspector. 'That what you wanted to hear?'

'Now sir, we have to ask these questions.'

'I tell you this for free, Inspector; I didn't kill him. My life and my family are too precious to waste on scum like him.'

'Very well, sir, thank you. We'll be in touch to verify your statement.'

'Don't you mean alibi, Inspector?' John stood up.

The Inspector kept an impassive face. 'Perhaps you could ask Professor Walker to come in, sir.'

John left, closing the door quietly behind him. The Inspector addressed his colleague who had been sitting quietly at the side of the room.

'What do you make of the set up, Sandy?'

The older man swung round in his chair, revealing himself to Inspector McInnis as slightly stout with grey hair and brown twinkling eyes. 'Well we've got a couple of nice motives so far. I mind the Professor from the last time;

178

you'll have read the notes. He's no fool, Bob.'

'No I don't suppose he is. I've only skimmed them so far but thanks for the warning. We'll hear what the Professor has to say.'

David making his entrance providentially at this moment, Sandy swung back and sat, pen poised, to take notes. David, however, was a bit shrewder than the last two interviewees. 'Morning, Inspector Bell. I see you're still working hard, glad to see you got your promotion.'

Sandy Bell swung round. 'Thank you very much, sir. Inspector McInnis is in charge of this case, however.'

'I bet you have your pennyworth of opinion though!' David pulled out the chair in front of the table, and the younger inspector, sitting down and folding his arms on his chest. He looked steadily across the table, returning the scrutiny of Inspector McInnis who was looking him over just as carefully. Eventually he spoke. 'We have your statement about last week's events to hand, Professor, could you just take me through the immediate events before you found the body?'

David paused a second to gather his thoughts and then ran through the morning's happenings ending with, 'I thought it best to send the team away as I told you, Inspector. There's nowhere on site for you to keep them before you can interview them. And they might have muddied up your forensic examinations if they'd been left to wander around.' He cocked his head, 'Or worse; someone might have been tempted to phone the press.'

'Ah! Yes, you've had experience of this before haven't you?'

'Don't be coy man! Your lot buggered up my site last time, and what you didn't wreck the press did. It cost me. I'm not blaming you, but it seemed like a sensible precaution.'

'Well I'm glad you can see it that way, sir. Of

course the real culprit last time is our *corpus delecti* this time, so to speak.'

'Yeah! And that gives me a thumping big motive doesn't it? Sorry, Inspector, I'm not your man.'

'You can of course account for your movements, sir?' It was put delicately.

'Fraid not, Inspector. I was at home and I could produce an alibi, but I'm not going to because I'm a gentleman. And before you ask it's because I'm a gentleman that I can't produce much of an alibi.'

He grinned wickedly and then switched off the grin as if someone had turned off the current, leaving his face bland. 'Seriously, I didn't kill the bastard, why would I mess up another site. Some of the money is mine and this will probably stop the work to the point where we've lost it. If I was going to do him in it would have been somewhere far away from here. Think about it.'

'Very well, sir,' he inclined his sleek head, 'but you may need to produce your alibi nevertheless.'

'Well gentlemen, have you done with me for now?'

Inspector McInnis nodded his head. 'I'll have a little chat with Miss Hamilton now if you don't mind sending her in, sir.'

'Fair enough.' David stood up and walked to the door, turning with his hand on the knob, 'Go easy on her; she's had a bad shock.'

He closed the door behind him and the younger man raised his eyebrows at the other, waggling them like Groucho Marks. 'So the professor has got a secret liaison. Wonder what she's like. I would have taken him for the archetypical crusty bachelor.'

Inspector Sandy Bell returned no answer for Kate had opened the door and entered, she stood just inside with her hands clasped before her like a child hauled before the headmaster.

'Come and sit down, Miss Hamilton.'

Kate came forward somewhat reluctantly and took the seat the older man was holding out for her. 'I…I d…didn't s…see anything.'

'Now wait while we ask you the questions.' He spoke soothingly.

'We have the statements of those immediately involved. We just need you to corroborate those; alright?'

Kate nodded, 'OK.'

Inspector Bell went and sat down and Inspector McInnis took up the threads. 'Now I understand you were in the office dealing with the record charts and notes; getting them out for the rest of the team. Is that correct?'

She nodded.

'And then Mr Williams came in and asked you to go out and help the Professor with Miss Gordon.'

'Uhhu.'

'Now did Mr Williams tell you why?'

'N…no he, he j…just said there was a b…body and Grace w…was in s…shock.'

'Fine and you brought her back in here and then you all waited for the police. Now did you see the body?'

Kate nodded and the Inspector saw her cheeks turning to the colour of skimmed milk.

'Did you recognise him?'

Kate shook her head, looking down at her hands.

'Nearly finished. Now it's just routine, but we need to know what you've been doing over the weekend?'

Kate gave a little gasp. 'I've been s…staying with a f…friend.'

'And can she confirm this.'

'H…He c…can.'

'Good.' he paused. 'So can we have a name then?'

Kate looked at the floor then at her clasped hands. Then at the Detective Inspector, 'D…do I have to s…say?'

'I'm afraid so.'

'B…but we d…didn't. Oh! Damn!' She raised a face on which tears were quietly sliding towards her chin. 'I was w…with David.' She sat waiting for the smirks.

The Inspector kept his face impassive. 'Ah! The professor wouldn't give us the name of his visitor. Thank you for being so helpful, miss.'

'You d…don't have to t…tell anyone d…do you?'

'No miss; only if it's pertinent to the case.' He watched her shoulders sag with relief.

'Now off you go. We'll have the Professor back for a minute if you don't mind.'

Kate made a hasty and precipitate exit calling, 'David', as soon as the door was firmly shut behind her.

David went across at her call. 'I gather they asked who you were with.'

She nodded dumbly, her eyes filling again.

'Don't fret, love. I just didn't want to compromise you if it wasn't necessary; I'm not ashamed of being with you.' He gently touched a cheek with two fingers, smoothing the skin where tears had left tracks. 'They want me again?' He nodded at the door.

'Yes.' the answer was a bit soggy.

'OK. Go over to Grace, I'll sort it out.'

He entered and stood just inside the door; shutting it but keeping his hand on the door knob as he turned to

182

face the two policemen, 'So my secret is out, gentlemen. But I'd be obliged if you'd keep it till I persuade the lady to marry me.' His mouth twisted into a wry smile. 'It may take some doing and I don't want too many spanners in my works.'

The two inspectors nodded, like a pair of dogs in the back of a car, travelling a bumpy road. 'Well I'm pleased to hear you say so.' And David turned around and left the room, closing the door softly behind him.

Sandy Bell turned to his younger colleague. 'Well that's a turn up for the books, Bob.' He scratched an ear, 'I seem to recollect some other woman though …' he said slowly, 'I can't just bring it to mind.' He shook his head, 'It'll come back to me.'

'Mmm.' McInnis picked up his notes 'We'd better see how they're getting on with the statements at the hostel, the forensics will be a while yet. I wonder how Jardin came to be in that hole.'

'Well when we catch the murderer you can ask him.'

GRACE WAS HUGGING KATE and drying her tears. 'Come on, it's alright, this will all be sorted out soon.'

'But they think D…David did it and it's all my f…f…fault.'

'I don't think they do at all.'

'He d…didn't tell them I was with h…him and they'll t…think he's c…covering s…something up.' Kate hiccupped.

'Oh!' For a minute Grace was bereft of words, 'Well I don't believe they'll think anything of the sort. I think they'll just think he was being a gentleman. Look here he comes now, see, not a manacle or leg iron in sight.' David

183

reached them at this juncture and took the sobbing girl into his arms.

'It's OK, darling.' He held her close and watched the incredulity flicker over John's face.

John opened and shut his mouth a couple of times then, catching David's eye, said, 'So can we all go home for now?'

'I believe so. There's nothing we can do here.' He shot back his cuff and looked at his watch, 'It's gone lunch time anyway. The police will be having theirs any minute now; they won't want a lot of spectators cluttering up their crime scene.'

The four of them walked around the energetically occupied police and made their ways towards their cars. Kate was tucked tenderly into David's Rover and they drove away before John's astonished eyes.

Grace exchanged a look with him.

'Actually I'm pleased for both of them.' John nodded at the spot where the car had stood. 'I just wish this mess wasn't happening. I'm going home to my wife; with any luck that little toe-rag will be asleep, and then maybe I can get some sleep too.' He grinned, then sobered 'I'll see you this evening, Grace, I'm bringing them to visit Millie.'

Grace nodded, 'See you there.'

She climbed into her car wishing that she had a strong man to lean on as well. If she had but known it, one was headed towards Millie's from the opposite direction. They met at her gate. Dan was pulling up, with a whiff of exhaust from his Jeep Cherokee, as she parked her more modest Mini Cooper outside the house gate.

GRACE HADN'T REALISED JUST how much she'd wanted to

see Dan until she did. He came to meet her as she locked her car door and she all but threw herself into his arms. 'Oh! Dan!'

Dan, absorbing her nine and a half stone of femininity on his soft shirt, took hold and held tight. He wasn't sure quite what had happened, but he wasn't going to look a gift horse in the mouth.

'Hey! Hey, lass!' He patted the tartan clad shoulder nearest to him and stroked the bubbly blonde curls while Grace clung on, shaking slightly. 'Let's away inside.' He put an arm around her shoulders and led her towards the front door.

Opening it with his key he ushered her in and closed it behind them. Then he took her back into his arms. 'Now then, lass, what's going on?'

'Oh, Dan, he's dead and he was in my well!'

Dan, justifiably mystified, continued to stroke her back.

'Ye aren't making a whole lot of sense, sweetheart. Who is dead, your Roman? And why shouldn't he be in your well?'

Grace, becoming aware that she was making a bit of a fool of herself, tried to pull away. 'Och noo, I rather like where ye are. Just settle a minute; then ye can tell me while we stand.' Dan pulled her firmly back and then held on, allowing her head to nestle against his shoulder.

Grace, taking him at his word, stood still absorbing the peace of the house; the faint smell of lavender polish mixed with a fainter undertone of antiseptic. The quiet tick of the grandmother clock on the wall bracket was a counterpoint to the clink of a radiator. When she found she was holding his collar with her left hand and stroking it, she stopped and looked up from the v of neck to the face above as he spoke.

'Noo then, tak' a few deep breaths and start frae

185

the beginning.' He spoke quietly, allowing her to lift her head but keeping a firm hold.

'You know the well I've been excavating?'

'Aye.'

'Well today when I went to start work there was a man inside.' She drew in a breath and continued softly, 'He was dead and the police think that he's been murdered. They asked me if I had an alibi.'

Dan looked down at her horror stricken face. 'Weel and that's how these things are done, sweetheart. I mind I've had to ask a few questions along that line my own self.'

'You?'

'Aye.' He smiled down at the face so close to his, ' Ye don't get to be in the army as long as me, with ma rank, and not have the little task o' sorting oot the defaulters, thrust upon ye occasionally.'

He gently brushed the hair off her face and rubbed a thumb down, just touching her lip. 'It's just routine ye ken.'

'But, Dan, I knew him!'

'Oh, and who was it then?' He could feel the shakes subsiding and turned her towards the kitchen as he spoke.

Grace was towed inexorably towards the back of the house. Dan pulled her through the door and shut it quietly, 'We'll mak' a cup o' tea and sit a minute. I dinna want to disturb Millie too much.'

Grace nodded, obediently sitting at the small kitchen table while Dan moved around the room; he was obviously familiar with kitchen duties, and Millie's kitchen at that. 'So who was this man, and how did ye ken him? Is he one o' the team?' He filled the kettle and switched it on, moving to the cupboard to get out mugs.

Grace watched him performing the mundane tasks and relaxed even more as he brought normality back to her. 'I'll have to go back a bit.'

'Aye.'

'He was a thief; and about fifteen years ago,' she paused, 'no it would be more. Anyway it was the summer I was sixteen; he tried to steal from a site we were working on. It was a summer evening and I think he thought the site was deserted for the night, but we were taking advantage of the light nights too. Anyway,' she paused and took the mug Dan offered, wrapping her hands around it and nodding her thanks, 'he tried to escape and John, the same guy I'm working with now, his best mate got killed. It was brought in as manslaughter.'

Dan sat down opposite to her, set his own mug on the table, and stretched jean clad legs out to the side. He reached across the narrow strip of board, just touching her hand for his own pleasure.

Grace smiled then raised the mug, sipping and grimacing slightly at the sweetness. Dan smiled across at her, 'Ye need just a wee bit of sugar, sweetheart.'

She set the mug back down 'I'll get fat.' It was said absently.

'For my sen I like a nice armful.' Dan smiled across the table, his blue eyes twinkling as he took in her figure, 'So yon corpse was known to this John too?'

'Yeah, and to David Walker, God help us! Apparently the police think this Jardin has been behind the disturbances at the site this last week.'

'OK, so ye all kent him, that doesna mean any of ye kilt him. It's probably thieves fallin' oot among their ain selves.' He nodded at her tea, 'Drink that up, ye'll need your strength, lass.'

Grace picked up the mug and sipped; she looked at him sitting so straight in his chair. 'She hasn't got much

187

longer has she?'

'Nae, lass.' His voice was calm and quiet; the eyes had lost their twinkle and were full of compassion.

'I wish …' She took another swallow in the hopes of shifting the sudden lump in her throat, 'I wish … we could find her James in time.'

'Aye, lass, I've been trying to do that very thing. My mate in America telt me he's still in receipt of an army pension and the last address was in New York. He's well to do apparently, but even money canna fetch him any faster, even if he will want to come. He'll no be sae young to be flying the Atlantic either.' Dan shook his head. 'My mate is in Washington so he was going to try if he might contact the man, personal like, and see if anything is possible.'

Grace looked astonished and Dan hastened to explain that Millie had asked him to help the previous week. 'Oh, Dan, how good you are to us.'

Dan looked somewhat embarrassed, 'Aye weel we a' do what suits us. I'm fond o' Millie, I'd like fine to mak her happy.'

Grace set the empty mug down and looked down her person, beyond the slightly grubby jeans to her work boots. She bent over, unlaced them, and started to tug them off; reflecting that she wasn't exactly making a good impression on this Scotsman, coming here in her working gear.

Dan came round and helped her pull them off, smoothing the thick wool socks back up her feet and ankles. He thought she looked delightful; he especially admired the snug fit of her jeans, but didn't think now was a good time to tell her so. Grace stood up, taking a deep breath as she turned towards the door. Dan was beside her even as she moved. 'She might not be quite conscious, Grace.' He uttered the warning quietly and took a hand, 'She's rousing now and now, but the periods are getting shorter.'

Grace nodded and without another word they went into the bedroom. Grace was surprised at how small Millie now appeared in the hospital bed. She was laying on her side propped up with pillows down her back, and the soft hiss of the oxygen dominated the room.

Dan squeezed Grace's hand, 'Do ye go and hold her hand a bit, and I'll just sit quiet over here.' He nodded to the high backed Queen Anne chair in the corner near the window where he could keep an unobtrusive eye on Millie.

Grace sat down in the green nursing chair and took one of the frail hands. Millie's eyes fluttered open and the echo of a smile passed over her serene features. 'Hello, darling.'

'Hello, yourself. Are you comfortable?'

'Oh yes. Mary's got me propped up nicely.' The voice was still clear, if a little breathless. 'I'm glad you've come. I wanted to say goodbye properly.'

'Grandma.' Grace found her voice was completely suspended by tears.

'Now, Gracie, be a brave soldier for me.'

'OK.' Grace tried to smile as she heard the familiar phrase.

'I'd hoped to introduce you to your grandfather, but maybe Dan can do that for me.'

Grace nodded and Dan, hearing his name, came soft footed into her line of vision, Millie smiled at him, 'You'll do that won't you, Dan.'

'Aye, Millie, I'll tak care o' her for ye.'

Millie closed her eyes again and Grace thought she'd gone to sleep until she suddenly opened them. 'At Gretna, Dan?'

189

'Aye, Millie if ye like.'

Grace, slightly mystified by these cryptic utterances, looked from one face to the other but Millie had closed her eyes again and Dan had returned to his seat.

The silence in the room wasn't oppressive, just peaceful. Grace sat trying to reconcile herself to imminent loss, and Dan sat wondering just when he'd fallen in love with the young woman sitting so close to the bed. He thought it must have been that giggle on Friday, or maybe it was when she'd cried all over him, or maybe it went even further back than that, he didn't know, he just knew she was his now. He'd promised Millie.

ANOTHER PAIR OF LOVERS was struggling with their destiny too, but they had slightly more insurmountable difficulties. David didn't know what to make of Kate's behaviour; she'd cried like one heartbroken all the way back to his house and he didn't know how to comfort her.

'Kate.' He'd sat down on the settee and set her on his lap. 'Come on, darling, you'll make yourself ill.'

Kate tried to stop but the tears just kept streaming down her face.

'What is it, darling?'

'It's a…all my f…fault.'

'You didn't kill him, darling.'

'I'm s…supposed to make it r…right for you and now it's all s…spoilt and it's all my f…f…fault.' Kate clung to him.

David tried the pat and stroke routine and, when that didn't work, turned up the blotched face which had been burrowing into his shirt. 'I love you; you know that don't you, Kate? I don't care what you think you've done, darling, I love you.'

Kate made a huge effort and tried to control herself. 'You won't, I know you w…won't. Nobody c…could when they f…find out.' She stopped and looking miserably into his eyes.

She scrubbed a hand across her own. 'J…just remember I love you t…too, David. I always h…have.' Then she got off his knee and walked away to the window in the big sitting room, looking out across the estuary. He could see she was trying to regain her usual calm and sat quietly waiting. He heard her blow her nose, and saw her take off her glasses and wipe her eyes. Presently she turned back to him. 'I'd like to go back to the h…hostel, David, if you'd drive me t…there?'

'But, darling!'

'Please, David.'

She left the room and he heard her moving about in the room she'd stayed in over the weekend. He shook his head. He would get to the bottom of this, but now didn't seem like a good time to try. She was too upset, and the whole business this morning had distressed him too.

When she returned he was pacing like a caged lion across his Ambusson carpet. 'David,' she seemed to have regained her calm, though he thought it was a rather unnatural one, 'I'd like to go n…now.'

'Look, can't you tell me what's wrong?' He spoke rather more impatiently than he'd intended and saw her flinch.

She shook her head and left the room. He followed her out and found her standing on the other side of the road looking at the sea as it ran noisily in front of them. 'I love your house D…David. I wish…I wish I c…could s…share it with you.'

'But Dammit! You can. You know that's what I want too.' He paced away and back again. 'Is it my age?'

He fired the question at her.

'Oh no, David, you're j…just r…right, it's me that's all w…wrong for you.' She turned and went to stand beside his car, her weekend bag at her feet, and not another word could he get out of her until he finally stopped trying and drove in a dark and brooding silence back to the hostel.

9

THE TEAM HAD BEEN incarcerated for quite a few hours in the hostel, where several Police Constables had taken their statements.

Doug, still pale, was answering questions of a young woman who sat efficiently jotting everything down on a large sheet of lined A4. 'So can you tell us your version of events over the last week then, sir?'

Doug looked at her; he might be married and in love with his wife but he wasn't dead, so he could admire her bust, which was quite spectacular, under her starched shirt, even while he answered. 'Over the last week there have been one or two discrepancies in the daily report sheets, and the Prof was a bit concerned about them. We couldn't find anything missing, but he was concerned enough to have me check out the finds with him and take the most important ones to his house.'

He scratched his head. 'I know there was some bother with Grace.' He looked worried, 'No, that's not what I meant to say.'

'Well what did you mean to say, sir?' The constable looked at him with wide sky blue, and very guileless, eyes which had fooled many a criminal.

Doug looked across the table, 'Something happened on Thursday morning, and Grace and the Prof were talking about it; and afterwards he called us all together and told us all to be extra vigilant.' He paused, watching her make strange squiggles on the page. She stopped and looked up at him.

'And?'

'Well later that night the Prof' came out to the hostel here because Kate had had a funny phone call and he wanted to talk about that.' He scratched again, 'And to warn us not to talk to anyone over the phone.'

She waited patiently for him to continue. 'Well then Friday we found someone had been on site overnight and the Prof' reported it to the police. But you must already know about that.'

'Yes sir. But we like to be thorough.'

Doug sighed gustily. 'Well David decided that we'd break early for the weekend and let the coppers have a chance to look over things. Anyway, today we all came back to work and then all hell broke loose.' He looked round the small room which had been commandeered. 'I didn't see the body or anything. David asked me to gather the troops and bring them back here, which is what I done.' He paused, 'Then we waited for you lot.'

'Thank you, sir, that's very clear. Would you like to send in the next person?' Doug nodded, giving one last look at the bust before walking with relief from the room. He decided he could face his dentist with ease now; it couldn't be worse than the last fifteen minutes.

INSPECTORS BELL AND MCINNIS were mulling over the statements taken that morning. 'Most of them have good solid alibis; they all live at that hostel and travelled in together this morning.'

'I suppose if one of them really wanted they could have gone to the site in the middle of the night, Sandy, but it would be more than risky. Starting a car would have been a noisy business in the early hours, in that remote spot. Someone was bound to have heard something.'

'Aye, you're right; which brings us to the handful who weren't in the hostel.'

McInnis ticked them off on his elegant hand. 'We've got the Professor. He certainly has a motive for killing if you look at the money angle, and he's got opportunity. If we're to believe he and the girl were in different rooms.'

'Well I'm inclined to believe that bit; he's old school, like me'. Sandy looked across at McInnis, 'We're inclined to offer marriage first, Bob. But that doesn't make him incapable of murder; it just gives him a better opportunity.'

'Right. I agree with you there. Now as to the girl herself …. Scared out of her wits, but no motive that I can see.'

They were in a small badly furnished room in one of the other huts. It was currently serving them as head of operations at the hostel. He pondered, resting his elbows on the folding card table and his head in his cupped hands. 'She might lie to cover up for him I suppose?' He cocked an eye at Sandy Bell.

'I don't think it. She's obviously smitten, it is right what you say, but, no, I don't think so.' He shook his head, making the cowlick of grey hair flop into his eyes. He pushed it back with an impatient hand. 'Though …' He paused again, 'I'm not sure.' he said slowly, 'she could just be painfully shy, Bob; but I wondered if she was lying about knowing Jardin.' His voice held half a question.

McInnis looked thoughtfully at the older man. 'I didn't see that. I don't know how she could, Sandy.' He frowned then shrugged, 'So we come to that young man John Williams. Do you believe his tale of falling asleep, Sandy? I find it hard to credit myself.'

'Ah well. That's because you have no bairns of your own yet, Bob. I could well believe it, being a father myself.' He grinned at the younger man.

'Well, he's got a whopping great motive. The criminal branch have been watching Jardin for a few weeks; since he swam back into our bailiwick. And they've

195

dug out his old records; you had a hand in the last go round, Sandy.'

He nodded across at the older man, watching him rasping a cheek with a callused hand, then Robert McInnis shook his head. 'A right little scoundrel he was. Not your violent type mind, but he did cause the death of Max Warner, John Williams' school mate.'

'Yes, I know, and so does somebody else here.' He looked significantly at his opposite number, 'One of the others said something about that; let me find it.' Sandy shuffled the papers. 'Here you are. Miss Potter; she claims she heard him say he'd like to break Jardin's neck only this morning.'

McInnis looked suddenly interested. 'Self-interest or spite, Sandy?'

'God knows, but I don't like witnesses who try to lay the blame. We'll have to look a bit closer at Miss Potter.'

'How about Miss Gordon? Reputable woman, seemed genuinely shocked at the death, and its true her grandmother is ill; though most of them seemed to think it was her great aunt.' He wrinkled his patrician nose as if he'd got a whiff of something interesting. 'Wonder which it is. Anyway I don't think she's got much of a motive Sandy.'

'Well she's worked for the professor for a good few years and she was present at the last incident'

'She can't have been very old?' McInnis raised an eyebrow.

'No, just a teenager. Howsoever she might have wanted a bit of revenge for wrecking that dig. She's obviously fond of the professor.' He made a moue, 'But I agree not much motive there. Though we'll have to follow up on this statement from the site foreman.' He tapped another sheet of paper with a stubby finger 'I want to know what happened Thursday morning. Professor Walker did tell us about the phone calls, but I think we need to know

196

what happened before then.'

'I agree, Sandy.' McInnis shuffled the papers together again. 'We also need to send a couple of likely lads round to ask a few questions of Frank Barker. Tell 'em to go careful. We don't want to upset such a fine upstanding citizen!'

Sandy snorted.

'Apparently Mr Barker's dumb friend Dennis Little, AKA Little Dennis, was seen trailing Jardin on Friday.'

'He's more likely to break shins than necks, Bob'

'Well mistakes happen. Will you do the search of Jardin's rooms?'

'Oh! Aye. There was a card in his wallet with a B & B address on it, along with thirty quid and a few coins. It wasn't a robbery?'

'No. Whatever it was it wasn't for the pathetic contents of his pockets.'

'I think I'll do that interview; Frank Barker and I go back a bit.' Sandy gathered his papers up from the table. 'What are you going to be doing while I check on these sterling citizens?'

'I'm going to do a closer run on the Misses Potter and Gordon. I don't like people who come off too clean.' McInnis picked up his own notes. 'And maybe a little look at Miss Hamilton too.

'Anyone who didn't know you, Bob, would think you were a suspicious soul.' He grinned and they left the room, laughing together and thus disconcerting several of the team who'd been hanging around outside the door in the hopes of hearing something interesting.

INSPECTOR SANDY BELL, WITH the aid of a very competent PC, was confronting Philip Jardin's landlady.

'Well I never, did!'

'Likely not, Ma', but we still want the key to his room and a look around it.'

'Well I ain't got it; he al'us takes his key with 'im.'

The Inspector exchanged a look with his young sidekick as the stout landlady looked at them triumphantly and said, 'Now what y' gonna do?'

'Well Ma', it seems we'll have to kick it in if you ain't got a key.'

''Ere, you ain't kicking my door in!'

'Well.' Sandy hid a grin. 'Surely you've got a spare; I bet folk are always walking off with the keys.'

The landlady admired a good bluff. 'OK, I'll go and get a spare, but 'ere,' she wagged a finger the size of a wiener sausage under his nose, 'don't you go a kicking my door in while I'm gone.' She waddled away, her thighs in her nylons apologising to each other as they passed and re-passed.

The two men leaned against the wall outside the door. 'Key wasn't on the body, Gareth, wonder if it's dropped out into that well? Remind me to check with the crime scene blokes.'

Gareth nodded his head and then it was his turn to hide a smile as the landlady came back, perspiring slightly and with a key in her ham-like hand. ''Ere you are; we 'as it for cleaning and such.' She handed it over and stood expectantly, waiting for them to open the door.

'You can go and Hoover or something now,' said Sandy, turning the key in the lock and opening the door.

'What and leave you to make a mess of the room! I'm coming in I am.'

198

'Oh no you're not!' The smile had gone entirely from Sandy's face. 'This is a murder investigation, not a bit of petty theft.'

'Oh! Ohhh! That's dreadful. Why didn't you say? Ooh! I feel quite faint.' She sounded more overexcited than overwrought.

'Well don't faint in here. You'll spoil my evidence.' He turned to the constable. 'Keep her out, Constable.' He pushed past and the constable swung his young bulk into her path and stood arms akimbo, watching her.

She eyed him with acute dislike but, since his bulk precluded her from seeing round him, she stomped away down the corridor muttering to her. He thought he caught the phrase, 'Bloody coppers!' and grinned, hastily changing it to a stern face as another resident popped his head out of his door to enquire what all the racket was about.

Sandy sniffed; he caught the faint odour of unwashed clothes coming from the pile in the corner and the undertone of marijuana. 'Hmm.'

He went across to the old fashioned wooden dressing table and started to pull out draws. The first two draws contained underclothes. None of them new but they did have the merit of being clean and folded. The third draw had shirts, unpressed but clean, and mixed socks, none of which appeared to have been a genuine pair for some considerable time.

The fourth draw was locked. Locked draws always got Sandy interested, especially when he could see that this lock had been fitted and wasn't part of the furnishings provided by the stout party in the hall.

'What have we here? Something you didn't want your landlady prying into, I'll be bound.'

He pulled a pen knife from his pocket and jiggled the lock, finessing until he heard the soft click. Then, putting the knife away, he pulled open the draw. 'Ah!

Treasure trove. I wonder where he picked you up.'

He carefully lifted out a small Egyptian statue, and then dived back in, removing a couple of scarab beetles and a rolled wad of soft felt. This, when opened, revealed a neat row of Roman coins lined up like buttons on a coat.

'Very nice! Still in the old trade I see. I wonder if he's got anything else.' He turned to search the rest of the room. The suit case contained a number of closely written pages obviously downloaded from a computer. Sandy scanned them hastily but, aside from the fact that they appeared to be archaeological site reports, couldn't make much sense of them. Nothing else of interest being forthcoming he went towards the door. 'OK Gareth. Put some tape on the door and we'll leave it for now.' He exited, the constable shutting and locking the door behind him, and then carefully tapeing the lock and stringing tape across the door jambs.

'If she's got another set of keys she won't use them.' Sandy grinned wickedly as they turned to walk away.

INSPECTOR ROBERT MCINNIS WAS conducting his own inquiries in a slightly more subtle manner. He was questioning a retired detective. He'd filled him in on the current investigation, as far as it went anyway. Now he said, 'Sandy said there was a woman in the case last time.'

His companion cast a look at the older woman sitting in a rocking chair by the empty grate. She didn't appear to be listening to their quiet conversation; in fact she seemed to be asleep. He stood up, 'I'll just be outside, mother.'

'Well, Yes and No, Bob' He opened the back door, looking back significantly at McInnis.

'Come and see my roses. It's a lovely afternoon and they've done really well despite the rain. Just a little powdery mildew on some of the leaves. You have to keep on top of that. It can spread terribly in the damp weather and infect the whole plant.' Bob McInnis looked curiously at the former Inspector but followed him out into the back yard of his council house.

He duly admired the Raspberry Ripple variety thrust under his nose for smelling. 'Very nice, Bert.' McInnis turned shrewd eyes on his father's former partner. 'What you getting at.'

'Just that. A little bit of mildew can spoil a whole rose and it isn't the rose's fault if the mildew blows its way.'

'Bert!' the tone was slightly exasperated.

'Alright. She was a nasty piece of work, and she was out to get what she could. He gave her the brush off but, being a gent, he wasn't quite firm enough and she tried to say he'd sexually harassed her. 'Touching her inappropriately'.' Bert shrugged. 'I'd say she did more touching than him; but the poor bugger was up against a teenager to his thirty something, so they tried to make a big thing of it.' Bert wandered over to a seat set back against the wall and sat down with a solid thump.

'It had all died away until that man Jardin came on the site. Then of course we started asking questions and everything got raked up again. She tried to claim her kid was his. Got a baby about a year old. Said he should pay maintenance.' Bert sighed. 'Wasn't true of course but the mud was bound to stick a bit, and she was banking on the publicity to force him into it.' He turned to look at the young man. 'He was a pleasant chap, but he got a bit embittered over the whole deal. I wouldn't say he was your man, for what it's worth.'

'This nasty piece got a name.'

Bert cocked his head on one side and scratched his neck in an effort at recall. 'Purvis or Peters, something like that. But it'll all be in the reports.' He looked over his garden, admiring the pagoda he'd put up that spring. 'Why do you want to know, Bob?'

'Seems Professor Walker has got himself another young thing. He says he's going to marry her.'

Bert grinned. 'What's she like?'

Bob rubbed his neck. 'OK I suppose; she won't turn heads, but she's pretty enough. A postgrad student, been with him about four years.'

'Well I wish him luck. Anything else I can help you with, Bob.'

'No,' Bob shook his head slowly, 'I don't think so.'

'Do you want to stay for a cuppa?'

'No, I'd better not thanks. I've got a couple of young ladies to investigate.'

'Oh! Nice work if you can get it.'

They parted; Bert to deadhead roses, and Bob to make sure no human flowers had been instrumental in the deadheading of Philip Jardin.

MEETING FOR A MUG of tea in the canteen at four thirty the two men exchanged information. 'Anything in the rooms, Sandy?'

'Got some nice artefacts that I don't think he came by lawfully. And some paperwork ditto. We need to ask the Professor whose reports they are.' Sandy sat back on the green plastic chair, dunking a ginger biscuit and expertly transferring the resultant damp morsel to his mouth. 'No keys found on the corpse or anywhere in its vicinity. Place was intact. So I don't think if it's thieves had a falling out, that they've profited; we seem to have got to his room first. He had a mobile 'cos I found a payment card, but we haven't found that yet either.'

He dunked more biscuit and spoke rather thickly through it. 'He got any relatives?'

'Ex wife. Hasn't seen him in years, she says. We've got her local branch to get a statement; they're going to fax it through ASAP.

Sandy grunted, 'What you got?'

'Well does Purvis or Peters ring any bells?'

Sandy cocked his head, 'Nope, should they?'

'Well Uncle Bert said he thought the female was called something like that?'

'Nope, wait!' He held up a hand like a man stopping traffic. Then shook his head. 'Nope it's gone. It'll come back to me if I don't worry at it.'

They sat drinking tea for a moment or two then Sandy said 'I'm going to see Frank Barker after supper. I'll take young Gareth with me. He's a good sturdy lad, got muscles that have had to learn to find space among the other muscles.' He smiled a bit grimly.

'Yeah he's a likely lad. But you be careful.'

'Yes, Dad!' Sandy's impish smile danced across his face.

Bob McInnis grinned at him as they stood up to leave a table littered with empty mugs, torn sugar bags, and white plastic spoons. The staff canteen was more utilitarian than understated elegance.

'WHY DON'T YOU SIT down?' Frank Barker was all friendliness. 'Have a scotch, Detective Inspector.' he said affably as he indicated with a sweep of the hand both a seat and the Bells whiskey sitting on the desk. This room definitely had a whiff of elegance about it thought the Inspector and, hard on the heels of that thought was that Frank Barker must be making a mint out of the gambling trade.

He pulled out the heavy oak chair in front of the desk and sat himself down. 'I don't think so, Frank; this is by way of being an official visit.'

'Ouch!' Barker shook a set of fingers as if they'd just been wrapped by a ruler.

''Philip Jardin', Frank, how much did he owe you?'

'Now now, Inspector, that's client confidentiality.'

'Not if your client's dead it isn't.' He watched carefully but Barker never batted an eyelid.

'When's the funeral? I'll send a wreath.' Frank Barker, lounging on the other side of the desk, shot the cuffs of his suit down and sat, pulling up his trousers to preserve the knife edge creases.

'You don't happen to know how he came by his need for a wreath do you.'

'Inspector, is that worthy of you?' Barker tutted, clicking his tongue against white teeth and frowning as he leaned back in the office chair, which emitted a faint squeak. 'A dead client doesn't pay his bills, now does he?'

'I suppose Little Dennis can tell me what he was doing last night?'

'Why Inspector? He was here, all the time.' Barker showed those teeth, putting Sandy forcibly in mind of a lion at the zoo. 'I won't have you defaming him that way.'

'Witnesses.' Sandy rapped out.

Barker frowned, shaking his head. 'I said he was here.'

'Aye and I want others to corroborate.'

Barker scowled. 'Why you picking on my man?'

'Because we know he was following Jardin.'

'Well that was very careless of Little Dennis. But you know, Inspector, he doesn't do the heavy stuff anymore. Proper gentle giant is Dennis.'

Sandy snorted inelegantly. 'Well I'll need more than your word for that. Where is he now by the way?'

'He's out doing a little job for me.'

'If he's gone to toss Jardin's digs you're too late.' He caught the flicker of annoyance crossing Barker's face. He smiled slowly with satisfaction. 'I'll expect him to report to the police station before the evening's done, so you'd better coach him well, Frank.' Sandy Bell stood up and nodded at Barker. 'See you around, Frank.'

He left, quietly picking up Gareth where he was propping up the door post outside the office. 'That went very well. Jardin owed them big time by the look of it, and we got there before they did.' He rubbed his hands gleefully 'I should like to know who told him Jardin was dead. You might ask about a bit, Gareth.' They left the building with satisfied smiles on their faces.

DETECTIVE INSPECTOR ROBERT MCINNIS wasn't smiling, and nor was Professor David Walker. David was looking at the site reports that the Inspector had proffered with an almost apologetic air. He stood now looking like a spaniel that had brought its master the morning papers; only to be reprimanded for slobbering on them.

'We need to establish if these are indeed from your current site.' He paused, looking longingly at the chairs in the study; he'd been on his feet for a good part of the day and resting his weight in one of those deep leather chairs would have been really nice. 'We'd also like to know whose reports they are.'

David, standing next to his desk, turned over the final sheet then lifted his head and removed his glasses. 'Yes, they're last week's. How did you get them, Inspector?'

McInnis ignored the question for one of his own. 'Who wrote them, sir?'

'You tell me where you got them and I might tell you who wrote them.'

McInnis moved from one foot to the other, rebalancing his weight. 'I'd rather not say just at the moment, sir.'

'Nor would I, Inspector. Which leaves us at an impasse?'

The Inspector redistributed his weight again, 'Ah!' He didn't think bribes or threats would sway the man in front of him, and he couldn't think of any anyway. 'Might we sit down Professor?'

David looked a bit startled. 'Sorry!' He pointed at the chair opposite the desk and sat heavily in his own seat.

'Look, sir, we don't want to accuse anyone wrongfully; but we do need to eliminate people. Those,' he nodded at the papers still in David's hand, 'where found in a place which might indicate someone was feeding Jardin information.'

'No way! There's no way the person who wrote these would do that.' He folded his lips and looked sternly at Inspector McInnis.

'If you say so. But we need to eliminate them all the same.' McInnis looked back, his face impassive.

The professor sat looking at him in the fading evening light. He sat for so long that McInnis began to wonder if he had forgotten the policeman's presence, 'Sir?'

David, coming out of his brown study, looked

across the table. 'Here's what we'll do, I'll take you to the person concerned and, if you'll let me ask the questions, I'll get you the answers.'

'I'm not sure I can let you do that, sir.'

'Then I'm not sure I can tell you who wrote them.'

They sat staring at each other. David implacable and the Inspector trying to think of some way of breaking the impasse.

'I could of course arrest you for obstructing the course of justice, but that wouldn't solve either of our problems would it, Professor?' He smiled grimly, 'You ask the questions while I'm there and I get to ask some more;' he paused, 'and you can stay in the room with me.'

He sat back, waiting, 'Or you could tell me why you're so sure this person is innocent?'

David looked at the clear brown eyes watching him. He stood up, 'I'm sure of her innocence but you have a point; you don't know her, Inspector. We'll go in my car and there'll be no arrests tonight, Inspector.' He wagged a slim and elegant finger under the Inspector's nose. 'I know my team.'

McInnis nodded and they left the room; David still holding the papers in his hand. He folded them carefully and went out to the car. David started the car and the Rover, with a muted roar of its engine, set the machine in motion, propelling them smoothly over the surface of the road. McInnis watched a heron take off at the noise and thought he might come out here bird watching in his time off.

He watched the estuary sliding by as they drove back towards the hostel along the one way road. 'You suffer much flooding?' He broke the silence that had sloshed in the car like the water in the estuary. He found it rather oppressive.

David glanced sideways at him. 'Not generally;

207

spring tides can be a bit scary when the wind's with them, but I love the land up here.'

They approached the turn off for the hostel and shot past. Bob McInnis looked back over his shoulder as they sailed on. 'Oh!'

'Yes, Inspector?'

'Nothing.' He subsided onto the seat. He thought he'd known who they were going to see. But it seemed the Professor wasn't just protective of Miss Kate Hamilton. Following this train of thought he said, 'Do you employ a secretary, sir.'

'No. Or at least not when I'm on site.'

'Oh.' McInnis sat quietly enjoying the comfort of the car. At least he was off his feet he thought. He'd find out soon enough who they were going to visit.

They pulled up in a quiet back street on the outskirts of Carlisle. 'Out you get, man; and keep your voice down.'

McInnis looking puzzled at this request, nodded. David strode confidently to the door and gave a quick rap.

'David! What on earth?' Grace looked from him to the Inspector with a puzzled frown on her forehead.

'Can we come in, Grace?' Grace stood back, allowing them both to enter. She eyed them both. 'You'd better come into the kitchen. I was just making a pot of tea.'

David walked in front of her and the inspector followed. When Grace came in she shut the door, looking from one man to the other. 'David?'

'Let's sit down, love, I've got to ask you some questions. But first …' he went across and gave her a hug, then stood back to look at her in the overhead lighting. 'How's Millie?'

Grace gave a tiny shrug, 'Not well, David. I've

decided to sleep over for the next night or two. John was here earlier with Sandra and the baby and I asked him to pass the message on.'

'Yeah! I guessed you'd be here after Saturday.' He sighed. 'I doubt if we'll be allowed back to work anyway, love.' He sighed again then patted her back and released her. 'Now, Grace …' he led her to a chair, 'sit down.' He pulled one out for himself and nodded at another, opposite, for the Inspector to take.

He leaned forward, taking her hands in a warm grasp. 'The Inspector brought some papers to me this evening; he wants to know where they came from and who wrote them?' David released her hands and pulled the folded sheets from his pocket; setting them down on the table and pushing them with a finger towards Grace.

Grace looked at him curiously then picked up the top sheet. She started to read the first line then gave a quiet gasp. 'Oh! But, this is my report. Where did you get it, Inspector?' she turned towards the silently waiting policeman.

'I'm not at liberty to say at the moment, Miss Gordon.' He looked steadily at her.

Grace looked at David. He shook his head. 'Can you tell us how someone has come by a copy?'

Grace shook her head slowly; 'I haven't even printed it out yet, David, it's still a rough draft but I've been so busy with Millie and …' she looked at him apologetically.

'That's alright, love, I know, but we do need to know how they came to be printed out and someone else saw them?'

Grace laid the papers down. 'David, I swear to you I haven't shown them to anyone.' She turned eyes beginning to cloud over with tears towards him.

'I know you wouldn't do it deliberately, Grace, but

209

might you have left someone in the room so that they could print it out.'

'But no one's been at my place. Not even the cleaner, the place is a tip.' She tried to lighten things, and failed miserably, looking sadly at the Professor.

'Alright, love. I believe you.' David took hold of her hands again.

Dan, entering at this moment, stood just inside the closed door, narrowing his eyes. He focused on her face and the tears sliding slowly down her cheeks, and then looked pointedly at the clasped hands resting on the table, and then his eyes went to David's. It was as well the professor was made of strong stuff; evidently the young red-headed giant who'd just entered considered little Grace his property, thought David. He wondered if Grace realised that.

He slowly released her hands, standing up and going across the small room holding out his hand. 'Hello, I'm David Walker. The Police came to ask Grace a few questions so I came along as moral support for her.'

Dan looked him over carefully before accepting the hand. 'Och Aye, I've heard o' ye, my Grace has mentioned y'r name, now and now.'

David didn't miss the possessive pronoun; he looked curiously at this man. Grace might have mentioned David to him, but David hadn't a clue who he was.

'I'll be the nurse, ye ken.' He came further into the room, making for Grace and taking David's vacated chair. He shifted so that he could put an arm around her shoulders. 'Dinna greet then, sweetheart.' He pulled a handkerchief from a trouser pocket and wiped her eyes as if no one else was in the room. Then turning to the two watching men he held her firmly in his arm.

'Noo then, lads, what is it you want with Grace; she's got enough o' trouble at the present without ye

210

bothering her.'

Inspector McInnis felt faintly intimidated and he didn't like it; however, the man now facing him had a different kind of authority to David Walker's. It was testosterone inspired and made him move carefully in his chair and in his conversation.

'My name is Detective Inspector McInnis; I'm with the police Mr er ...' He looked enquiringly at Dan.

'My name would be Sergeant Major, Daniel Alexander Campbell.'

'Ah! Right.' The Inspector absorbed the steely glint without flinching, much. 'Miss Gordon was just helping us to fill in a few blanks in our enquiries, Sergeant Major. Some information she, er, she had, has been found under er, suspicious circumstances, sir.' He resisted the temptation to come to attention under the force of the look now boring into him.

'Is that so, Inspector? Well and there's no need to mak' the lassie cry while ye do it is there?'

The Inspector tried desperately to regain some authority. 'It's important she explain herself, sir.'

'Aye,' he turned Grace away from the Inspector, cuddling her close, 'Tell me all about it, Inspector, and we'll see what's happened.'

The Inspector looked desperately at David; this hadn't been their deal and he didn't want to give too much away, but both men continued to look at him without speaking. He mentally shrugged, he actually rather liked the look of the soldier before him. 'It's like this, sir, the man who was found dead at the site today ...' He stopped. 'You do know about that?'

Dan nodded briefly.

'Right, sir. Well he's a known criminal. He was found in possession of a report which Miss Gordon admits

211

she had written. We're trying to establish how he got it.'

'Well and ye only had to ask the lass. I'm sure she can tell ye if she knows,' he paused, 'and if she dasant a'm sure she'll tell ye that too.'

He turned to Grace who was sitting quietly now that he was holding her. She felt that nothing much could go wrong if he was there, and had been slowly realising that love came in some odd packages and hers was in the shape of a six foot two, red-headed, Scotsman.

She had been leaning her head against his chest, and now straightened up. 'But that's the trouble, Dan; I don't know how he got it. It was on my computer at home and I certainly haven't let him in,' she looked squarely at the Inspector, 'or given it to him.'

'Well, Miss, if that's what you say, how the H…,' he paused, 'Have you any idea how he might have got it?' The Inspector braved one pair of blue eyes and one of green.

David shook his head. 'She'd have told me about that.'

The Inspector swung round to the professor, 'Yes, sir, I understand she tells you about things. What exactly did she tell you on Thursday morning that was so significant?' McInnis suddenly felt in control again.

David looked at him blankly. 'Significant.' He shook his head, 'Do you mean about the padlock being off, but we told the police about that.'

'That and something else, sir. It caused you to, and I quote, 'speak to the troops about being extra vigilant.'

David frowned in an effort of concentration.

'If you found the padlock off when you came to work, why did you have the talk with Miss Gordon first before talking to your team?' McInnis' attitude said, 'get out of that.'

212

While the other three watched, David began to smile. 'Oh dear, er, Grace, I'm going to have to tell you know.'

Grace looked back at him, an answering smile dawning in her sad eyes. She nodded slowly, looking at the inspector, 'OK, David, but try not to laugh too much, Inspector.'

David came forward and pulled out the remaining chair. 'It's like this, Inspector; our Grace has hunches. She would never reveal her secret, but last Wednesday she went to the site at about, well it would be three on Thursday morning, right, Grace?' He looked across at her. 'Anyway she apparently uses dowsing to locate artefacts.' He shrugged as one failing to understand but willing to accept. 'After she'd done, she sat down to look at the stars.' His lips twitched, 'And then she fell asleep and rolled into the main excavation.'

He smiled across the table, 'The gate was un-padlocked when Grace arrived and she accused me of failing to lock up properly.' He turned to the inspector, 'I'd say your man had been there that night.'

'It's to be hoped he wasna still there when you were, Grace, Sweetheart.' Dan dropped a light kiss on the soft hair tickling his chin.

David and Bob McInnis exchanged a glance as the same thought came to them. David beat the Inspector to the gun, 'Did you see anyone there, Grace? I know you said the place was deserted, but could he have been around watching you?'

Grace shook her head, 'I don't think so, David.'

'Did you go home, or to the hostel, after you left the site that morning Miss Gordon?' The Inspector was doing some thinking of his own.

'Home.' Grace suddenly saw the import of the question. 'Oh! Oh! That's creepy.'

213

The three men exchanged glances. Then the Inspector spoke. 'If you wouldn't object very much, Miss Gordon, I'd like to get your fingerprints,' he held up a hand as David would have spoken, 'just for elimination purposes, then we'd like to fingerprint your house.' He stopped, grimaced, and continued, 'Jardin was too good a lag to have left any, but you never know.'

He touched the papers, 'These are copies, if there are none of Miss Gordon's prints on the originals then we can …,' he was about to say probably, but changed his wording after a glance at the two men watching him, 'I should imagine, eliminate you from that branch of our enquiries,' he ended.

'Right then, Inspector, if ye've done I'd be obliged if ye'd go; I've a patient to nurse and Grace is worn to the bone this day.' It was dismissal, pleasantly but determinedly put. The inspector stood up and so did all the others. 'I'll need to come back, Miss Gordon, and speak with your grandmother. It is your grandmother isn't it?'

'Ye'll no be disturbin' Millie, Inspector.'

'It is police business, Sergeant Major.'

'Aye, and that's as maybe; but ye'll no disturb her all the same.' Dan stood looking at the other two men, his blue eyes shooting sparks.

The Inspector shrugged, tonight wasn't the time to fight this battle. He followed David down the corridor and they left the house, Dan closing the door behind them. Then Dan returned to the kitchen where Grace had reseated herself at the table.

Dan went straight across the room. Pulling her up into his arms, 'When we're marrit ye'll no go roaming about excavations in the middle o' the nicht.' He gave her a gentle shake. 'And the only falling ye'll do is inta my arms, do ye hear me.'

Grace looked first astonished and then indignant.

214

'Who said we were getting married. I don't remember being asked?'

'Grace,' he said chidingly, smiling down into her face, holding her close a minute, and preventing her struggles by angling her head just as he wanted it and planting a kiss that she might have fought if she'd had more warning. He lifted his head, observing the swollen lips and slightly glazed look with some satisfaction. 'We burn for each other, sweetheart; I think we'd better wed soon before we go up in flames entirely.' He shook her again gently as she didn't speak. 'Did ye no hear me tell Millie I'd wed thee a' Gretna?'

Grace looked at him, licking those lips so that he wanted to kiss her senseless, 'I thought that was to meet my grandfather.'

Dan gave in to temptation; kissing her so that both of them had to cling to stop themselves falling. Her body arched against him and Dan shivered with need. 'Sweet mercy woman, we have to get marrit!' He went back for a third kiss so that Grace, by this time totally dizzy with her own needs, allowed him to pick her up and sit her on his lap at the kitchen table. He raised his head to mutter. 'Dear God it had better be soon.' before he went back to her lips.

How long they would have indulged is open to wide conjecture; however, the clock sounding eleven seemed to bring Dan to his senses. 'Millie!' He allowed Grace to breathe, resting his forehead against hers, and with his eyes closed said, 'Please Grace?'

Grace wasn't in any better condition. 'Yes, Dan.'

'OK, I have to go and be a nurse. I canna do it wi' ye sitting on ma lap.' He smiled his slow smile at her and allowed her to stand up. 'Though how a'm to concentrate wi' ye upstairs in yon bed God only knows!'

Grace took his hand, 'We'll keep watch together.' They went hand in hand into the quiet room. Dan pulled up the Queen Anne chair next to the nursing chair and they sat down.

'Can I do anything, Dan?'

'No, lass, just maybe hold Millie's hand. She's sleeping but it's the drugs, not natural sleep ye ken. I'll just do a set of obs' and turn her in a minute. She might wake then and it'll be a comfort to her to have you there.'

10

IT WAS AN UNEASY awakening for several people. Grace had fallen asleep in the nursing chair and awoke to find herself well wrapped in a blanket. She stirred and sat up, wincing as several areas of her spine objected to the straightening process.

She looked sleepily around to find Dan. He was standing next to the open window with a hand on the sill and the other outside feeling the rain fall, a curious expression on his face.

'Dan?'

'Hello, sweetheart. You sleep sound and ye don't even snore.' He came towards her, a tired smile on his face. 'A kent ye would be the ideal wife.' He leaned over and put a soft kiss on the bubbly hair while Grace wondered what on earth she looked like.

'And you're beautiful too. What more could a man ask for.'

Grace, struggling to extricate herself from the blue folds surrounding her, gazed at him with some astonishment. 'You have obviously lost your mind.' But she said it with a smile dawning on her tired face. She finally managed to stand up and walked round the bed to look down on her grandmother's face. 'She looks peaceful.'

'Aye, lass. Will ye mak' us a drink while I see to her. And then you can sit a bit longer. But I want ye to go and get some fresh air. You're no to sit all day by her side, for that would be bad for both of ye.' Dan looked down at the pale face before him, reaching out almost unconsciously to hold her hands.

'Aye, lad.' Grace smiled up at him, squeezing his hands before letting them go and leaving him to his ministrations.

INSPECTOR MCINNIS HADN'T HAD much rest; he'd written several reports, deployed men to track down the whereabouts of Dennis Little, who hadn't arrived as requested, and waded through a mass of paper from the last archaeological dig in the area in which Jardin had been involved.

The net result of this was a headache, but also a surprising depth of knowledge about the various *dramatis personae* of this case and appreciation of his father's abilities as a policeman.

By nine he was ready to tackle some more interviews. He rang through to Sandy Bell's office. 'Sandy, good morning, can you come through? I'd like to compare a few notes.'

Sandy presented himself a few minutes later bearing coffee in pottery mugs, and with a thin file under one arm.

'What you got there?'

'This is information on the things we found in Jardin's room. The professor is recommended for the source of the Egyptian stuff; but guess who the university thinks we should show the coins to.' Sandy's brown eyes twinkled with amusement.

'OK I'll bite. Who?'

'Miss Grace Gordon or her aunt.'

'Well, well. I suppose we'd better go and see her then.' McInnis gave a wolfish grin. 'Perhaps we'll manage a bit better without her two Saint Bernard's standing guard.'

'Eh!'

'I'll fill you in on the way, Sandy, but first I've got some surprising news for you. Look at this!' He thrust a copy of the report from the southern branch under Sandy's nose and watched it twitch with interest while he polished off his mug of coffee.

'Well I'm damned, and we didn't think there could be anything to connect that one.'

'First stop the hostel then, Bob.' The two men headed out, nodding at one or two colleagues as they went.

They arrived to find the place swarming with students in various stages of casual wear and David Walker, moving furniture with a great deal of energy and grim determination, in their midst.

'Professor Walker.' Bob McInnis smiled sleekly at David, a tiger sighting potential prey, as they came through the entrance corridor of the communal rooms. 'We'd like a few words with you when you have a minute; but first we'd like a word with Miss Hamilton.'

'Kate?' David look surprised. 'Alright, but she really isn't involved you know.' He turned away and went down the corridor to the main sitting room, two policemen following him. Kate was helping to set up a large trestle table down the centre of the room; a number of cardboard boxes sat on the floor next to the wall and several youths appeared to be bringing in bowls of water.

'We thought since we weren't allowed back on the site yet we might sort and catalogue the finds so far. It's rare to get the opportunity to do it before you've finished digging but then,' David shrugged, 'I should imagine we have, haven't we, Inspector?'

'We're working as quickly as we can, Professor. However, not all your girls have told us everything they know.'

'Kate!' David shouted above the din and Kate's head came up like a spaniel hearing its master. She came towards him apparently calm; however, David was aware of the extra tension in her body as she came to a stop next

219

to him.

'D…David.'

'The police need to have another word. Don't worry just tell them anything they need to know and answer all their questions.' He smiled down at her.

Kate paled, 'But I t…told you everything y…yesterday, Inspector.'

'Not quite, Miss. Could we step into the little room we had yesterday do you think?' Sandy stepped back, then forward, to avoid yet another large box apparently approaching under its own two legs. The legs where shapely and he appreciated them, clad as they were in short shorts and hiking boots and socks. The expanse between was long and brown.

Kate looked from the two inspectors to David. 'Would you like me to come with you, Kate?'

Kate shook her head, making the curls bounce. 'N…no it's OK.' She led the way down the corridor again against the flood of human traffic and crossed into the next hut, waiting quietly while the Detectives came in. Then she shut the door and stood waiting beside it.

'Sit down, Miss Hamilton; it is Miss Hamilton isn't it?'

Kate nodded, but her hands clenched and they could see the colour bleaching from her skin.

'Funny but that's not the name we were given.' Bob look sternly at her, 'It's an offence to lie to the police you know.'

'I didn't.' Kate, looking more frightened by the minute, started to shake. 'Its m…my m…mother's m…maiden name, I've used it,' she caught a breath, 'I've used it s…since s…school.'

'And your mother's married name was Jardin wasn't it?'

Kate nodded; they could see the tears starting to well up in her eyes.

'And Philip Jardin was your father, wasn't he?'

Kate nodded again. The tears were making long streaks down her face now but she didn't make a noise; just stood there, all the misery she was feeling revealed on her face.

'When did you last see him?'

'W…when I w…was fif…fifteen.'

'And you haven't seen him since? Do you really expect us to believe that, Miss Hamilton?'

Kate shook her head, she spoke passionately and for once with hardly a stutter. 'I hated him. Do you know what it's like to have a f…father in prison and all the kids know about it Inspector? Do you know how cruel they can be? Do you know what it's like to know your father is a t…thief and a m…murderer and wonder if you might be tainted like that?' She rubbed her face with the backs of her hands. 'I k…know, and he's dead, and he's still s…spoiling m…my l…life.'

Sandy Bell went towards her and gently took a hand, leading her towards one of the seats. 'Why didn't you tell us, Miss Hamilton?'

Kate sat because her legs didn't feel as though they would support her, but she was still in fighting mode. 'To a…avoid this. I knew you'd s….suspect m…me, but I didn't k…kill him. I'm not a m…murderer no m…matter what my f…father was. I tried to h…help.' She sobbed out the last word, bowed her head, and gave in to the silent tears.

Inspector McInnis shook his head at Sandy. 'No-one has accused you of murder, Miss Hamilton.'

Sandy patted the nearest shoulder and proffered a handkerchief. Kate blew prosaically and wiped her eyes, but still the tears fell. 'We need to know if you knew he was up here in the North, Miss Hamilton.'

Kate raised pansy brown eyes swimming in tears which dripped under her glasses and ran down the side of her nose. She nodded. 'My m…mum wrote and t…told m…me, she was worried I m…might m…meet him accidentally. I thought,' she gulped, 'I thought if I left some s…signs at the s…site David would b…be on g…guard and it would be OK.'

The two men looked at each other. Bob opened his mouth to ask another question but it wasn't uttered. David, after a perfunctory knock came into the room, took in Inspector McInnis seated at the desk and the sobbing girl and said, 'Good God, man do you bully all your witnesses?'

He went across to Kate, squatting down next to her. 'Here, darling, it can't be that bad.'

McInnis, stunned by the accusation of bullying, hadn't quite rallied when Sandy Bell came into his own. 'We haven't quite finished with Miss Hamilton yet, Professor. There are one or two questions we still need to ask.'

David gave him a savage look 'Well ask them, blast you!' He turned back to Kate, taking hold of the hands twisting the handkerchief and stilling them 'I'm here, Kate, and here I stay.'

Kate, looking if anything even more stricken, shook her head violently, 'No, No, you have to go.' She tried to push his hands away, raising eyes that looked haunted to his face.

'Kate.' There was a wealth of hurt in David's face and voice.

'I'm s…sorry, so sorry D…David but,' she bit her lip, 'please, please go.'

David stood up slowly, releasing her; he looked

like a man who'd just been told he was dying. The other men looked at him sympathetically as Kate lowered her head and resumed her mangling of the cloth.

He turned on his heel and left the room, closing the door with a quiet click. The silence was fragile. Sandy and McInnis exchanged looks that spoke volumes about women.

'Now, Miss.' Finally McInnis broke the stillness, 'What did you mean by, 'tried to help'?'

Kate looked up. Her face was streaked, and her curls were badly tangled and damp as they stuck to her cheeks. She sniffed, wiping a hand over her eyes. She took a deep breath 'I t...thought if there was something really wrong on the s...site David would have to b...bring in the police and p...people would be careful. So I uncovered Grace's skeleton and took away the l...ladder. I went before b...breakfast on Thursday m...morning.'

'And why did you think there was a need to bring the police in?'

'The site r...reports didn't always a...add up. And one or t...two t...things had gone missing.' She was calming as she explained, only taking the occasional deep breath. 'Grace found a P...pontin on the site and it shouldn't have been t...there. In fact it was on the s...surface. I wondered t...then if,' she sniffed again, 'if m...my father was about, he likes coins, and then it disappeared.'

'Yes, Miss.' Sandy looked significantly at Bob McInnis, 'One final question for now. Just how did you get to the site without anyone hearing your car leave on Thursday?'

'Oh, I used one of the b...bikes.' Kate looked surprised.

The two detectives swallowed; it was that simple, any of the crew could have travelled the same way and no-one the wiser, and their suspect list had just filled out again.

Kate blew her nose again, looking down at her hands. Sandy came around to the front of her chair, crouching in front of her as David had done. He looked into her face 'Professor Walker is an honourable man, Kate, perhaps you should tell him what you've told us.' He stood up and the two men left her sitting at the table, and quietly closed the door behind them.

GRACE WAS SITTING AT a table too; she'd gone back to her own small flat to collect a change of clothes and gather up her laptop. Now she sat in the quiet kitchen of Millie's house gazing at the screen and trying to concentrate, without much success, on her preliminary report of the skeleton.

She sighed, casting a glance at the ceiling. Before she'd slept the night before she had been talking to Dan. He'd looked so tired and had admitted that he was finding it increasingly difficult to sleep in the motel. The solution had seemed obvious to Grace but Dan had taken a bit more persuading. However, he was now ensconced in her old bedroom upstairs, hopefully asleep.

He'd gone to fetch some spare clothes and his own laptop when Mary arrived for the day shift, returning an hour later with a smile crinkling his eyes. They'd sat in the kitchen drinking tea while he told her the news.

'Sweetheart, there was an e-mail waiting, from Washington.'

'Oh, Dan!' Grace looked at his tired face, 'What did it say?'

'It would seem our Millie's beau is over in England just noo. My mate was told he was on a business trip.' Dan sipped tea, 'He's trying to track the man doon and see would he be willing to come north.'

Grace hugged his arm as it rested on the table.

'Don't get your hopes too high, Grace,' he warned.
'But I'll grant it's a good start to the day.' He set the mug
down

'And you need to rest, Dan.'

'Aye a' do, tell Mary she may call me if she has
need. I'm going to enjoy sleeping in your bed, Grace.' His
eyes twinkled and he smiled down at her as he stood up.

'You're being provocative again.'

'Aye,' he tilted his head, looking like a pathetic
puppy, 'do ye think it might earn me a good night kiss,
sweetheart?'

'More like a thump.' But Grace was already
moving into his arms and offering her lips, so that now she
couldn't concentrate for thinking of Dan upstairs. She
sighed again; perhaps she'd better go out and get that fresh
air he'd talked about.

She'd barely got outside the gate when the jam
sandwich pattern of a police car drew up in front of her.
She looked back at the house as Inspector McInnis got out;
he spoke softly to the driver and moved across the
pavement. 'Miss Gordon, perhaps I could have a word.'

'Certainly, Inspector. Have you come for your
fingerprints?'

'Well Miss, I'm not denying it would be helpful if
you could provide them today. But actually I came to ask a
few more questions.'

'Do you want to go inside, Inspector?'

McInnis considered a second and came to a rapid
decision. 'Not really, Miss, perhaps you could get in the
squad car and we could go to your flat while I talk to you.'

Grace nodded, stepping forward. When they were

225

both safely strapped in McInnis leaned forward and gave her address the driver.

'Now, Miss,' he turned in his seat, facing her, 'we need to speak to your Grandmother. By the way is it aunt or grandmother?'

Grace pressed her lips together. 'It's grandmother, Inspector. Why do you need to speak to her?'

'We have to confirm your statement of your presence on Sunday for one thing, and we've been given her name as a source of information for Roman coins for another.'

Grace looked out of the window for a minute until she was sure her voice was steady, 'Well I'm sorry to have to refuse, Inspector; my grandmother isn't expected to live much longer. She has neither the strength nor the energy to answer questions, either about my whereabouts or coins. Roman or otherwise.'

The Inspector looked slightly disconcerted, 'But ...'

'I'm sorry, Inspector, we're talking days, I can't let you bother her.'

'Oh, I'm sorry, Miss. You said she was ill, but I hadn't realised how ill.' McInnis was a compassionate man really. 'Well where did you go shopping after you'd been visiting? Maybe someone can confirm that bit.'

Grace named a local precinct and he scribbled it down in a notebook as they pulled up at the door of her flat.

'We have some coins that were found in Jardin's possession. We would like to try to establish were they came from.' He looked hopefully at Grace. 'Perhaps you ...'

'I don't know, Inspector; I'm a bit busy at the moment.' She smiled without humour, 'I wouldn't have thought you'd want a suspect dealing with evidence anyway.'

Bob McInnis grimaced behind her back as he followed her up her path and waited for her to open her door. She was right, but he was a bit stuck; she was apparently the best in the north of England. If he could only eliminate her he could use her. 'Mmm, yes, Miss.' He followed her in and promptly rapped his shins on the umbrella-stand, knocking it flying so that it jammed the door open.

'Blast!' Grace bent to extricate man from umbrella, 'That happened last week as well; it's got a mind of its own.' She pulled it free and set it back in the stand. 'In you come, Inspector. You'll forgive the untidiness; I'm really a closet member of slut's anonymous.'

She stood up, a curious expression flitting over her face.

'What have you just thought of, Miss?'

Grace shook her head and she spoke slowly. 'It's probably nothing Inspector, but the umbrella fell down last week and jammed in the door just like that, but,' she frowned, 'I could have sworn I'd shut the door. It did it all by itself.'

'What day, Miss Gordon?' McInnis resisted the temptation to grab her and give her a shake as she stood thinking in the hall.

'I can't quite remember. The days have been a bit blurred just lately.'

She turned and walked into her front room. 'What do you need to do, Inspector?'

'If I could use your phone, Miss Gordon, I'll arrange for a team to come and dust while you're here. That'll save us considerable time.'

He picked up the phone at her nod and spoke crisply into the receiver. 'Right, they'll be here shortly.'

'Would you like a coffee?'

227

He nodded and followed her into the small kitchen.

Grace picked the kettle up and began to fill it, 'What about your young man out there?'

McInnis smiled sourly, 'He's just watching our backs, Miss. I'd rather he stayed outside for now.'

Grace shrugged, setting the kettle down and switching it on. She started to put together the coffee things and slowed her movements, 'It was the day it rained, I put the kettle on and went to get changed.' She blushed slightly as she followed in her mind the sequence of events. 'But before I got the kettle switched on the umbrella fell and I went out to the hall with it in my hand to see what had happened,' she paused, 'and the door was open so I closed it and went back into the kitchen.' She smiled suddenly. 'It was Thursday, because I went to look at the bruise on my…' She stopped abruptly and felt her cheeks growing hot.

Bob McInnis would love to have asked just where the bruise was but didn't quite have the courage when he caught her eye.

'Yes, Inspector, it was Thursday last week. And what's more,' she said triumphantly, 'my computer was on and it shouldn't have been. But I just thought I'd been careless again.'

'Well, Miss, that's been very helpful; it's surprising how often people don't wear gloves to use a computer, we might get lucky.'

'Yes and so might I, Inspector.' She finished making the coffee and handed him a mug. 'Can you tell me what these coins looked like or would that compromise the evidence too much?'

The Inspector weighed up the girl before him; his instinct was telling him he could trust her but his training was saying something different. Instinct won. 'They were a bit odd actually, Miss, with little brackets on the sides of them.'

He shrugged, 'in for a penny' or a Roman coin anyway, he thought. 'I can draw you a bit of a picture. I only knew they were coins when Sandy showed them to me because they had heads on the with those leaf things around them.'

He pulled out his notebook and sketched rapidly. 'There, Miss.' He handed over the paper.

Grace looked at the rough drawing, she looked excited. 'They had laurels and these little handles on the side you say?'

'Not all of them, but some did. Is that good then?'

'If they're what I think they are its fascinating. They're called 'Pontins', Inspector.'

'Kate said you found one of those at the site but it got stolen.'

Grace looked a bit sheepish. 'Er, no. I took it to show Grandma, but we couldn't figure out why it should be on the site in the first place, they come from around Kent. David knew I'd got it.' Grace suddenly looked worried. 'I didn't steal it. He's got it back now, you ask him.'

'Yes, Miss, I'll do that. So you say they don't come from around here?'

'No.' She frowned at him, 'Just how many have you got?'

The Inspector scratched an ear and sipped his coffee, 'I think there were ten.'

'Oh I do hope you can clear me, I'd so like to have a look at them and so would …' She stopped as if she'd hit a brick wall.

'And so would …?'

'And so would Grandma. Only she can't.' Grace looked incredibly sad and Bob McInnis wished he'd kept his mouth shut. He was relieved to hear a tap on the door. 'That'll be my team.'

The forensic team was thorough and left streaks of grey powder on doorknobs and windows and around her printer. Despite herself Grace was actually quite fascinated by their investigations. She'd submitted to fingerprinting without a qualm. 'my laptops back at grandma's, Inspector.

'We'll print that later then,' McInnis nodded at one of the team to follow up on the laptop.

Now in the aftermath of their ministrations she looked around her small flat and grimaced. 'It's a good job I'm not house proud Inspector.'

'Er! Yes, Miss Gordon; it's an unfortunate side effect.'

'Well have you finished with me for now then?'

McInnis nodded his head; he looked her squarely in the face, 'Thank you for your cooperation, Miss Gordon, you've made my task a lot easier. If we can clear you, are you willing to look at the coins?'

'Certainly. I look forward to it.' She smiled a trifle sardonically, 'I know I'm innocent so I can say that.' her lips twitched as she caught the slight smile on his face.

The Inspector was about to take his leave when her phone rang. She stretched out and lifted the receiver off the hook. 'Yes.' She held it out to McInnis, 'It's Inspector Bell for you.'

She walked away into the bedroom to give him a bit of privacy and poked at the dust around her desk. Then walked to the bed and sat down. He found her there several minutes later. 'Thank you once again, Miss Gordon. I must go. Can I give you a lift anywhere?'

Grace stood up, looking at him thoughtfully; the man seemed rather strained all of a sudden. 'No its fine, Inspector. I'll walk back to grandma's, the fresh air will do me good.'

The Inspector left speedily. She heard the front door slam and the silence of the place descended on her. It was the first opportunity she'd had to think since the night before. She pondered the words of Dan as she perfunctorily tidied the bedroom, fetching a hover to suck the dust off her printer and make the bed.

Did he really mean it when he said he wanted to marry her? He could just be feeling sorry for her. Or it might just be a sexual thing; after all he'd said he wanted to bed her, he hadn't said he loved her. She looked at the covers she'd just tucked in and felt herself blushing.

She knew she loved him and, now she came to think about it, she'd been rather open about her feelings; she felt herself blushing even more as she sat down on the recently straightened duvet in the bedroom. Had she forced the man into declaring things because of what she'd said? 'Oh Lord.' She almost groaned the words out loud.

She sat thinking of the last time she and Dan had been together, until her stomach began to growl at her like a small puppy demanding a meal and she looked at her watch. Almost one, she'd better get back to Millie's. She stood up and gathered her things, walking away from the chaos of the sitting-room and closing the door on it, her mind as muddled as the mess she left behind.

INSPECTOR BELL HAD HAD the fiddly task of cornering David Walker and asking him if he was willing to look at exhibits a. through m. that had been discovered in Jardin's rooms. He wasn't too happy to have been assigned the task but quite understood Bob McInnis' reluctance. McInnis felt he'd got off on the wrong foot that morning with the Professor, and then the painful scene with Kate had made him even more reluctant to have too much to do with the man.

'I don't think he likes me, Sandy, and I can't say I blame him. Even if it isn't my fault.' His nose wrinkled. 'I think you'd do better to tackle him while I go and see Miss Gordon. At least that way we'll know he's occupied and not likely to come barging in on that interview.'

Sandy Bell had nodded. He had a great deal of sympathy for David Walker; it was obvious to a blind man that the professor was smitten badly, and badly hurt by Kate's rejection that morning. However, a crime had been committed and they had to solve it while the trail was still hot.

He'd discovered the professor as he was supervising the placing of several trays of potshards on the table. The professor's face was bland to the point of being devoid of emotion altogether.

'Professor, a word with you if I may?'

'Yes, Inspector.'

'Can we speak in private a moment?'

David nodded and led the way to another room which Sandy discovered was a dining hall. It was, however, empty save for one older woman dressed in the ubiquitous jeans and flannel shirt of the team member. She was busy stirring something on the stove in a large steel saucepan. Sandy sniffed appreciatively.

'Carol, if we could have a moment?'

Carol looked at the two men, took in their expressions, and nodded her own head. She turned down the gas, 'Give it a stir, David.' and she left the room, closing the door behind her.

David went across to the stove and picked up the

wooden spoon, beginning to stir the contents of the saucepan. 'Well, Inspector?'

Sandy leaned comfortably against the work surface, watching him. 'It's like this, sir, we found some artefacts in Jardin's rooms and your name was one of those suggested to us as a means of identification.'

'Does this mean I'm not suspect number one then, Inspector?'

Sandy shrugged. 'We haven't eliminated you yet, sir, but, so far, as you say, it doesn't make sense; you hardly want to lose time on the site.'

'Huh! Thanks for that, I don't think.' David knocked the spoon against the side of the pan and laid it on a convenient saucer. He turned and looked squarely at the older man. 'What makes you think I'd want to cooperate with the law at this particular time, Bell?' He looked the Inspector over sardonically, hands in his pockets as he leaned against the side of the stove.

Sandy shook his head, 'I don't, but I have to ask.'

David turned back, picking the spoon up again, and stabbed at the contents of the pan. He sighed, 'I'd be cutting off my own nose to spite myself if I didn't, wouldn't I, man?' He stirred for a minute in the silence. Then sighed again, 'Fine. Bring your bits and I'll cast an eye over them; though I'm not promising to be able to give you their provenance, which is what I suspect you want me to do.'

Sandy nodded. He coughed and stood up from his leaning pose and then he fidgeted with the money in his trouser pocket. He pulled a hand out and touched David on the sleeve; stilling his movements, 'Look I know it's none of my business but Miss Hamilton ...' He trailed away at the steely look in David's eye. The hand gripping the spoon had gone white and Sandy could feel the muscles bunching under his hand.

'You're right it is none of your business.' David ground the words out.

Sandy Bell held up both hands in a sign of peace. 'OK. But the lass loves you, and I …' He stopped again.

'I know she does. And before we're finished she'll know I love her.' David stirred vigorously. 'Now is that all, Inspector?'

Sandy Bell nodded. 'Thanks, we'll be in touch about the things.' He turned and left, finding Carol standing outside the door leaning against the wall and looking out of the open doorway to outside, where a squad car waited with a driver. She straightened as he came out of the kitchen. 'All done?'

'Yes thank you, Miss.'

He went outside and got into the squad car, driving to the excavation site to see how the team were getting on there.

KATE HAD SPENT TEN anxious minutes in the quiet little room after the two detectives had left, worrying that David might come in, but the door had remained firmly shut. She pulled herself together, scrubbing vigorously at her cheeks with Inspector Bell's handkerchief, then stood up and went to the door.

She opened it quietly and peered cautiously round it, but the corridor appeared deserted. She crept along it, her heart beating like a set of tom-toms, but encountered no-one before she reached the sanctuary of her bedroom. Hastily she slipped in and shut the door. Then she pulled her large rucksack from under the bed and began to pack.

She wasn't alone in packing; another member of the team was engaged in the same activity, and almost as stealthily. Alice Potter had had quite a shock that morning

234

when the police had turned up again. She'd overheard one of them saying something about the girls not having answered all the questions yesterday. She didn't fancy another round of questions.

If that stupid man hadn't been threatening her, she wouldn't be in this situation, she thought. She shoved clothes into her own rucksack with far less precision than Kate was using. She looked at the little mobile phone in her hand and buried it in her shorts pocket. That would have to go as soon as possible; she hadn't been able to dispose of it yesterday morning; people had arrived at the site too early.

She shuddered. Thank God Jardin hadn't been found before a lot of them had arrived; no one seemed to have realised that she'd come earlier to the site. She had been horrified to find him there snooping around. She shivered as she replayed their conversation and its aftermath.

'What the hell are you doing here?'

He'd stood smugly on the edge of the tarp covered hole and looked across at her, 'I came to get the loot before anyone was around.'

'I'm around you fool.'

'Yeah, well, miss clever, you can't tell. I know your secret now. You'll never make him pay up you know, and you aren't gonna rat on me 'cos I know too much about you.' He'd smirked at her.

Alice had stopped her forward movement, 'What do you mean.' She'd tried to bluff but she'd seen the glitter in his eye that said he knew and was sure of his facts.

'I mean I know about the old scandal.' He shook a finger at her, 'You're not the only one who can ask questions and find things out.'

Alice had stood watching as he lifted the tarp and began to peer underneath, totally ignoring her as if she didn't count. She sidled around the side of the well, coming nearer to him and gathering up a heavy stone.

He'd glanced over his shoulder at her but hadn't noticed what she had in her hand. He went back to peering down the well, his stringy hair flopping into his face, 'It's the creepiest site I've ever been on,' he remarked as he continued to look downwards. 'I reckon that soldier is guarding this damn place still.'

She'd raised the stone and hit him hard on the side of his head. He'd tumbled down, half under the tarp. She'd only planned to knock him out while she got away; at least that's what she'd told herself. She'd stood appalled for a few seconds looking at him laying in the mud caused by the rain the night before; then panicked and shoved him right under. Climbing under herself she had pulled him down the serried steps that Grace had so carefully cut.

He'd still been breathing, though it was a funny sort of breathing she thought. She'd moved the well cover half off and shoved him down; after she'd rifled his pockets for his mobile. She eyed him down in the hole and pulled the ladder out. She didn't want him climbing back and telling everyone about her before she'd managed to get away. Scrabbling out herself, she had taken the ladder over to the small store near the portaloos. She wasn't sure what she was going to do then.

She shuddered; she thought she might have left the site and made a run for it, but others had started to arrive. She'd played possum until she could mingle and no one would know whose car she had come in. Then she hung around, sweating, waiting for everyone to be occupied so that she could leave without attracting undue attention, knowing that any minute Grace was going to find him and he'd start to talk.

Well now she was going to run. She'd seen Kate creeping along the corridor and guessed her intentions. The girl obviously had a guilty secret that the police had ferreted out, and now she was going before anyone else should know. Well that stupid girl could take the fall, and while they hunted her Alice would be out of there and out of the country, but not before she'd got what was due to her. She slid open the window in her room and threw her bag out and then, checking that it was clear, climbed out herself.

SANDY BELL WAS TALKING to his colleague; it was late in the afternoon, 'We've got the results of the autopsy, Bob, and I don't like it, not one bit.'

'OK spill the beans, man, don't keep me in suspense.'

'He died of a broken neck all right; but he was bashed on the head first. He wasn't dead when he went into that well.'

'So we can rule out a covered up accident. Damn, I rather wanted it to be that, Sandy, because I think I know who did it.'

'You think it was the lass Kate.'

'Well yes, Sandy, I do. She has the biggest motive, she loves David Walker, and she hated her father. If she'd seen him at the site she might have tried to get him to leave and there might have been an accident but this, this is definite intent, unless ...' He spoke slowly, 'Unless she was working with him and it was an accident.'

Sandy shook his head, 'The report says he was hit on the temple with a blunt instrument, they think a stone. There are traces of grit and soil in the wound. Incidentally, that was one hell of a wallop, Bob, cracked the temple like an eggshell. Could it not have been John Williams?'

'No, his alibi checks out all the way. The foreman woke him up and he says he definitely was asleep in his car.'

'Worse and worse, Sandy. We're going to have to go back out to the hostel, and I'm not looking forward to arguing with Professor Walker again.'

'I'll get the team looking for a stone.' He pulled a comical face as they stepped outside, looking across the excavation site and all the heaps of spoil. He headed purposefully towards one of the forensic team and Bob watched him talking as he stood waiting at the side of the squad car.

As Sandy came back he said. 'All set?'

'Yes, they are not amused.'

'No, I don't suppose they are. I wish we could find his mobile, Sandy. I don't like loose ends.'

'Maybe the lass has it, we'll soon find out.'

'What about the forensics; anything there?' McInnis set the car in motion.

'Plenty of footprints and, thanks to the professor's actions, there's only one pair unaccounted for. We've got him, the two girls, Williams, and Jardin's shoes all matched, but that doesn't eliminate her, just puts her at the scene even more firmly.' Sandy shifted in his seat. 'Have we tracked down Little Dennis?'

'Not yet. He appears to have gone to ground, but what that proves is nothing much. He's probably guilty of half a dozen things he doesn't want us to question him about.'

THE PLACE WAS STILL noisy, but the noise seemed to be confined to one room as the two policemen arrived. They headed in a purposeful way towards where they'd seen the worktables being set up that morning.

'Oh! God! It's the Rozzers again, David.' John was less than complimentary.

David Walker looked up from his position at the end of the table and gave them a harsh look from his green eyes. 'So I see, John. Perhaps you can direct operations for a bit while I see what they want now.'

He walked the length of the room and came to a halt as they stood next to the door. 'Gentlemen?'

'If we could just step outside for a minute, sir.' Sandy had cast a look among the assembled company and hadn't seen their quarry in the room.

'What can I help you with now, gentlemen?' David sounded and looked weary.

McInnis sounded and looked apologetic. 'I'm afraid we need to have another word with Miss Hamilton, sir.'

David shrugged. 'Help yourself. I haven't set eyes on her since this morning. She's in her room as far as I know.' He turned away, and then back, 'It's in the next hut down the corridor.' He turned and went back into the big room currently serving as a cleaning station, but not before Sandy had seen the utter misery in his eyes.

The two inspectors exchanged looks. 'I never did like a sulky girl.' McInnis remarked as they headed to the door David had indicated.

He rapped smartly and stood back, waiting. Sandy looked at him and the door then said, 'I've got a nasty feeling, Bob.' He stretched out a hand and opened the door to reveal an empty and tidy room. 'Oh damn!'

They hurried back out and up the corridor and into the big room again.

David, raising his head, took in their expressions and moved swiftly towards them. 'What?'

'She doesn't appear to be there, sir.'

239

'She must be here somewhere.' He looked round as if expecting her to pop up beside his arm.

The other two shook their heads.

'Damn! I knew I shouldn't have left her alone; but when you're told in no uncertain terms to go, that's what you do. She's got to be somewhere around.'

He turned back to the assembled team who, by this time, had ceased talking and were looking at the three men. 'Can you go and look around please. We need to talk to Kate and it seems she isn't …' He stopped.

John came forward, turning to face the men and women. 'Search carefully; she been upset since we found the body. She might just have gone for a long walk to sort herself out.'

He looked at David standing so silently beside him. He'd never seen David so totally lost before. The big man had always seemed in control of any situation. 'David?' he touched an arm, 'Come down to the small sitting room.' He gave the Inspectors a totally unwarranted look of dislike.

They stood watching as John half led the professor away. John returned a few minutes later; he caught the young woman called Carol by the arm, 'Make the prof' a coffee, there's a love, while I deal with this.'

He turned to McInnis, 'How can we help you, Inspector?'

Sandy answered. 'We need to know who saw Miss Hamilton last and when.'

'She your latest suspect, Inspector?' He shook his head in disbelief. 'She couldn't hurt a fly and you'll never convince me different.'

One by one people were returning to the room shaking their heads. Doug touched John's arm. 'Her car's gone, John.' John heard the incredulity. 'And we can't find

Alice either.'

John turned back to the policemen. 'They've probably both gone shopping together. Retail therapy, Inspector.' But he sounded doubtful.

Doug shook his head. 'Their clothes have gone, and the cot is stripped in Kate's room.'

John stilled the chattering group now surrounding them. 'OK think. When did any of you see Kate or Alice last?'

McInnis turned to Sandy. 'Take statements. I'll go and speak to Professor Walker.'

He left the room, shadowed by John. 'I don't need you, sir.'

'You might not, but David does.'

They entered the small room to find Carol sitting next to David, a mug of coffee on the small table in front of him. 'Thanks, Carol.'

She nodded and got up, leaving the three of them and quietly closing the door.

David seemed to have got himself back under control, in fact, thought McInnis, he was like a tightly wound bow. He shrugged slightly; he had to do his job.

'I'm sorry, sir, but I need to know when you last saw Miss Hamilton?'

'You were present, Inspector. The young woman told me to go away so I did.' He spoke quietly, his voice devoid of all emotion and his focus fixed on the coffee mug. 'I don't force myself on women.'

'No, sir, I didn't think you did.'

David gave him a very surprised look, then looked back at the mug steaming on the table. 'I knew she was upset about all this business, but I thought she trusted me enough to know I wouldn't hurt her. I thought she just

241

needed time that's all.'

John looked across at the Inspector. 'What exactly did you need to see Kate for; maybe we can answer your questions.'

David Walker spoke harshly into the silence that followed. 'They think she killed Jardin, John, can't you see it on his face.'

John looked from one man to the other; indeed he could read it on the policeman's face.

'And now she's run away they're certain of it. Dammit, Kate hasn't got it in her, man.' David's fist clenched as he stood up and looked at McInnis.

There was a quiet knock on the door and Sandy came in. 'Miss Hamilton hasn't been seen since we left, Bob, and nor has Alice Potter.'

'Alice, what the hell has she got to do with anything?' David looked from one Inspector to the other.

The policemen looked puzzled. 'Did you get a report back about her, Bob?' Sandy cast his colleague a long look.

'Nope, but then I wasn't that concerned.' McInnis looked a trifle guilty.

David eyed them belligerently. 'Well you should have been; I'm almost positive Alice told me a thumping great lie on Thursday. The trouble was it didn't make any sense so I decided I'd better keep my mouth shut. I wondered if she'd been doing something she shouldn't on the site.'

Three pairs of eyes settled on him, 'I think you'd better clarify that, sir.'

David shrugged, 'For God sake sit down the lot of you.' He suited his action to his words, picking up the coffee and taking a sip. 'When I came out here on Thursday evening, to find out what the phone call was all about,

242

John.' He nodded at John who was seated on the arm of a chair opposite, 'Kate said she'd had a phone call and so did Alice. Now Alice said she'd had hers in the site office; but I was in there all afternoon. I know she couldn't have answered the phone. The fact that she'd lied didn't connect until Friday evening; and I wasn't overly concerned, even then.'

He shrugged again sipping more coffee. 'I knew she'd wanted to work under canvas on the site and I'd vetoed it. I thought she'd maybe sneaked off to do a bit of unauthorised digging and if anyone had noticed she wasn't working on cataloguing, she was covering her butt.'

He swung round, catching a sceptical expression on McInnis' face. 'Just why do you suspect Kate so firmly, Inspector, or can't you tell me?'

McInnis, caught in the twin headlights of David's angry eyes, found himself almost squirming. 'I'm afraid I can't tell you, Professor, except that she had a hell of a good motive for wanting Jardin dead.'

'Kate! Don't be bloody ridiculous man.'

Sandy, looking from his colleague to David, opened his mouth then caught the warning glint and quick shake from Bob McInnis as he looked at John Williams. 'I think I'd better go and talk to the rest of your team in the light of this new information. Could you come with me, Mr Williams?'

John, after a cautious look at David and a nod from that man, left, followed by Sandy Bell.

'So what didn't you want John to know, Inspector?'

'Yeah, Sandy said you were sharp.' He hesitated.

'Come on, man, out with it.'

'I'm not altogether sure I'm not betraying a confidence.' He looked apologetically at David, 'In fact I know I am, but you have to know, sir. Kate Hamilton is

Philip Jardin's daughter.'

He watched as David Walker stilled, his eyes fixed on Bob McInnis' face. He watched as that clever mind assimilated the facts; he could almost see the man totting up actions and behaviour in the light of this new knowledge.

'So you see, sir, we have reason to suspect her of either, as she says, hating the man, or of being in league with him.'

David shook his head. 'I don't believe you.'

'Sir, we know she was…'

He was interrupted. 'Oh I believe she is his daughter. I just don't believe she would have anything to do with stealing from my site. What's more, Inspector, I never will if you question her till you're blue in the face.' He smiled grimly. 'No, we have to find her, but not for your reasons, man. Poor kid must be torturing herself with all this, blaming herself; we'll have no sins of the father's around here, Inspector.' He stood up. 'Let's see how Inspector Bell is getting on.'

11

AT ABOUT THE TIME Kate's disappearance was discovered Grace was to be found sitting beside Millie's bedside. She'd been sitting there holding Millie's hand and watching her face for nearly an hour, but Millie hadn't stirred. Mary had gone for a meal but she would be back shortly. She was doing a twelve hour shift too now.

Grace hadn't seen Dan. He'd risen and gone by the time she arrived back at Millie's house at lunchtime. He'd left a brief note saying he wanted to get a change of clothes and check his e-mails, but he hadn't returned during the afternoon. Grace first worried that he was avoiding her, and then worried that she'd put him in a position where he felt he had too.

Then she'd told herself he was entitled to come and go as he pleased and she didn't care. She knew she was being irrational, but she couldn't seem to help her mind running around in circles thinking about their relationship, if they had one.

Mary's return was a welcome relief, in that it stopped her thinking so hard; but it meant that she had to shift while Mary did her job, and that gave her time to worry again. 'Don't worry, Miss Gordon, she'll be safe while you go and have a meal.' Mary, mistaking Grace's expression, tried to reassure her.

Grace offered a tight little smile. 'I'm not really hungry.'

'People often aren't, Miss Gordon, but starving yourself won't help you, or Miss Armstrong.'

'No I don't suppose it will.' Grace spoke wearily, but after another long look at Millie she turned and left the room. She dimly realised that she was in the way and that Mary had nursing cares to perform, but she didn't want to leave in case Millie should die while she was gone.

She wandered into the kitchen and filled the kettle, switching it on and sitting down at the table. She laid her head down on her hands on the table and closed her eyes; Dan found her there ten minutes later.

'Sweetheart!' There was a wealth of love in the word. He went across the room, dumping a bag of groceries on the table and pulling out a chair before sitting next to her, and then he leaned over and scooped her up onto his lap. 'You're worn out, Gracie. Did I no' tell ye not to sit with Millie all the long day.'

Grace, half asleep, found herself enclosed in arms that were both comforting and familiar. She gave a half sob, half chuckle. 'I didn't.' Then she woke up a bit more and struggled to move.

'Och let a man gie ye a bit of comfort, darling, I'm in need o' a bit my ain self.' He pulled her close again and kissed the soft hair tickling his face.

'Dan?' Grace spoke against his soft linen shirt.

'What, sweetheart?'

She gulped, 'Dan.' She turned up a face full of misery. 'I love you. But I don't want you to feel you have to marry me just because of what Grandma said.'

'I've told ye before, I please my own sen. I dinna do what a' dinna want. Now what is this?' He eased her back so that he could look at her.

'Millie asked you to marry me, and you might want me but ...' she paused, blinking tears off her lashes, 'But you don't have to marry me for that.'

'I've said I'll marry ye, because that's what I want. Don't ye dare suggest we do anything else.' He gave her a gentle shake, then kissed the mouth so close to his own. Grace felt her insides melting with needs she didn't know she was capable of. 'Sweet mercy girl; we ha' to marry for I willna take ye any other way. A' love ye, do ye no ken that yet?'

Grace shook her head, 'You didn't say.'

He pulled her close for another long kiss, 'And is this no saying it another way?'

'I'm sorry, Dan, I'm stupid tonight.'

'Nae, darlin', you're just grieving and I shouldna be pushing ma sen on ye. Save that,' he held her close, 'a'm doing a wee bit o' grieving ma' own self.'

Grace put her arms around him and kissed him softly on the cheek.

He smiled into her eyes, the slow gentle smile she loved. 'Ha ye eaten this day.'

She shook her head.

'I thought as much, you're much too pale. Come on, sweetheart, let me make a drink and ye shall eat then go and rest for an hour, a'll call ye if there should be need.'

He allowed her to stand up and then went over and switched the kettle back on again. Turning, he rummaged in the grocery bag, bringing out a loaf. 'Hot buttered toast and warm sweet tea are what ye need.'

'Oh, Dan, I don't like sweet tea.'

'Like or not it's what ye need and what ye'll get. Let a man spoil ye. A' canna go into the bedroom, Mary will be insulted and think a' dinna trust her.' His hands were busy even while he spoke and presently the pair of them were eating toast with butter melting into it, and drinking tea that was both hot and sweet. Grace pulled a face but Dan shook his head and she picked the mug up and drained it.

'Right, sweetheart, off to bed with ye.'

Grace opened her mouth to protest only to have him lean over and settle his lips on hers. When both their

247

hearts were pounding, and Grace's head was spinning, he released her to say, 'Dinna argue.' He took her hand and led her along the corridor and up the stairs. 'I havena changed the sheets but I made the bed. Will that be alright, darlin'?'

Grace nodded and Dan smiled down at her. 'Go to bed, I love ye.'

He left the room and Grace looked around the space which had been hers since childhood, seeing it afresh through Dan's eyes. The row of books abandoned as she'd moved on - a comment on the many hours Millie had spent reading to her. The set of chess men still half-way through a game she'd been playing with Millie last time she was home, and the rag rug on the floor that Millie had taught her to make the winter she was ten. She went across to the bed and lay down, allowing the tears to seep out from behind her closed eyelids.

Dan came to wake her in the early hours. 'Grace,' his hand was gentle on her shoulder, 'I think ye'd better come down, lass.'

She looked at him sleepily and then in some alarm at the clock. It was almost three. Then she discovered that she had a blanket draped across her. She scrambled off the bed.

'Steady, lass, take your time.'

'Dan, is she…?'

'Nae, but the time's no sae far off.'

Grace followed him down the stairs and was installed tenderly in a seat beside the bed. She took hold of the soft cool hand and looked sadly down at Millie. Dan appeared at her side bearing a mug of tea. 'Drink it up, lass.' He moved to the side of the bed and sat down carefully on it, resting a hand on Millie's shoulder. He looked with compassion at Grace, 'She may wake again or she might not, but I promised ye both ye should be

248

together if it were possible.'

As if she'd heard him Millie opened her eyes. They were still bright, the hand holding Grace's squeezed softly. 'I love you, Gracie,' the words were hardly audible. Millie turned her head slightly. 'And you, Dan.' She closed her eyes and sighed deeply. The two who were watching reached out and completed the circle, joining their hands, waiting.

The silence in the room had been profound for nearly an hour; Grace refused to take her eyes of Millie's face. Dan had sat, dividing his watch between the two women both now so dear to him. Now he gently squeezed Grace's hand drawing her attention towards him. He stood up, raising Grace and turning her into his embrace, 'A' have things a mun do for her.'

'Dan?'

'Aye lass, she's gone.'

He held her while the first storm of weeping passed then took her out of the room and up to the bedroom again, settling her under the cover. All the while whispering words of comfort and love. 'Hush, sweetheart, lay your head a wee while. I'll bring you down and ye can keep watch, if ye must, till the dawn comes in.' Grace curled up, her head resting on the pillow, lying hollow eyed as he left the room, closing the door quietly after him.

THE TWO PEOPLE WERE sitting on a grassy bank looking down on the Roman fortifications of Vindolanda. Despite the fact that it was only the beginning of August they both had jeans and waterproofs on. Dan had an arm around Grace's waist as she sat gazing down on the activity going on below them under the lowering grey skies of late afternoon.

'Warm enough, lass?'

'Yes, Dan. You were right; I needed to go away from the house for a little while.' She turned her head, looking at him. 'Thank you for bringing me here. Grandma brought me here many times when I was young, showing me things and peopling the place for me.' She looked back at the activity of the archaeologists busily excavating down below.

'She used to make me close my eyes and then she'd say, 'Can you hear them?' and she'd talk about the fort as it was. The noise of the parade ground as the soldiers did their marching, and the ringing of metal as the men worked at the forge making the horseshoes, the bellowing of the cattle and the baaing of the sheep in the Vicus, the crowing of cocks and the chatter of the people in the township outside the fort.

'She'd say, 'What can you smell? Can you smell the dung and the hot metal and the animals, can you smell the corn and the cooking? She made me experience it all.' Grace looked at him. 'And I'd forget that it was so quiet up here. Then she'd make me open my eyes and see the landscape, the vastness of it and the freedom of a sparrow hawk on the wing and she told me the people might have gone away but while we listened to them and talked about them they always lived, soaring over the land like that hawk.'

She sighed, 'That's why she was fascinated by archaeology and encouraged me. She told me people had so much to teach us and their lifetime wasn't long enough, so we had to learn from them after they'd gone. That they had a right to be remembered as people, not just things.'

Grace moved against him and Dan cuddled her close. 'Aye, lass, she's still teaching us both, even now.' They sat in silence, absorbing the quiet until Grace gave a shiver.

'Come on, sweetheart, you're cold. Let's go and get a warm drink.' He pulled her up and they made their way towards the café.

He stopped just outside its doors, looking across to a small slate inset with brass writing. Grace, prevented from moving by his hand, looked in the same direction. 'It's in memory of the fallen Roman soldiers who died while serving on British soil, Dan. David says everyone should be remembered for something, not just be nameless skeletons for archaeologists to dig up.'

She walked with him as he went to look closer and read the inscription. 'I like yon idea.' He nodded at the plinth. 'Though ye've brought them to life already, Grace.'

They made their way indoors and sat with cups of tea in front of them in the all but deserted tea rooms. Grace looked across at the strong face of Dan. 'Thank you, Dan; you've been so good to me today. Helping me to arrange everything, and phoning round people with the news, and looking after me.'

'I ken ye could have done it your own self, lass. But I needed to help, for me.' He smiled lopsidedly. 'What will ye do now?'

'Now.' She looked down into her cup absently, stirring her tea. 'Now, I'll …,' she paused, returning his smile, 'I'll greet, then get mad, then get sad, I suppose'

'Aye, then ye'll accept.'

'Aye.' she gave him a small smile which barely touched her grey eyes. 'What will you do?'

'Oh I've a mind to tak' a holiday. I'd like it fine if I could spend some of it wi' ye.' He reached out and stilled the busy hand. 'I'll no rush ye, lass, but I would wed thee.'

'I know, Dan, but I'm …' she looked sadly at him, 'I'm not wanting to rush you either. I don't want you to feel you're committing yourself because of …Oh damn!' She brushed away the tears springing to her eyes again.

'That's alright, lass.' He passed a handkerchief

251

across the table, and waited patiently while she wiped her eyes. 'I'll no' change my mind. I'm dinna want thee oot o' pity or promises. I'll no' change ma' mind,' he said again, 'but ye tak' all the time ye need.'

Grace, listening to the Scots becoming increasingly broad, looked across at him, noting the deepening dark circles under his eyes. 'You're exhausted, Dan. I'm a selfish woman.'

'What gave me awa'?' He smiled crookedly at her.

'Your accent.' She stood up, abandoning the tea-cups and taking his hand. 'I think it's time I took care of you.'

They walked away from the site and Grace drove the big Jeep back into the town; Dan was nearly asleep when they pulled up outside her flat. He looked puzzled as they stopped.

'You need to sleep, Dan. You can sleep in another of my beds.' She unbuckled her seatbelt and climbed down. Dan met her on the sidewalk. 'A'm no sure this is sic' a guid idea, lass.'

'Oh it is. I don't like your car and, anyway, how would I get back home if I take you to the motel?'

'That's no just what a' meant.'

'I know exactly what you meant, Dan, and we're consenting adults; but you're too tired, and I'm not going to let you do anything you might regret, just at the moment.' She held out a hand and he put his in it as they went through her door.

THE POLICE HAD SPENT a long and fruitless day searching for their missing suspects. They had issued pictures of both girls to members of the force and a statement had been given to the press. The local news had picked the story of the murder up and ran a three minute slot on the six o'clock news. Grace had glanced at it with the sound turned down, while she scribbled notes at her sitting room table.

She was still sitting at the table when Dan came through at half past eight; he brought coffee in pottery mugs and mingled that aroma with his own freshly showered and shaved person. He smelt of the imperial leather she kept for days when she'd come home filthy from the dig. He'd put on the clean, but outsized, sweatshirt she'd left on the bottom of the bed. Grace grinned at him despite her grief. 'That looks better on me.'

'Well I'm no sure I care t' go about proclaiming I'm an idjit.'

He looked down his chest at the white lettering emblazoned on the front. 'Where did ye come by such a thing?'

'David bought it for my last birthday.'

'Ye've kent the man a while, lass?'

'Yes. Grandma met him when I was about six or seven; he was a young and very eager archaeologist and she was a brilliant amateur. He used to bring me sweets and sit me on his knee while he asked her questions.' She smiled softly, 'I adored him, he was the father figure I so desperately needed.' She looked at Dan. 'It's no wonder I grew up to this trade.' She touched the books in front of her.

'A weel, I'll no' be jealous o' him then.' He leaned over, stealing a kiss and sitting down next to her at the table. 'What are ye busy wi'?'

Grace grimaced, 'I'm trying to distract my mind by writing up what I've learned so far about my skeleton.' She showed him a sketch.

'Well now that would be the humerus with a large attachment site.' He admired the sketch; 'Ye've a pretty hand at sketching, lass.'

Grace found she could still blush. Dan admired the pink stealing into her cheeks then looked back at the drawing. 'So what does this tell ye?'

'On its own not a lot, many of the spearmen had extra muscle in the throwing arm. But taken with these finds,' she pushed two other sketches across the table, 'I'd say he was either a capsari or a seplasiari. Probably the later.' She grinned at his frown. 'They're both kinds of nurse in the Roman army; one for wounds and fractures, the other for ointments.'

Dan picked up the other sketches, 'These would be a pestle and mortar?'

'Indeed they would, and they were buried with him inside that well, along with a stone engraved with the caduceus. You'd have recognised that, Dan, being in the trade so to speak; even lay people seem to recognise the snakes twisted round the stick as having something to do with medicine. I would hazard a guess that he got that muscle attachment grinding ointments.' She watched as Dan looked again at the attachment.

'He was about twenty-five or thirty and he'd had his head bashed in. There were a few early signs of healing; so he was either in a fight or a skirmish and didn't die immediately, but probably within the following forty-eight hours. I also know the poor soul had the beginnings of osteoarthritis, but then a posting to Hadrian's Wall wasn't just calculated to give you a suntan.'

She smiled across at Dan, thinking he probably didn't tan either. 'What I don't know is why he was buried in the well. I think actually that it was a reburial because I think I found his stapes in a different area, but by whom and why is still a mystery.'

'I've barely scratched the surface yet though.' She pushed the papers into a pile. 'It's weird that he should have had a head injury, Dan, since that's how Philip Jardin died. It was on the news earlier, but I wasn't taking much notice. Do you want to see it?'

She reached for the control and turned the sound up, 'I recognised Inspector McInnis looking very stiff in front of the microphone, and some pictures of the site investigation van.'

They both fell silent watching the headlines and then tuned in to the police report. Dan grunted half way through, but kept his peace until the end of the slot. He reached for the control, muting the TV. 'I ken yon lassie.'

'Eh!' It wasn't elegant but it expressed Grace's surprise.

'Yon lassie, Kate Hamilton, the one they're asking about. I havena' seen the other but the red-heided one, she's staying at the motel.'

'Are you certain?'

He nodded.'Oh aye.'

'What's she doing there in God's name? Here give me that phone; I want to know what's going on.' Grace punched in a row of numbers.

'David, what gives, why are they looking for Kate and Alice? What's been happening?'

She held the phone, listening intently to the voice at the other end, nodding occasionally. 'Well I've got some news for you; Kate's at the Motel at Gretna.' She held the telephone away from her ear as the receiver squawked at her.

Then she put her hand over it. 'What number, Dan, do you know?'

He shook his head. 'My corridor, but after that I couldna be sure.'

'David, have a word with Dan will you?' She

passed the receiver over and watched as Dan listened intently.

'Aright, man, ho'd thee whist a minute.' Dan sounded exasperated. 'I tell ye the lassie was at the motel yesterday afternoon when I was leaving. She'd been greeting for her eyes were red, and she booked in somewhere down my corridor, of that I'm certain. I'm in twenty two.' He nodded a time or two and then gave some directions before stopping to listen again.

'Aye weel we a' must do what we must. But my advice would be to tak her to the polis' and if need be ye can offer bail and good conduct, but if ye keep it quiet it mak's it worse.'

He listened quietly for a minute longer then handed the phone back. 'He'd lak a final word.' Grace took the phone.

'Grace.' The voice at the other end was calmer now, 'You don't know how grateful I am, I've been out of my mind worrying about her. I'm going to go and fetch her back to my place. Can you let the police know? Not where she is, where she'll be in about an hour.' He paused, thinking. 'Tell Dan thank you, and Grace …' She heard the smile in his voice, 'When's the wedding?' She opened her mouth but heard only the quiet click, and then the buzz of the disconnected line.

'Well really!' She replaced the phone and looked at Dan. 'He wants us to phone the police and fill them in.'

'I thought he might see sense.' Dan smiled, stroking her curls for the pleasure of touching her. 'I ken how he feels; I'd be beside mysen an I lost thee, my darling.' Grace found she couldn't look away as his blue eyes blazed his love for her.

DAVID GOT INTO HIS car and shot off along the road. He

hoped to God Kate was still there. He only slowed for the villages he passed through, then put his foot hard down on the pedal. He was going to get Kate and make her see some sense. He wasn't going to leave her alone again. God knows what mischief she'd be up to next.

The receptionist confronted by nearly six foot of elegance simmering with temper and anxiety kept her head admirably. She was sorry she couldn't provide him with information about who was staying there, it was confidential.

David, green eyes glinting, took a step forward and she thanked her stars she had a counter between them. What might have happened next is anyone's guess; but Dan and Grace came through the door.

Grace went across to David, who enfolded her in a bear hug. 'Gracie,' he looked down at her face, 'are you alright, petal?' It was a pet name not used since her childhood and Grace swallowed hard and smiled mistily up at him.

Dan, meanwhile, was dealing with the receptionist. She was looking with disapproval at him, 'Mr Campbell, you know I can't tell you that.'

'You might be upset if a' go and knock on every door till a' find her.' He smiled across the counter. 'For God sake lassie does he look as though he's going to hurt her?'

The receptionist stood indecisively for a minute, 'Well it's twenty-seven; but I didn't tell you.'

She stood back as the three people walked through the fire door and down the corridor. David, with an arm round Grace, looked down as they followed Dan. 'Why are you here?'

'I thought she might open her door to me if not you; you can be a bit intimidating, David.' Grace was following Dan's progress with her eyes. He stopped in front of twenty-seven and motioned for Grace to knock.

257

The two men stood back as she knocked and waited for Kate to open the door.

Kate, opening cautiously, looked incredulously at Grace. 'What?' her eyes travelled from her to Dan and then settled on David; the colour drained from her face and she would have fallen if David hadn't grabbed her and lifted her up. He carried her into the room and laid her on the single bed just inside. The other two followed him in.

Dan moved forward, 'Here, let me ha' a look.' He checked the pulse at her wrist and turned, looking at David. 'Probably lack of food and too much worry; she'll come round in a minute.'

David sat heavily on the bed next to Kate, pulling her into his arms and cradling her against his chest.

'Thanks.' He nodded at Dan who, with Grace, had gone to sit on the settee under the window. 'Has Grace filled you in on what's been going on?'

Dan nodded briefly. 'I canna see that slip o' a thing murdering anyone.'

David shook his head. 'She didn't.'

Kate stirred in his arms and he turned his whole focus on her. 'Darling, come on, it's alright.' Kate was struggling against him.

'Its alright, you didn't have to run away. Didn't I tell you I loved you?'

'But D ...David, you don't know ...' Kate was still trying to stand up, he eased back slightly but didn't let go.

'Oh yes I do, and I don't give a damn. Do you think I care? I don't care if your father was Jack the Ripper. I love you.' He smiled down at her with such a look of longing that the watching couple exchanged glances and stood up.

'We'll be in ma' room if ye should want us.' Dan, holding Grace's hand, left the pair sitting on the bed. Neither apparently registered their exit.

They walked quietly along the corridor, 'We were a bit superfluous to requirements there, Dan.'

'I'm no sae sure, yon receptionist might ha called the police if we hadna arrived when we did.'

He pulled her through his door and closed it behind him. 'Ha' I told you I loved ye recently?'

Grace smiled up at him. 'Not for hours.'

'Oh good! I like telling ye.' He bent his head.

They had progressed to the settee and were sitting quietly talking when there was a rap on the door. Dan went and opened it to find David and Kate standing there. He pulled it wider and they came in.

'Thank you, Dan.' David went and sat on the bed, pulling Kate down next to him. 'We've decided that we'd better go and speak to the police tonight.' He held tightly to Kate's hand. 'I've rung the Inspector and he suggests we meet him at the station in the city.'

'Kate thought if she left I could get things sorted out in my mind.' He smiled down at the white-faced girl sitting silently next to him. 'Of course, I couldn't sort anything out if she wasn't there. But we'll manage now.'

'I'm sorry, Grace, it was me that went into your well, but I didn't s…spoil the site except for uncovering the s…skeleton and I was very c…careful.' Kate spoke slowly with the odd hesitation and few stutters.

Grace smiled across, 'OK, but why?'

'I thought it would convince David t…' She looked at David and they saw him gently squeeze her hand, 'to take p…precautions; because I knew my father was around,' she finished.

'Father?'

'Philip Jardin.'

'Oh!' Grace looked at David then back at the

259

younger girl. 'I'm glad he's convinced you it doesn't matter who your father was.' She watched the faint colour wash the younger girl's cheek's as David dropped a kiss on her hair.

'So now we're going to visit the Inspector and then Kate is going home with me.' David stood up and so did the others. Dan looked at them. 'Will ye want us to come wi ye?'

'No, I don't think so. If they want you they can find you themselves. But thanks again.' He held out his free hand.

David turned towards Grace and, under cover of Dan's instructions to Kate to get some food inside her, spoke quietly, 'I like your Dan, Grace.'

'Aye.' Grace smiled, 'So when's the wedding?' Her lips twitched.

David leaned forward and hugged her, 'She's a little thing but Minoan,' he whispered in her ear.

Grace gave a choked chuckle as he stood erect and stretched out a hand to Kate.

INSPECTOR MCINNIS WAS TIRED. However, when one of your missing witnesses reappears you don't sit at home. He looked at the pair sitting in an interview room at the main station and sighed. 'So you left because you couldn't face upsetting Professor Walker, Miss Hamilton. I understand that, and if you weren't watching the television you naturally wouldn't realise we needed to speak with you again. But you have to see it from our viewpoint. It all looked very suspicious.'

'I'm s…sorry, Inspector.'

'Why Gretna, Miss Hamilton?'

'I was s...scared if I went home he'd f...follow and talk to my mother and, to be honest, Inspector, I was t...too upset to go f...far. It seemed a s...safe place to be.' She smiled wryly.

'So,' he sighed tiredly, 'when we went to speak to you yesterday afternoon we had just one or two more questions to ask you.' He shook his head then looked at the constable on the door. 'Fetch us some coffee, lad, I need some caffeine.'

'Now.' He turned back to Kate.

'Yes, Inspector.'

'Why did you suspect your father and no one else of being on the site? I know you said your mother wrote to you, but that doesn't explain you leaping to the conclusion that it was definitely him. How did you know he was at the site?'

'It was the Pontin. It was his l...lucky one he always carried it in his p...pocket. My mother told me. It had a nick in the t...top. I recognised it from her description when Grace f...found it last week.'

'Ah that explains it!' The Inspector smiled grimly. 'Now, what happened when you were fifteen when you met your father?' He held a hand up as David would have spoken. 'Sir.'

David put an arm around Kate's shoulders. She smiled at him. 'It's OK, David.' She turned back to the Inspector. 'He came to visit. He t...told my mother he had the right to s...see me and I s...suppose I was curious and a bit f...flattered that he cared. My mother wouldn't say much about him at all. She'd t...told me the bare f...facts of the t...trial. He brought me some books he said I might be interested. I was. They were archaeology b...books. One was 'Vegetimus' Epitome of Military S...science', David.' She looked up at him. 'It got me hooked.'

Inspector McInnis looked enquiringly at the

261

Professor. 'It's a sort of how to build a fort by numbers, Inspector.'

Kate sat back as the constable brought in some mugs of coffee and a plate of digestives and then went to stand by the door again. 'I t…thought it was a wonderful s…subject, and I decided then that I wanted to go to university and study it. My mum wasn't very happy about t…that; but then she said we owed David. He'd lost money because of my f…father. I t…thought I might help David, but then I met him.'

Her hand came up to her shoulder and rested on his hand. 'I fell in love with him, Inspector.'

The Inspector coughed and looked away, gazing down into his mug then back up. 'So you didn't have any more contact with your father?'

'Unfortunately I did.'

'Miss, you said you hadn't seen him since you were fifteen.'

'I hadn't, but he rang me after I f…finished Uni'. I thought he was being nice, congratulating me, but he w…wanted me to act as a, I don't know, informer I s…suppose.' She shook her head. 'I hated him for that, he ruined all the p…pleasure I'd had in p…passing. I was reduced to nothing more than a,' she waved her free hand, 'Mata Hari.'

David gave a small chuckle. 'Mata Hari. Drink your coffee, darling.' He looked at Inspector McInnis. 'Are you convinced she's not your murderer, Inspector? She doesn't exactly hide her feelings for the man.'

'Well, sir, she does have a wonderful habit of incriminating herself,' he smiled grimly, 'but I think we're done for now.' He shook a finger at Kate. 'Don't you go disappearing again.'

David set his mug down, 'She'll be out at my house, Inspector.' He put an arm under Kate's and she

262

stood up. 'We can go?' he raised an eyebrow. McInnis nodded, and the couple left Bob McInnis to wonder if having a girlfriend was a good thing or a bad one.

McINNIS AND SANDY BELL were in the office on Thursday morning. Bob McInnis was filling the older man in on the events of the previous evening. 'At least we know where one of them is. But what caused the other one to run, Sandy, that's got me puzzled. She didn't strike me as the nervous type.'

'Dunno, Bob, but we've found Dennis Little. He ain't the nervous type either.'

'Where?'

'Gone to earth over the border in Annan. He's got relatives there.'

'Damn stupid to go to them if he thought we might be looking for him, but that's Dennis all over.' Bob McInnis scratched at a nick on his chin. 'Remind me to get some new blades when we're out, Sandy, blasted razor's so blunt I could ride to London on it.'

Sandy grunted an acknowledgement of the request then said, 'Are we bringing him in?'

'Yeah, he might as well 'help the police with their enquiries'.'

'What about the other girl, Bob? Any nearer finding her?'

'Well we were being a bit cautious there. Thought she was an Aussie and didn't want to offend our colonial cousins.'

'Bob haven't you ever heard of PC?'

'Yeah, it's what I call my computer; I haven't got time for that political correctness stuff, Sandy.'

263

McInnis shuffled some papers on the desk. 'Anyway it turns out she's British; see for yourself.' He pushed a flimsy file across. 'Why these girls must put everything in new files beats me. I've got a stack of them all with a sheet or two in each.'

Sandy vouchsafed no comment; he was busy reading the two despised sheets. 'Does this get us any further?'

'Haven't a clue, you can see for yourself. Single parent, took the child out there in search of a better life, mother died of a drug overdose when the girl was thirteen, she's been in foster care ever since. Got brains and used them; qualified for uni' but seems to have decided to enjoy the 'great OE' whatever that is.'

Sandy grinned, 'Overseas Experience', Bob. My eldest is trying to persuade me to pay her passage to go over there. Says all the Aussie kids do it.'

'Whatever! She came over in the spring and has been working on the site for the past month. Seems to have got on with everyone, but no one knows that much about her for all that.'

'Young kid, maybe she took fright for all her bravado.' Sandy laid down the flimsies.

'Well at the moment she's disappeared into thin air. Douglas Stirland, the foreman, reckons she took one of the bikes. But why did she go and where?'

Sandy shrugged. 'So, what do we do next?'

'I'm going back to Jardin's rooms; I want to see if there might be clues to his buyer. I know you looked, Sandy, but I'm stuck; there must be something somewhere.' Bob rubbed at the nick again. 'He can't have been buying on speck; not if he'd owed Barker big bucks. You can have the inestimable pleasure of interviewing Dennis Little.'

'Gee thanks, Dad. Just what I always wanted.' Sandy grinned as Bob stood up and swiped at his grey hair in passing.

THE INTERVIEW WAS CONDUCTED on strictly legal lines. Dennis, however, wasn't happy, 'I didn't do nothing.'

'Good, you keep doing nothing, my lad.'

'I ain't saying nothing.'

'Even better.' Sandy was 'Mr Geniality' himself.

Dennis gave him a puzzled look. 'If I ain't gonna say nothing, whatya want to keep me here for?'

'Oh I like looking at your sartorial elegance, Dennis.'

Dennis took a moment to process this. 'Ere don't be so smart.'

Sandy shrugged. He decided to take a shot in the dark. 'So how come you told Mr Barker that Jardin was dead before you came and told us.'

'I ain't nobody's grass.'

'Quite right, Dennis, I shouldn't let anyone tell you what to do.'

Dennis' brow furrowed in perplexity, then he smiled. 'You're playing hard copper and easy copper. I seen that on TV.'

'But there's only one of me, Dennis; unless you count Gareth standing by the door there.'

Denis swung his bulk round in the plastic chair, making it creak ominously, and regarded Gareth who had hastily hidden a grin. Gareth looked back at him blank faced.

Dennis swung back. 'I work for Mr Barker; he pays me to tell him things.' Dennis was nothing if not tenacious

265

when he got hold of an idea. 'He's entitled to tell me what to do.'

'So you told him about Jardin because he pays you to tell him.'

'Yes.' Dennis looked triumphantly at Sandy. Then thought about what he'd just said. 'Or I would have if I'd known.'

Sandy grinned, 'Too late, my lad. The first statement stands.' He looked across the expanse of table at a face only a mother, or those involved in the wrestling trade, could love with any sincerity. 'He told you to keep watch on Jardin to make sure he didn't do a bunk with the money he owed.'

'If you knows so much why you asking me?'

'Well, Dennis, my young friend, I like to have my facts confirmed. So when did you see the body then?'

'Who says I saw Jardin's body?' Dennis being cunning reminded Sandy forcibly of Wily Coyote just before he fell of the cliff, or had the boulder drop on his head.

'Well you must have seen his body to be able to earn your pay.'

Dennis cocked his head in deep thought. Sandy could almost see the wheels meshing. 'That's true.' Dennis nodded sagely.

'So I'll ask again. When did you see his body?'

'When she throwed him in the hole.'

'Ah,' Sandy had to repress the instinct to jump up and down. He continued to look at Dennis calmly. 'And did you tell Mr Barker who she was?'

'Course I did.'

Sandy waited him out in silence.

'She was the bird Jardin was shouting at in the street.'

'That would be on Friday?'

'Yeah,' Dennis was now so unsurprised by the depth of Sandy's information that he continued unprompted. 'She met him Friday afternoon near the Town Hall and they was shouting at one another. Then I follows her to see where she went, but she got in a car with a lot of other young kids and I couldn't follow her any longer.' He paused for breath. 'Mr Barker said I done right following her and not Mr Jardin, but I found him again. He said I was clever to do that.'

He scratched his head, 'I dunno though.' He subsided.

Sandy looked at him, a lurking pity at the back of his eyes. 'And he told you to go and take a holiday with your relatives did he?'

'Yeah. Said I deserved a holiday for being so bloody clever losing Jardin to a girl.

'Hmm. Well you can go for now, Dennis, but we might want to talk to you again. So don't leave town.'

Dennis looked at him cautiously and stood up. 'You ain't going to arrest me?'

'Not unless you want to confess to a murder, Dennis?'

'Nooo, not me. I ain't murdered nobody.'

'Off you go then.'

Dennis walked to the door, glancing back once or twice as if he expected to feel the hand of the law on his collar. The constable opened the door and he walked out, still with a puzzled look on his face.

Sandy shook his head as Gareth shut the door smartly on Dennis' heels. 'Shouldn't be let out without his

267

keeper. That was informative; I think we'll just check up on our chief female suspects and ask them what they were doing Friday afternoon.'

'How did you know it was Friday, Chief?'

'Because that was the day the first report came in of Dennis shadowing Jardin. I just took a guess.' He grinned at the constable, 'I got lucky.'

DAN WAS SITTING ON an easy chair, his laptop on his knee, watching Grace stacks books haphazardly on the table as she searched for a particular reference. He was a tidy soul himself but he supposed he could live with her chaos. He'd come from the motel to her flat in time for breakfast and had whisked her out and away to a local MacDonald's. 'Ye need food.'

'I eat plenty; you're always feeding me, Dan.'

'Aye weel, it looks as if it might be ma' job for life. A' need t' get in practice.' He'd grinned, sneaking an arm around her and kissing her soundly.

'What shall ye do this day?' he'd pushed a plate of bacon and eggs in front of her. 'A've a mind t' keep ye company, if ye'll ha' me?'

'Of course I'll have you.' Grace blushed as he chuckled, and gave him a gentle thump on his arm. 'Not like that!'

'Noo is it right to get a man's hopes up only to dash them doon agin.' Dan was quite pleased with himself. Not only was he keeping her distracted and the deep misery that turned her eyes to pewter, at bay, but he felt he was getting to know her as well.

That morning they'd finished the meal and come back to the flat, and he'd pottered in her kitchen, then read a book while she sat at her computer. He wanted to keep her away from Millie's for a bit longer. He knew she would have to go and sort the house out eventually but he wanted her emotionally strong for that task.

As he worked on his own computer he was considered the twin merits of tea and biscuits, augmented by kisses, as a further distraction. He was about to put the lid down on the laptop when he noticed he'd got a flag for an e-mail. He grunted quietly and flicked buttons.

He scanned the screen rapidly, 'Grace, I've got an interesting e-mail to show you.'

Grace looked up and across. She found she was comfortable with Dan; he was the first man she'd found she could share her space with and not feel he was intruding. She abandoned the books and walked over, looking down at the screen and reading ...

'Sorry to hear about the lady's death, Dan. Do you still want the man? I've got a phone number if you want to contact him? He's in Newcastle!! Is that North England?' The phone number was printed out and the name of a hotel. 'Look after yourself buddy. Robin.'

Grace looked at Dan; watching as he scribbled the name and number down and closed the laptop. He looked up at her, 'Do you want to phone or go?'

12

INSPECTORS BELL AND MCINNIS were pouring over the evidence and interviews they had collected so far. 'OK so I think we can eliminate Professor Walker and John Williams on the evidence of Dennis Little. Do you agree, Sandy?'

'Aye.' Sandy rubbed his chin. 'I'd rule out Dennis Little as well, he might have done it but his story rings fairly true. I'm going to have another word with Barker later this morning. Just to confirm a few facts if I can.'

'Hmm, well I didn't get any more information out of Jardins' room. Except this.' He held a pair of small saint's medals on a gold chain up for Sandy's inspection. 'It was inside the money pocket of his jeans. The ones sitting in the pile of dirty washing.'

Sandy gazed at them. 'Och I'm sorry I missed them, Bob.'

'Don't fret, Sandy; I was lucky to find them myself.' McInnis grinned. 'Want to guess who they are?'

Sandy shook his head, flicking back his hair.

'Let me introduce you to St Antony of Padua.' McInnis flicked one silver medallion, 'Patron Saint of lost items.'

'Oh yes.' Sandy's lips twitched. 'And t'other'

'St Jude; patron of lost causes.'

'He was a superstitious sort wasn't he? Believed in keeping his options open, if what you say is right about the coin Kate Hamilton claims belonged to him.'

'Well now, this morning I rang the prison where they had the delight of housing him for five years and they confirmed that one. Only time he got into a row was when

270

one of his cell mates tried to nick it from him.' He looked across at Sandy. 'And you're right. Very superstitious, wouldn't go to church in clink, said God talked to him there.' McInnis sniffed as one who attended confession, whenever his mother nagged him into it. 'I can sympathise with that.'

'Kate's story does check out, Bob. I don't like her for chief suspect.'

'Well who do you like for that role?' He sounded a bit exasperated.

'Dunno. We need to check out Grace Gordon and her for their whereabouts Friday afternoon; see if either matches Dennis' young woman in the street. Pity the constable didn't get a good look at her; he was focusing on Jardin and Dennis. He wasn't even watching specifically; just noted in his events book and reported that the one was following the other.'

Sandy Bell rubbed a finger over one eye, then leaned his hand on his chin, looking at McInnis. 'Anyone of them could have ridden a bike to the site Monday and nobody any wiser. I've tried to find out who went in what car but none of them seem very sure. I'm going to have to ask them all again on that point.'

'I wish we could find that damn mobile, I know he had one; the copper who spotted him saw him use it. I've got a feeling it's a major clue to solving this case, Sandy.'

'Well I think it's got something to do with that girl's disappearance.'

McInnis shook his head, not in disagreement but in puzzlement. 'It doesn't make any sense; she's only been in this country for ten weeks. She doesn't know anyone well enough,' he paused, 'unless it really was an accident.' He looked at his opposite number. 'I think I'll go and have another word with the professor, Sandy, I've had an idea. I'm putting my trust in St Michael the Archangel, Patron

Saint of policemen. I'll see you out at the hostel.'

THE TWO MEN SEPARATED to their self-appointed tasks. Sandy was shown into the same office with the same ceremony as the previous time.

'Well, Inspector Bell, and how can I help you this time.'

'Frank,' Sandy Bell took the proffered seat and sat down in a seemingly casual manner, 'I was just wondering if you've thought about telling me how much the late unlamented Jardin has left you short for your holiday trip.'

'Enough, Inspector.'

'Hmm. I was also wondering if you'd like Detective Inspector Josephs to visit?' He offered a patently false smile. 'He's so fond of you.'

Josephs was head of the Drug Squad, as they both knew. 'That sounds remarkably like a threat, Inspector.'

'No, I'm not allowed to threaten suspects.' Barker's head came up sharply, 'Oops sorry, I mean helpful citizens.'

Barker looked him squarely in the face. 'I don't deal in drugs.'

'No-one accused you, Frank; it must be the company you keep that gives us a totally false impression of you.' He grinned amiably across the desk, noting the clenched fist gripping a paperweight on the blotter. He looked at the fist pointedly.

'You haven't got any call to check out my clientele that way.'

'So you won't mind a visit from an old friend then?'

Frank suddenly lost all his urbane charm, revealing his true and rather nasty personality. 'He owed nearly ten K; that what you want to know?' he said savagely.

'That's a big sum to let him run up, Frank.' The voice was chiding but the eyes were watchful.

Frank Barker held his gaze, 'He was an old and valuable customer, Inspector.'

'Hmm. If you say so.' Sandy sounded sceptical. 'And when was he going to pay you this ten k back?'

Barker picked up a pencil, turning it over and over as he weighed his options. 'It was due today as a matter of fact. He promised he'd be able to pay on the dot, said that's when he'd get paid for a little job. Anything else you need to know, Inspector?' He raised eyes that promised murder if ever he got the chance. 'I'm rather a busy man; I haven't got time for visiting policemen, if you follow me.'

'Oh I follow you. I'll tell Josephs you're busy just now.'

'You do that, Inspector.' Barker stood up and watched the policeman walk out the room, closing the door behind him. Then he picked up the paperweight and hurled it at the door. Sandy, hearing the crash as he walked away, smiled grimly. 'Now that's a man you don't ever want to turn your back on, young Gareth.'

INSPECTOR MCINNIS WAS ONCE again looking at the doorway of the hostel. He was looking at the door because John Williams had stopped him at the entrance. 'What do you want now, Inspector?'

'I'd rather like a word with the professor.'

John raised an eyebrow. 'Not here. You'll have to

go to the site; he's gone to fetch the rest of the artefacts with Kate. Is there any chance we might get back to it before our time is up, Inspector?'

'I don't know, sir, we're doing our best.'

'Hmm.' The look and the voice were sceptical.

'I'll go to the site then.' He turned on his heel, climbing into his car and driving away as John watched. He in turn was being watched also, if he'd only known it.

PROFESSOR DAVID WALKER WAS a happy man. He didn't give a damn about the site except in the sense that people would be disappointed, and he'd possibly be slightly out of pocket; archaeology had finally been usurped as number one in his affections. He strolled down to the site from the main car park, holding Kate by the hand and grinning like a small boy out for a special excursion.

They'd sat up much of the night talking. Everything from where his next excavation would be, to discussing what family they both wanted.

The devastation that met his eyes as they turned the corner and viewed their current excavation didn't dim his mood very much at all, but Kate was horrified, stopping to look around.

'Oh! David, look at it.' Even though the police had done their best, the fact remained that they'd had to walk over digging areas in their pursuit of the regulation blunt instrument.

David shook his head. 'True, my beautiful one, it is a mess.' He continued to walk, towing Kate along. 'Let us repair to the site shed and drink tea while we consider our options.'

Inspector McInnis found them there twenty minutes later, seated at the table with the report books in front of them. 'Ah! Inspector, have you come to tell us we can have our corner of a foreign field back?'

'I'm afraid not, sir.' McInnis was genuinely sorry. 'I've actually got to ask both of you a few more questions.'

David raised an eyebrow. 'Alone or in company.'

'That's up to Miss Hamilton and you, sir.'

'Well, all things considered, I think you'd better take us as a couple, Inspector.' He stretched out a hand and Kate gripped his firmly. 'Will you take tea, Inspector? I'm feeling benevolent.'

McInnis shook his head, but did sit down across from them at the long table.

'Miss Hamilton, can you tell me where you were on Friday afternoon?'

The mobile eyebrows twitched together but David held his peace. Kate looked at McInnis with some astonishment, and then shrugged. 'I was with D...David; we went f...for a meal and t...then to his house. We w...were sorting finds from Grace's well.'

'And you can confirm this, sir?'

'Certainly, Inspector. It is indelibly fixed on my mind, Kate allowed me to kiss her for the first time; you don't forget such a glorious experience like that in a hurry.' The two men watched the colour flood Kate's cheeks.

'David, sshh!' Kate turned, swinging her hair forward and looking down at their clasped hands.

'You will note, Inspector, that she doesn't stammer for me. This indicates a level of relationship which might cause you to have doubts about my impartiality; however, I can assure you that we were together.' He smiled and dropped a kiss on the down bent head. 'Friday? The murder hadn't happened, Inspector.' He looked squarely into the brown eyes, his own green ones glinting with curiosity.

'No sir.' He looked again at Kate's down bent head and the clasped hands. 'You may not want to answer my questions with Miss Hamilton present, sir.'

'I don't think we'd better have any secrets, Inspector. We've had enough problems with those,' his lips twitched.

'Well, alright sir, but …' he paused, 'you may not like it.'

'Out with it man, she'll be thinking I'm an axe murderer or a bigamist soon.'

'Funny you should say that.' McInnis wrinkled his patrician nose. 'When we were investigating Jardin the first time, eighteen years ago, you'd been having some trouble with one of your students, a female.'

'Ahh!' the syllable was drawn out.

'I did ask, sir.' McInnis cast a look at Kate; he was beginning to sweat slightly. He had no desire to dim the glow on the girl, but he did need to ask.

'Yes, Inspector.' He tightened his grip on Kate's hand then spoke to her, 'What the nice policeman is trying to say, darling, is that I was accused of sexual harassment and worse; and fathering her child, by one of my students. She'd worked the site the two years before and asked if she could come and work with me again. I knew she'd dropped out of Uni' to have a baby and she wanted to continue her studies, she said. I was a bit sorry for her actually, Inspector,' he swung back to the Inspector.

Kate gripped his hand and he looked back at her. 'It's one of the reasons I wouldn't allow myself to care for you, Kate. You also have been one of my students. No man likes to be accused of that sort of thing; once in a lifetime is once too many for me.' He looked quietly at her and saw her shy smile, the pansy brown eyes reflecting her love for him.

The Inspector coughed quietly, 'Sir.'

276

'Yes, Inspector. So what actually do you want to know that causes you to drag up all this old history?'

'It's just a theory; but what was her name and what happened to her, Professor? The old notes only mention it in passing, so to speak, because it wasn't relative to the case as such.'

David looked blank. 'I'm damn if I can remember. I was so relieved to be shot of the whole business I allowed her to disappear from my life.' He sat pondering while the other two watched his brow furrow in thought. 'Patterson? No, Potter, that's what it was.' He smiled triumphantly at the inspector; then focused on an inspector hastily rising from his seat, like a grouse sensing the beater's approach. 'Oh! No, she's too young. Wait a bit,' He looked at McInnis as that man stopped at the door, looking back at him, 'The baby?'

'Possibly sir, it would give us some sort of a motive.'

'What, for murdering Jardin? How does she link in with him, man?'

'I can't stop to explain now, sir. I must go and make a few phone calls.' He left the door to swing on its hinges, and the couple sitting in the surprised silence like a pair of birds huddled together in the aftermath of an autumn wind.

DAN WAS HELPING GRACE to set the front room to rights at Millie's house. The funeral was scheduled for the following day and Grace had some old fashioned notions about providing people with a wake. 'It's not that there'll be a lot of people, Dan, but she'd want me to do things properly.'

'Aye, lass, I ken that.' He was busy unscrewing the base of the hospital bed. He flexed a few muscles and pulled the components apart with a small grunt of satisfaction. 'Right, I'll put it in the back of the car and take

277

it away for ye.'

He leaned it against the wall and came towards her as Grace folded bedclothes in a neat pile. 'Ye'll be alright, lass?' He took her hands, stilling her and smiling down at her serious face.

'Yes Dan, I'll be OK.' She raised silver grey eyes that flashed her determination at him.

'I'll no' be long. Then we can finish up here and go and get some fresh air.'

'Taking care of me again, Dan?'

'Aye, it's my new mission in life.' He leaned over and took the offered lips in a long kiss. Grace felt her stomach whirl and clench in delight, and wrapped her arms around his waist.

'Be good, sweetheart.' Dan put her from him, going to pick up the bed frame. He'd just managed to heft it when the doorbell rang. He gave Grace a startled look and she edged by, giving them both a quiet frisson of pleasure as their bodies came into close contact.

Inspector Bell stood on the doorstep. 'Miss Gordon.'

Grace looked from Dan to the Inspector. 'If you'd just step aside a minute, Inspector, I'll give you my attention.'

Sandy Bell skipped out of the way and Dan swung the frame out of the door. 'Here lad, I'll give you a hand.' The two men manoeuvred the bed frame down the path and into the car and walked back up the path together.

Dan gave Grace a careful look as she stood by the opening and then went into the sitting room to fetch more pieces of bed. Inspector Bell followed him and they accomplished another two journeys before either spoke anything more than, 'To ye, man', and 'Straighten her up, lad.'

278

'I'm obliged to ye.' Dan stood back and let the Inspector through the door, he brushed a hand over his hair, 'How can we help ye, Inspector is it?'

The Inspector nodded at him, absently looking around at the stripped room.

'My grandmother died Wednesday, Inspector; we're sorting things out a bit.'

'Yes, Miss.' He looked at the young couple, 'I'm sorry to hear it, Miss, and I wouldn't intrude if I could help it but I need to know what you were doing Friday last week.'

Grace looked puzzled, 'I was at work.'

'No, Miss, in the afternoon. Can you account for your movements then?'

Dan moved protectively towards her, 'She was wi' me most o' the afternoon and evening, Inspector.'

'And who are you, lad?'

'I'm her fiancé.'

Grace smiled slightly; it had been said with such firmness. She looked across at the Inspector, 'We …' was as far as she got. Bell, looking slightly embarrassed, pulled a mobile out of his pocket. 'Damn kids keep changing my ring tones.' He stilled the relentless playing of 'great balls of fire.' ''Scuse me.' He held the machine up to his ear.

'Yes, Bob. What? Are you sure?' The pair watched as he shook his head in astonishment. 'OK, I'll get a bulletin out.' He flicked the machine off. 'Sorry I've got to go, thank you anyway.' He left, leaving another couple standing astonished.

GRACE HAD SPOKEN TO David late on Thursday afternoon and he had suggested that it might be easier for all concerned if she held the wake out at the hostel. He argued that it was bigger than Millie's small house and, though Grace said she didn't think there would be that many there, David persuaded her to use the place anyway.

Grace had been stunned as she recognised a couple of eminent professors and senior government officials that had turned up for what she thought would be a simple funeral service. David, coming into the chapel, settled himself next to Grace as she stood dry eyed, and somewhat amazed, next to Dan. 'Where have all these people come from, David.' David briefly hugged her. 'I'll tell you later, love.'

He'd ushered her out of the chapel at the end of the simple service, pausing to speak to a tall distinguished man, 'Sir Henry, if you'd like to gather the troops and bring them out to the hostel?'

The man addressed as Sir Henry inclined his head. 'See you out there.' He spoke in a rich fruity voice.

'David, who are these people?' Grace asked the question even while she looked about in a faintly distracted way.

'Your aunt was greatly respected, Grace, a lot of big names consulted her in a purely private capacity. If she'd had the opportunity to go to university she'd have been as famous as many of them.' He smiled sadly down at her. 'She never understood how well she was regarded.'

'Oh!' she looked back at Dan following quietly in their wake, and held out her hand as they reached his big Jeep Cherokee. She'd looked around in the throng but there were several strange male faces. 'I'm expecting someone but I don't know what he looks like. I'll go ahead in case he's already at the hostel if you're sure your Sir Henry can get them all there?'

David raised an eyebrow. 'Alright love, I'll see you out there.'

Dan stowed her away. He started the big machine and they set off. 'Ye'll ha' to tell me where to go in a bit, sweetheart.' He reached out his left hand, resting it on her two clasped in her lap where they gripped her bag. 'I dinna see him but there were so many strange faces there.'

'I don't know, Dan. He said he would come.'

'Aye, well, dinna fret. Yon man will round them all up; if he should ha' come your David will see he gets to the right place.'

They drove along the back roads out of the city and, with Grace giving directions, pulled up outside the hostel.

Dan parked neatly at the side of the collection of huts.

'When I was a student I used to stay in the huts with the rest of the team, I thought it was great fun. Now I wouldn't swap my own bed for one of those cots for any price.'

She looked up at Dan's face as he gave a small chuckle. 'Ye'll no get the chance, lass.'

They went inside to find the women of the team had set the big trestle table with the customary baked meats. Grace went and sat on the sagging sofa to await the arrival of the hordes that weren't far behind.

She had been handed over like porcelain china from the care of Dan to David, when he'd arrived. She was vaguely aware that Dan was mingling with the members of the team even while he kept an eye on her progress round the room with David.

David took her round and introduced her to several men she had only heard of and she listened to praise heaped on her grandmother. They had nearly completed the circle when David stopped in front of a tall, slightly stooped, old man who'd just entered the door. Grace felt her mouth dry up as she looked at him. 'I'm sorry, Grace, I don't er...' David looked surprised.

Grace smiled shyly into eyes the same grey as her own. 'I er, think I might be able to introduce you, David.' She looked into the old face, 'I believe this gentleman is Mr James Belsham.'

David held out a hand, 'How do you do, sir.'

The two men shook hands as Dan came over, at Grace's frantic look, to stand behind her, placing his hands around her waist and pulling her back against him. He looked the old man over carefully: the good black suit and the heavy wool topcoat, the impeccably tied, silk tie, and concluded that his buddy was right when he said the guy was loaded.

'Howdy.' The elderly man turned to Grace. 'We've only spoken on the phone and I'm having a bit of trouble fitting all the facts, little lady. But if what you told me then is true I'm desperately sorry. I would have married her you know.'

'Grace?' David eyed the two standing looking silently at each other. 'Good grief!'

'Aye, man.' Dan looked across at David. 'A' think we mun find a bit o' quiet for a minute.'

David led the way out and across to the sleeping quarters, courteously showing the way to the older man as Dan and Grace followed. They went into one of the small unused bedrooms. Three of the walls were lined with empty bunks, their wooden slats white in the reflected light of the naked bulb hanging from the centre of the ceiling. A small table and four chairs were placed squarely under the light.

They filed in and sat down. David looked again at the two faces: one so familiar to him, the other a stranger's face and yet familiar. 'I must admit I've been puzzled, Grace; when you said Grandmother to the police the other night I didn't like to say anything. I gather you were

282

Millie's secret, sir.' He looked into eyes the same grey as Grace's.

James Belsham sat gazing at Grace, almost drinking her features in one by one. He dragged his gaze away to answer the implied question. 'I was such a secret, even I didn't know about me.' His lips twitched. 'I wish I'd know earlier. I've been in this country for nearly a month this trip and I could have visited. I shall always regret it.' He turned back to Grace. 'Damn Girl! But you're beautiful!'

David continued to look from one face to the other. Grace sat holding tightly to Dan's hand. Her stomach was quivering, her mouth dry. The precipitate entry of Alice held the tableau still and then shattered it like a stone in a calm lake.

'You owe me,' Alice all but spat the words at David. 'You wouldn't pay then, but you'll bloody well pay now!'

David rose slowly, looking as if he'd been struck in the face. Dan rose at the same time, hastily moving Grace out of the way. James Belsham sat quietly, unmoving, and cautiously watching the byplay. David stepped around the table. 'I don't think this is the place to discuss this, Alice.' He paused, reached out a hand towards the girl and then withdrew it. 'Shall we step into another room?'

'Ashamed of me are you?'

David shook his head and walked past her, forcing her to follow if she wanted to speak to him. Dan looked at the other two, for once undecided as to his course of action. He made up his mind. 'Yon man might need a witness.' He received a nod from Grace and quickly followed David out of the door.

'I think we'd better put off this discussion until later, Grace. Can I take you out for a meal or meet you somewhere else?'

Grace, who had been listening to the steadily rising

283

voices coming through the thin walls, nodded her agreement and they both rose and left the room, going outside as the voices ceased.

AS THEY WALKED THE short distance, a squad car pulled up and the two inspectors climbed out. David and Dan stood outside; there was no sign of Alice. The two men stood quietly; David was pale and angry looking, his breathing heavy. He was obviously making an effort to control his temper. They turned as the approaching officers came up to them. David snarled at them, protesting. 'For God sake, can you not leave the girl alone for one day! She's just buried her aunt.'

'Sorry, sir. 'McInnis frowned. 'We didn't expect you here, I understood you were going to be at Miss Gordon's house.'

'Well I'm not.'

'We came to ask a few more questions of your team.'

'I should be grateful you didn't turn up at the chapel.' David looked at them with something verging on disgust.

'A very quick word, Miss Gordon,' Sandy spoke apologetically.

Grace nodded, 'I won't be a minute, David.' David gave her a long look but she seemed to be holding herself together. 'OK, but it better only be a quick word or I'll be back here.' He walked away, his back stiff, headed to the main recreation hut.

Dan didn't move away, he placed a hand around her shoulder, 'Yes, Inspector?'

'I was just wondering when you could come and look at the coins, Miss Gordon.' Sandy refused to be intimidated.

Grace opened her mouth to tell the man to go to blazes when they all became aware of a female voice shouting in the hut David had just entered.

'What the hell?' McInnis headed rapidly towards the open door, just in time to catch Alice full in his arms as she hurtled out of the doorway. He grabbed hold and held tight to the struggling girl as she swore viciously at him.

'Hear, hear, that isn't any way to talk.' Sandy was almost as quick off the mark as Bob McInnis. He caught her arm as it was in danger of clawing out Bob's fine brown eye.

'Now, Miss.'

David, coming back out, narrowly avoided catching the hand on its downward swing. He laid a gentle hand on the girl only to have her snarl at him. Kate, emerging from the dining hut, stood looking at the struggling group and then, with a good deal of forethought, shut the door behind her and held it shut.

Dan, carefully placing Grace behind his back, stepped forward to lend his aid to the two policemen as they put a pair of handcuffs on Alice; more in an effort to restrain than to arrest her.

'Will you stand still, Miss?' Sandy was going red in the face.

'What so he and his whore can blacken my name the same as he did to my mother.' She swung round and spat at David.

'Look at him, all supercilious, showing round the big-wigs and him no better than a molester. Well I hope you lose a mint at this dig. It's what you deserve; it wouldn't have hurt you to give her an allowance, but no, you're too good for that and she died, and it's all your fault.'

David stood in stunned silence while the two officers held her arms securely. Dan stepped forward; 'I think she dropped this, Inspector.' He handed over a small cell phone. Whereupon Alice started cursing and swearing, struggling to escape the iron grip of Bob McInnis.

James Belsham stepped around the struggling trio. He observed the police squad car with some trepidation but schooled his face to remain bland. 'Careful, sir, perhaps you'd better wait inside.' Dan proffered the suggestion even while he watched Sandy Bell looking over the cell phone.

Bell flicked it and looked through the keypad of most often used numbers. 'I think it's Jardin's, Bob.' He keyed in the first on the list waiting expectantly for it to connect. 'I'll look silly if this is Barker.' he said in an aside to McInnis.

The shock was profound, as was the silence, when James Belsham put his hand in his pocket to bring out his own ringing phone. Everyone turned to look at him, and Alice burst into hysterical laughter. 'Oh! Gawd, that's rich. Who the hell is this old geezer?'

Inspector's McInnis and Bell were wondering the same thing.

'Sir.' Bell had a great respect for age, but an even greater respect for the law. He looked steadily at Belsham. 'Why has this phone got your number?' He held up Jardin's mobile phone.

James Belsham looked at Grace. 'I'm sorry, my dear. I thought it was safe to come, but you see our sins always find us out.'

He walked away and climbed in the back of the squad car before the astonished eyes of the assembled company.

Bell, after a barely perceptible pause, said, 'I'll get a separate squad car sent out, Bob. Which one do you want?'

McInnis, holding manfully onto the hysterical female in his arms, said slightly breathlessly, 'I take this one. But tell 'em to make it quick will you.'

Dan moved and took Grace in his arms; she was obviously having some difficulty keeping up with events, and no wonder. 'Come away, sweetheart, a'll tak ye home.' He looked across at David. 'Ye'll see t' things ower there?' He nodded across the space to the communal hut before which Kate still stood sentry.

David nodded; Grace wasn't the only one having problems. 'I'll see you as soon as I can.'

Dan shook his head, either in refusal or because he didn't know if it was right, but he didn't speak. He half carried Grace to his car, putting her in the seat, belting her firmly in, and driving away.

JAMES BELSHAM WAS SEATED in a small interview room with a cup of coffee in front of him. Inspector Sandy Bell, with due regard to the man's obvious age and his genuine desire to help the police, had ensured his comfort. He came in now, satisfied that McInnis had secured their prisoner. He'd also taken time to trace the other numbers on the mobile phone.

'Now, sir, perhaps you might like to explain why a man like Jardin should have your private phone listed as his top number?'

'That's easy. I have employed him sometimes.'

Sandy ran a finger round the inside of his ear as though he couldn't quite believe what he'd heard. 'You were employing him?'

'No, Sir.'

Sandy scratched his grey locks. 'I think you'd better explain, Mr Belsham.'

'I collect Roman antiquities, mostly honestly, but I was put in contact with Jardin nearly twenty years ago. He's supplied me with the odd thing since. I'm aware he's a bit shady and I must admit I didn't always check the origins.' Belsham sipped coffee and smiled rather tiredly.

'In other words you knew he stole things and you've received his stolen goods?'

'Well that's putting it bluntly but, in essence yes, that would be correct.'

Sandy shook his head and paused to take a gulp of his own coffee. 'So why were you out at the hostel today?'

'Because, Inspector, Miss Gordon is my granddaughter.'

Sandy opened and shut his mouth a time or two, then gulped more coffee under the twinkling eyes of the old man. 'Right, sir!' He pondered his next question.

'Perhaps you can answer one of my questions, Inspector.' The grey eyes looked seriously at him.

'I might,' said Bell cautiously.

'How had that extraordinarily vituperative young woman got Jardin's phone.' He paused, watching Bell's face. 'I know the man was murdered, it's been all over the news. I thought I might be able to see Grace and disappear again. There shouldn't have been anything to tie me to your crime.'

Bell looked the man over, noting the suit, gold cufflinks, and Swiss watch. A signet ring glinted on his right hand. 'Strictly speaking, sir, unless you've got stolen goods on you, there isn't. Employing the man hardly leads to murdering him. Even if I thought you were capable.'

'Oh you'd be surprised how capable I am, Inspector.' He brushed the comment aside, 'The young woman?'

'We think she probably killed him, sir. We're not

288

sure of her motive, but I think we'll find her foot prints match the pair we haven't identified at the scene. She had Jardin's mobile and her mobile number was on it. So she knew the man, and we have a somewhat dubious witness that saw her push Jardin into the well, where he subsequently died.'

Belsham nodded slowly. He sat silently assessing the information. 'I have no stolen goods on me, Inspector, nor have I received any in your fair country,' his lips twitched, 'this trip. And you'd have to prove what I have in New York wasn't come by honestly.' There was a definite drawl to the words that caused Bell's own lips to twitch slightly.

'So really I'm just, 'helping you with your enquiries,' as you say over here.'

'Mmm.' Bell looked at the shrewd eyes watching his. 'Quite, sir. Unless we can prove he was employed to steal for you at the site.'

'Oh I don't think you'll prove that, Inspector. I said I employed him occasionally; I didn't say I was employing him at the moment. I deeply regret the manner of his death, however.'

The two men sat watching each other cautiously as they drank the remains of their coffee. Bell was the first to break the silence. 'I think you've helped us all you can at the moment, sir. I'd be obliged if you wouldn't leave the country; but of course I can't stop you if you do.'

Belsham stood up, gathering his topcoat from the back of the chair. 'I'll be going home next week, Inspector. Now,' he paused, looking Bell squarely in the face, 'I'm sure you'll be pleased to hear that my collection is complete.'

Bell nodded in perfect understanding of what he was being told, verbally and otherwise.

'Perhaps you could furnish me with Grace's

address? I should like to make her acquaintance properly.'

'I'll have a car take you there, sir. Thank you for being so helpful.'

REPORTING THE INTERVIEW TO McInnis he summed up with. 'We haven't got anything on him and he knows it. He was employing Jardin, I'm positive of that but …' He shrugged, 'He's unlikely to try again in this country either. As to being Miss Gordon's grandfather, I'd like to hear the story behind that, but I don't suppose we will.'

McInnis, smiled grimly. 'Well you're welcome to hear Miss Potter's.'

Bell shifted more comfortably in his seat. 'You'll make a fine police chief one of these days, Bob my lad. Tell me all about it.'

'It's rather sad really. Miss Potter was brought up believing Professor Walker was her father. Her mother was stoned most of the time and blamed him for deserting them. When the girl got the chance to come to this country she searched him out intending to make him pay for said desertion.' He sniffed, 'I don't think she'd quite figured out how.'

Bell shook his head. 'I don't know which to blame, Bob, the drugs or a society that doesn't care.'

'No.' McInnis looked sadly across the table. 'Anyway, she was snooping around the site when she saw Jardin on one of his sorties and linked up with him. If I understood her correctly, but I wouldn't swear to that, she became a trifle …' He rubbed a hand over his face. 'Er, foul mouthed about nearly everyone. Jardin was threatening to expose her because he didn't like working with amateurs.'

'So I suppose she clocked him one to shut him up.'

'Yeah, she said he was still breathing when she

290

pushed him into the well in a panic. I had to tell her that the push broke his neck. I don't know, Sandy; we've got to prove malice aforethought.' He shrugged. 'If she sticks to her story of trying to shut him up while she made her get away; its only manslaughter.'

'Why did she take the phone?'

'Says she didn't want him ringing for help before she'd managed to leave the site. Which could be true of course.' McInnis rubbed a palm across his cheek, 'Or she could have been shrewd enough to know that her number on his phone would incriminate her.' He sighed, 'The first makes it manslaughter; prove the second and we might have her for murder.'

Sandy sighed as well. 'We'll charge her with murder and let the lawyers fight it out.' He stood up 'I'm going home early, Bob. I'll be in to write up all the reports tomorrow.'

As THE SQUAD CAR deposited James Belsham at Grace's small flat he admitted privately to himself that he'd been damn lucky, and that he wasn't looking forward to this meeting as much as he ought.

Dan opened the door to him and Belsham could see it was only the Scotsman's innate courtesy that got him into the house. 'I'd like to talk to Grace.'

'Aye.' Dan led the way to the sitting room. He went immediately across the room to Grace, who was seated at the table, and stood behind her chair placing a comforting hand on her shoulder.

James Belsham examined afresh the young woman. 'I wish I'd known.'

Grace was looking at him. 'You'd better sit down.'

Belsham came further into the room and settled on a dining chair in front of the couple. 'I owe you an

291

explanation, Grace.'

'No, no you don't. I don't know you, you see. Until last week I didn't know you existed.'

'I didn't abandon Millie.'

Grace put her head on one side. 'She didn't say you did.'

'Nay she never said that, just that ye'd argued' Dan spoke slowly, "Beyond bearing', she said; and I had a sneaking sympathy for a man trying to explain to women the reasons why men kill men.'

Belsham acknowledged the statement. 'But I could have come back couldn't I'

'Aye.'

'I was so mad with her and myself. And then, I don't know, it was so far away and a different world was opening up; but that's not a really good excuse.'

'Nae it's not.'

'Dan.' Grace spoke softly, looking over her shoulder at him.

'Aye, sweetheart, I'm sorry.' Dan lightly squeezed her shoulder.

Grace turned back to her grandfather. 'She asked us to tell you she was sorry she'd quarrelled, that she'd loved you, and, whatever your reasons, she forgave you for not coming back.'

James Belsham sighed deeply. 'I wish I'd dared to come and see her, I knew where she lived. But the longer I took the more impossible it seemed, so I didn't come. I didn't know about the baby.' He looked across at the eyes so like his own. 'I swear I didn't, your phone call was the first I knew about her having a grandchild, and even then I didn't know you were mine.'

'She's no' yours. She's mine noo.'

'Dan.' Grace reached up a hand to still the fierce grip. 'Go and make us a drink, darling, I'll be alright.'

He looked down at her, seeing the strength and the love in her face. 'Alright.' He went out, leaving the door open.

'What a fierce young man you have as your protector. I should marry him quickly; love like that doesn't come to us often. I wasted my chance out of greed and laziness.'

Dan, coming back, stood in the doorway. 'She'll marry me soon.' He gave her a look loaded with all the love he had, seeing the same love reflected back.

'I should like to explain.' Belsham looked at the books still stacked haphazardly on the table from the day before.

Dan raised an eyebrow. Grace kept her gaze steady on the old face, saying nothing.

'I, like you, love archaeology, but you serve the dead honestly. I've always wanted artefacts for their possession, not to share. Jardin was working for me.' He shuddered. 'God help me, if I'd known where all this would lead I wouldn't have touched the man with a barge pole. He worked for me for twenty years except when he was in prison. He was as brilliant and as crooked as me. And I'm sorry for it, because I can see that it's lost me the most precious possession of the lot. Family.' He stood up, 'I'll not stay for a drink if you don't mind.'

He reached into his inside pocket, pulling out a wallet and extracting a piece of card. 'If you should find it in your heart to forgive me, then you can contact me any time, day or night.' He turned and left the room before either of the others could stop him, disappearing out the door.

Grace looked across the room. 'Dan?'

'Aye, a'll fetch him back for ye.'

293

He returned with the old man. What had passed between them Grace didn't know but Belsham sat down heavily in the recently occupied chair. Grace stretched out a hand. 'I'm sorry too, Grandfather. We'll get to know each other shall we?'

James took the outstretched hand, his touch at first tentative. Then he grasped it firmly, closing his eyes for a minute. Dan moved quietly out of the room, returning with three glasses of single malt which he set on the table. He went round the table and sat next to Grace.

'Let's start again. I'm sorry, I ken we're a' a wee bit tense.' He stretched out a hand over the table, 'Ma name is Daniel Campbell, a'm aimin t' marry Gracie, such time as she'll ha' me. So you mon get used t' me to for I'll be kin o' yourn too, soon.'

James Belsham took and shook the proffered hand. 'I shall be proud to know you if I get the chance.' He turned back to Grace. 'I'd like to offer an explanation. It's not an excuse, but it might help you understand a little.' He paused then said, 'The war affected people in a lot of different ways. Some of my mates clung to every one of their surviving relatives. They were so grateful anyone had survived.' He shook his head and Dan pushed the whisky closer.

Nodding his thanks to Dan, James took a small sip. He rolled the small tot glass between his hands, watching the contents coating its sides. 'I went the other way. I'd lost so many mates I got so I wouldn't allow myself to have any deep feeling for anyone in case they weren't there the next week. Then there was Millie. God! How I fought from loving Millie.'

He looked up at the young couple. 'She was so sweet and kind and she moved into my heart before I knew she'd done it. Loving her was the best thing, making love was …' He took another sip of liquid. 'When I realised what I'd done, I looked for excuses to escape from her.' He

294

shook his head. 'I can't explain; except to say I was so scared of loving anyone in case they died on me I tried to freeze her out, arguing with her and staying away. It's gotten to be a bad habit. Eventually I stole something from her; I thought it would make her so disgusted with me she'd leave and I could blame her instead of myself.' He shrugged, grimacing.

Dan moved his hand and took Grace's. 'Aye man I ken what ye mean. Loving is frightening.'

James looked at the younger man, seeing the compassion on his face. 'Yes, well I've paid for it. I've got money and loneliness as my reward. Along with some coins I've never dared to display, or even look at, and a pile of regrets.'

Dan nodded, 'We all pay for our choices. Millie made hers as well, she dinna ha' t' keep t' bairn, or Grace. She dinna ha' t sleep wi' thee, man. It was her choice as well.'

'Yes I suppose it was. I nearly picked an argument again today. I wanted to see you, Grace. But I was so scared you'd make demands on me. One's I don't, didn't, want to fill.' He gulped the rest of the whisky. 'I wanted to stay and run at the same time. Can you understand?' His eyes pleaded as he looked across the table at his granddaughter. 'I chose a crooked path because it was easier to love things than people. I find it very unpalatable to be rejected by someone else; I'm getting a taste of my own medicine and it has a bitter taste.'

'Aye, man, most medicine has.' Dan squeezed Grace's hand and picked up his own tot. 'I'm thanking God for Grace, for I could ha' been standing where ye are if she hadn't happened along.' He knocked back the whiskey and set the glass down. 'Millie asked would I wed her at Gretna, ye ha' the choice o' being there.' He stood up, putting a hand on Grace's shoulder, 'I'll gie David a ring, lass, while ye talk a wee while more.' He paused. 'Millie told me she found a Roman hoard, would it be that?'

James looked squarely into the stern face. 'Yes.' He looked down at the empty glass dull colour washing his cheeks. 'It was part covetousness, but mainly because I thought she'd never forgive me for that.'

'Aye well, she did, and she loved you, so all ye have to do is forgive yoursen.' Dan walked out of the room and the two left, sat quietly thinking. Eventually Grace pushed the other glass of whiskey towards him. 'I won't be a moment.' She got up and went across to her bedroom, returning with a small box.

'Millie gave me these when I was sixteen. She said I might learn a lot from them. Not just about coins or Romans but eventually about the value of things. I think you might learn a lot too.' She pushed the small box across and watched as James, after a glance from under neat eyebrows, carefully took off the lid to reveal two Roman coins.

He pushed the box away, looking down at the tabletop. Grace watched him for a thoughtful minute. 'You're welcome to them. I don't want the bloody things.' It was said fiercely but quietly. 'I want Millie.'

'So do I.' Grace gritted her teeth for a second to gain control. 'She's gone, but I'll share her life with you if that's what you want.' She took a deep breath. 'She was better at forgiving than I am, so you'll have to help too.'

James raised eyes full of fear and haunted by regrets. 'Perhaps we can help each other. You're more forgiving than you know.' He stretched out a hand and Grace gripped it firmly.

'SO WHAT WAS THE end of it then?' Dan and David sat talking out at David's house, both of them leaning back in comfortable leather chairs sipping good Glenffidich.

'They've come to an uneasy peace at the present. Nae doot it'll all settle its sel'.' He looked across at David. 'Has the stramash settled aboot yon lassie?'

'She'll stand her trial.' David shook his head. 'I blame myself. I never checked her mother was OK.'

'A' weel we can all be wise after the event, man. Dinna fret yersen too much, everyone makes their ain choices,' he looked up as Grace and Kate came in, 'and she's mine.' He grinned across at Grace, holding out a hand. She came and settled on his knee.

'I love you.' He whispered the words as David moved to the settee and Kate snuggled down next to him.

Printed in Great
Britain
by Amazon